Claws for
Alarm

*St. Martin's Paperbacks titles
by Cate Conte*

CAT ABOUT TOWN
PURRDER SHE WROTE
THE TELL TAIL HEART
A WHISKER OF A DOUBT
CLAWS FOR ALARM

Claws for
Alarm

CATE CONTE

St. Martin's Paperbacks

For Katsi, my newest furry angel.
And for all his brothers and sisters who became angels before him.
Love and miss you all.

This is a work of fiction. All of the characters, organizations, and events portrayed in this novel are either products of the author's imagination or are used fictitiously.

First published in the United States by St. Martin's Paperbacks, an imprint of St. Martin's Publishing Group.

CLAWS FOR ALARM

For information, address St. Martin's Publishing Group, 120 Broadway, New York, NY 10271.

www.stmartins.com

ISBN: 978-1-250-76155-2

Our books may be purchased in bulk for promotional, educational, or business use. Please contact your local bookseller or the Macmillan Corporate and Premium Sales Department at 1-800-221-7945, ext. 5442, or by email at MacmillanSpecialMarkets@macmillan.com.

Printed in the United States of America

St. Martin's Paperbacks edition published 2021

10 9 8 7 6 5 4 3 2 1

Acknowledgments

Getting to write about cats and cat rescue is such a dream come true. I love that I can draw so heavily on a passion of mine, as well as many years of experience, to bring these books to all of you. So a huge thank you to the team at St. Martin's—Nettie Finn, my editor, the graphics team, the editors and production team—for all your work in bringing this book to life. And for my agent, John Talbot, for helping me make this series what it is today.

Special thanks to my assistant, Jen McKee, for helping me keep my life on track! Pretty much nothing would get done without her. Jen, you are invaluable.

I have some wonderful friends who helped make this book what it is—Jessie Crockett, the most masterful plotter I know; Jason Allen-Forrest, my first reader; and Sherry Harris, whose keen editing eye always makes my books better. And Riham El-Lakany, my mentor and best friend, for always cheering me on.

Jessie and Sherry are also my blog mates, along with Edith Maxwell/Maddie Day, Barbara Ross, and Julie Hennrikus/Julia Henry. They are my favorite women in the world to be with on this writing journey. The mystery community as a whole is simply amazing and I am grateful every day to be part of it.

And most of all Aime—the one who puts up with me when I'm on deadline and keeps me caffeinated and fed. Thank you babe—and thanks to Shea, Lena and Isaac for keeping me entertained in between writing sessions. Love you all.

Chapter 1

"When I said I wanted sand between my toes, this wasn't exactly what I meant." I stared down in dismay at the cat litter that was supposed to be in the litter box, but somehow had managed to cover half the floor of my cat café instead.

Adele Barrows, my star volunteer and fellow crazy cat lady—dare I say maybe even a little crazier than me—handed me a dustpan without even looking up from where she was scooping cat food into bowls with her other hand. "They're cats. Whaddaya expect?" she said with her pack-a-day rasp. I'd been trying to convince Adele to quit smoking for a year now, to no avail.

I took the dustpan, biting back my retort, not wanting to sound like a complainer. After all, Adele normally did most of the cleaning here at JJ's House of Purrs, Daybreak Island's first and only cat café and me and my partner Ethan Birdsong's brainchild. We'd soft-launched a year ago when I'd moved back to the island on a whim after a decade-long absence, turning my Grandpa Leo's huge home into part cat shelter, part expanded residence and giving Grandpa a starring role as co-owner. JJ's was named after Junkyard Johnny, the stray cat I'd adopted upon my return. He'd found me at my grandmother's funeral and we immediately became besties. He'd also been the inspiration for the café. And while we'd seen much success in our first—and mostly rushed—iteration, this new summer season was going to be epic, in my opinion.

Last year we'd opened with our dining room as the cat café and Grandpa's kitchen as our coffee and baking base. It had worked, but wasn't ideal for, you know, living in the actual house. This year we were in a much better place. We'd done extensive renovations, which were now complete, the food operations had moved to the garage-turned-food-service-area—Ethan's dream since we'd moved here—and my accompanying store with JJ merchandise was fully stocked. I'd also opened an online store that was getting a lot of traction. JJ was a superstar on the island and his reputation had already spread far and wide thanks to the great publicity we'd gotten since our opening. What better way to keep promoting that than putting his adorable face on sweatpants, coffee mugs, tote bags, and other souvenirs?

"I know," I said now, in response to Adele's comment. "But it was easier to manage with ten cats. Which was my limit, if you recall. Then I let Katrina guilt me into another five. Pretty soon we'll all have to move out to make room for the cats." I motioned to the more-crowded-by-the-second café area, where a family of kittens currently wrestled, tumbling over one another in that flexible kitten way they had. I'd had to add two cat trees just the other day, and even though we'd just expanded the café space, I felt like it was already too small again.

They were stinking cute, though.

When I'd opened the café in response to a need on

the island after the only other rescue center had closed
due to lack of funding, I'd been firm in my limit. It was
Grandpa Leo's house, after all, and he and I, along with
Ethan, JJ, and my sister Val, had to live here too. And
for the last few months my boyfriend Lucas and his dog
Oliver had pretty much moved in, so we were kind of a
full house. But Katrina Denning, my good friend and
the town's animal control officer, had worn me down. She
knew I could never say no to a furry face in trouble and
she took full advantage of that. Now we were up to fifteen. And the latest residents were the messiest. Adorable, but messy. A mom and her litter of six kittens. No
foster homes had been available, so they showed up at
our door.

"Budget cuts," Adele said with a shrug. "You know
how it is. Katrina's in a rough spot."

"I know, I know," I sighed. The police department
as a whole was facing budget cuts at the start of the fis-
cal year, which meant the animal control budget would
take the hardest hit. It just wasn't that important to
some police chiefs. When Grandpa Leo had been chief
he had been different, but his replacement wasn't of the
same mind.

"Anyway, I wouldn't care, but today of all days I want
the place to look good." I sank to my knees and began
dutifully sweeping as Tommy, our orange and white
triple-pawed kitty, watched with interest, hanging over
the side of the tree with his face on his paws.

"That's right, your fancy-pants rescue lady is coming."
Adele made a face.

"What fancy-pants rescue lady?" Mish Warner, one
of my newer volunteers and a childhood friend, walked
into the room with a stack of freshly washed litter boxes.
Mish had started volunteering with me a month or so ago.

She said she needed something fulfilling to do when she wasn't running her pet supply store, A Pawsitive Experience. She and her husband Stevie both loved cats and were looking to adopt a feline friend for their Yorkie, Pebbles. Mish, Stevie, and I had all gone to school together since kindergarten. But unlike me, neither of them had ever left the island. They'd been high school sweethearts and gotten married in their early twenties. And as far as I knew, they still liked each other. It was cute.

"That woman from the rescue league that doesn't really rescue anything," Adele said with a disdainful sniff.

"What woman from the rescue league?" Mish asked, looking at me.

"Adele! That's not nice." I wagged a finger at her.

"It's true!" Adele protested. "They have no shelter. They like to run fancy parties and get their names in the paper, is all."

"They use their funding for spay/neuter clinics, foster home networks, and lobbying for animal rights." I frowned at her then turned to Mish. "She's not that fancy. She just happens to run a well-known rescue league. One that does a lot of good work raising money," I added with a side-eye to Adele.

Adele snorted. She wasn't one to suffer fools easily—or anyone she deemed rich and pretentious. I wasn't sure my impending guest fit either of those categories, but once Adele had something in her mind, there was no getting it out.

"Really," Mish said in an odd voice. "Which one?"

"Shoreline Animal Rescue League in New Jersey," I said. I had to admit, I was a tiny bit starstruck by this request. I'd been following the League since I was a kid. Granted they weren't our neighbors—we were out here on a little island off the coast of Massachusetts—but they had a presence that seeped all the way into the northeast corner of the country, well beyond the tri-state area. They always had compelling marketing materials and excellent tug-the-heartstrings stories about animals they'd helped save and policies they'd helped implement, both federal and statewide. Their fundraisers were legendary and attracted all kinds of celebrity endorsers, and they had extensive reach and influence around the entire East Coast when it came to effecting change for animals.

So when Jillian Allen, the executive director, called me out of the blue and asked to meet with me, I immediately said yes. She said she was coming to the island on business and wanted to see this "famous" up-and-coming cat café for herself—and meet JJ, of course. Which had won me over, but hadn't sat well with Adele.

"On business?" she'd snorted. "Like what? Scoping out her new summer house?"

I had no idea, and I honestly didn't care. I was flattered that they'd taken notice of us and our café and certainly wasn't going to look for an ulterior motive. I also figured maybe they wanted to start a foster network out here or something.

"What's her name?" Mish asked in kind of a strangled voice.

I took a closer look at her. She looked funny all of a sudden. Her lips were twisted in a weird shape and she stood frozen as a statue, still clutching the litter boxes. "Jillian Allen. You okay?"

"Hmm? Oh, yes of course. Just kind of hungry." She smiled, but it seemed forced.

I could sympathize. When I was hungry I turned into a beast. "Why don't you go grab something from Ethan? You know he's always cooking or baking some kind of deliciousness." Now that our café was open, Ethan spent most of his time out in the newly converted garage making all kinds of treats. Including vegan and gluten-free options.

"Good idea," Mish said. She dropped the stack of litter boxes where she stood with more force than I thought necessary, sending the more skittish cats scrambling for cover, and headed out the door.

Adele shook her head and bent to pick up the boxes. "So how does this woman know about you anyway? No offense," she added. "It's just that New Jersey isn't right down the street."

"She heard about us through some research into new East Coast rescues," I said. "Said they want to start helping smaller places throughout the region. We'll find out more today."

Adele was clearly still skeptical. "They *should* help more places. And stop paying people fancy-pants salaries when they could use that money to save more animals. I have no respect for places that don't get their hands dirty, Maddie. You know that about me."

"I do know that about you. And I get it," I said. "But different places run differently and it doesn't mean they care any less about the animals. They just have their own way of getting things done."

"Yeah, without doing the hard work," Adele shot back. "Anyway, what time is she coming?"

I glanced at my watch. "Around three, she said. I have to make sure this place is in tip-top shape." I winked at her to let her know I was kidding. With Adele, it was always in tip-top shape. While I wished she was better at taking care of her own health and well-being—i.e., quitting smoking and cutting back on the boxes of wine—when it came to the cats, she was a complete perfectionist.

"Grandpa is looking forward to doing his thing and showing the place off. You can stick around and help too if you want. That's part of the shelter-manager role, after all."

Just last week I had offered Adele a real, paying job as our full-time café manager, and I was over the moon about it. Although she was probably going to keep at least one of her three other jobs, this might help take some of the load off her. It would definitely take some off of me.

"'Course I'll stick around. I wanna see just how full of crap she is." Adele grinned at me. "Now. Why don't you go get some coffee and I'll finish here. You do a lousy job with a dustpan anyway."

Chapter 2

Half an hour later I was showered, freshly caffeinated, and ready to show off the café to the fullest. I'd traded my litter-cleaning sweats for a cute new summery dress I'd ordered online last week and felt much more presentable. I picked up my phone to text Lucas before I went into the café. My boyfriend—I still loved saying that—had a full day of grooming appointments today at the salon he owned, Diva Dogs and Classy Cats, and he'd taken Oliver to work with him knowing we'd have a full house. His place was the only full-service, year-round grooming business on the island, and it came in handy for me with all the cats who needed freshening up after their rescues. Of course, I'd been able to negotiate a good rate given that I knew the owner and all.

Getting ready for the big visit, I texted. *Wish you and Ollie were here*.

Figuring his hands were deep in a sink full of dog hair and it would be a while before I heard back, I stuck my phone back in my pocket and whistled for JJ, who immediately came running. The two of us headed toward the café. On the way, I glanced out the back window and caught sight of Mish, outside on the phone, holding a cup of coffee. I paused to watch her walk around talking, waving her cup around. At one point the coffee splashed out onto her shirt and it didn't look like she even noticed. Her jerky, stiff movements told me she was agitated. I wondered if she was having a fight with Stevie. I hoped not.

I pulled open the French doors separating the main house from the café and let JJ in ahead of me. He bolted right for the kittens, squeaking non-stop. He loved the little ones.

The cats' portion of the house was an expanded version of our former dining room. We'd taken down walls, added on a few hundred square feet, and opened up this whole west side of the house into an expansive cat haven. We'd added multiple built-in shelves for them to climb, beams coming off the ceiling where they could walk over everyone's heads, hidey-holes—everything and anything to create a veritable feline playground. They had beds and toys galore, of course, and we'd built a cabinet along one wall to hide the row of litter boxes. It served a dual purpose—we had beds on top so they could hang out. Then of course we'd added seating for the visitors, both seats as well as beanbag chairs, floor pillows, and—my personal favorite—a couple of those cool Moon Pod chairs. Each wall was a different color— hot pink, orange, green, or blue—and we had colorful pillows scattered around the room.

I loved the atmosphere we'd created. It was super fun and comfortable. And today, crowded. Adele was cleaning. Again. Someone must have kicked more litter around—probably the kittens. Adele was funny. For all her skepticism about our visitor today, she wouldn't stand for the café to look less than perfect, no matter who was coming. One of our volunteers, Harry, a retired widower who I thought was sweet on Adele, was also there. He held a feather toy high in the air, coaxing Murray, one of the more playful cats, to jump for it. Although I noticed him sneaking adoring gazes at Adele whenever she wasn't paying attention. Which she usually wasn't, as long as there were cats around.

Ethan and Val were in the corner trying to coax one of the more shy residents, George, out from under one of the cabinets. The more curious cats were out and on alert. They even looked anticipatory, many of them watching the activity around them intently. There wasn't usually this much activity all at once. We spaced out visitors so as not to stress the cats out and to make sure they were showing up at their best for our guests, and we usually only had a few people working in the café at once depending on the amount of appointments we had.

Grandpa sat on one of the couches, looking comfortable and relaxed in one of his cat café outfits. Every time he worked the café or did any publicity for it, he had a special wardrobe. Sometimes it was silly and fun, like his cats-in-yoga-poses button-down shirt. Other times it was more serious. Today he'd gone the more serious route, with jeans and an Arm the Animals T-shirt—the classic design, featuring a cat with a hand grenade. He wore a JJ's House of Purrs hat over his bushy white hair. Seventy-five years young and he had more hair than most guys I knew in their thirties. I loved that he was a walking advertisement for the café. He hardly ever set foot outside without some branded gear, even when he was in private investigator mode.

"So do you have a spiel ready for our guest?" Grandpa asked Adele.

Adele shot him a look over her shoulder, but couldn't keep the smile off her face. "Yeah. It'll be all about how we do actual rescue work here and not just dress up in fancy clothes and have parties."

"Adele. You better not," I warned.

"Is that really all they do?" Val asked, absentmindedly rubbing Ethan's arm. He responded by taking her hand and squeezing it tight. They were still in the cutesy, in-love stage of their relationship. They'd gotten together after Val and her loser husband Cole Tanner had split up last year shortly after I'd returned home. Val had moved back to Grandpa's, and we'd all ended up living together like one big happy family. Or hippie commune. Some days I wasn't sure which it was.

"It is *not* all they do," I said with a sigh. "For the last time. What are you all doing hanging around in here anyway? She's not coming for a while."

"Just spending time with the cats," Grandpa said defensively. "Is that not allowed?"

"Maddie, I have to go." Mish poked her head around the door. She looked distracted at best. "Is that okay? I'm sorry."

Adele was about to protest, but I shot her a look. "It's fine, Mish. Harry's here. And everyone else, apparently. We're in good shape."

"Thanks." She left through the café entrance, the door slamming behind her.

I wondered again what was up with her, but the doorbell to the main house rang abruptly, followed by a banging on the door. Then it crashed open, and my friend Damian Shaw's excited voice rang through the house.

"Maddie! Leo! Are you guys here?"

I opened the French doors and frowned at him. "What's up?"

Damian's eyes were wide and shining and he motioned manically. "Come with me. You have *got* to see this."

Chapter 3

Grandpa and Val followed me into the living room.

"What's going on?" I asked Damian, just as he was getting ready to shout again. Damian owned the Lob-stah Shack down the street, right next to the ferry. He'd bought it just under two years ago, and no one thought a guy from the Midwest would ever be able to make a go of life on a northeastern island. But he'd proven them wrong—his business was doing awesome.

Damian shook his head impatiently. "Can't explain. You've just gotta come with me. Come on." He grabbed my arm. "What are you waiting for?" he asked, looking back at Grandpa.

"I'm invited?" Grandpa asked, amused.

Adele came in with JJ tucked under her arm. "What's all the ruckus?" she asked, looking annoyed.

"We're going out for a few minutes. You too," Damian said to Adele. "Let's go." He dragged me toward the door.

"Damian, I really don't have time—" I started.

"It won't take long. Promise."

Adele looked at me and shrugged. "Whaddaya say, boss? Can I get a break?" she asked with a smirk.

"Just go," I muttered, pushing her ahead of me and grabbing JJ's leash off the hook next to the door. He squeaked excitedly—he loved going out—and waited for me to put it on.

Grandpa, Val, Damian, Adele, JJ, and I piled into Damian's Honda Pilot, the only vehicle with enough room for all of us, and headed toward town. We were lucky—Grandpa's house was in a prime spot, right down the street from the ferry dock in Daybreak Harbor, the largest of the island's five towns. The house had been in our family for generations, which was why I had to step in last summer when he was being pressured to sell it after Grandma died. I had grown up in that house. There was no way I was going to see it torn down and replaced with a transportation center. We'd kept it, and now I'd come full circle to live there again with him.

But instead of going all the way downtown, I was surprised when Damian made a sharp left past the ferry dock and down the winding road that broke off into a fork. Stay right and we'd head into the downtown area. Left kept us on the coastal road. A minute later, we pulled into the Daybreak Island Marina parking lot.

I immediately saw what he was so excited about. You couldn't miss it. One of the largest boats I'd ever seen was parked at the dock. The word *boat* didn't actually apply. It was more like *yacht*. Or *cruise ship*.

Growing up where we did, my sisters and I were no strangers to ocean life and the people who lived it. They had beautiful boats and spent much of their time on the water, they took sailing trips around the world or competed in regattas, or ran businesses involving cruises or charters. In the summers our parents took us to Newport, Rhode Island, where the *really* fancy boats and people congregated. I used to walk around the marina and try to guess who would own a boat three times as big as Grandpa's house, which was pretty darn big.

And only once or twice had I seen a boat like this. The sleek, black yacht parked at the dock had to be five stories tall and spanned as long as the entire marina and dock combined. The back of the boat had an outdoor kitchen on the third level that rivaled my mother's remodeled indoor one, her pet project from a couple years ago and her pride and joy. We all piled out of the SUV and stared at it.

"Wow," Grandpa said. The king of understatement.

"Whose boat is that?" Val asked Damian, her eyes wide. "That's amazing."

Adele sniffed, crossing her arms over her chest. I knew what she was thinking—more "fancy" people who swarmed to our island every summer. She called them "elites" and held mostly contempt for their fake tans and excess amounts of money. In addition to working at the café, Adele's recent slate of jobs included taxi driver. If it were up to her, she'd never drive a tourist anywhere—her services would be saved for the locals. The rest of us were happy to take whatever money the tourists wanted to leave us, because it would make our winter months easier. When only residents were on the island, it was hard to run a business.

"This is what ya dragged us out here for?" she scoffed now. "To gawk at some rich person? I got work to do." But despite her tone, I could see her sneaking looks at the boat when she thought we weren't watching her.

Damian could barely contain his excitement. "Of course. This is the biggest boat that's ever docked here. I asked the marina guys." He pointed vaguely in the direction of the office. "Who do you think it belongs to?" he asked me.

I laughed. "Why do you think I would know?"

He shrugged. "You know everything."

"I appreciate the sentiment, but I think you're exaggerating." I walked toward the dock, hoping for a close-up and maybe a glimpse of whomever owned this thing. "It's probably a CEO of some financial company. You know, a banker. Or a tech company," I said over my shoulder.

Val fell into step next to me. "You think? Not some famous person?"

"No way," Damian said, pulling up on the other side of me. "It's gotta be someone cool. Not some stuffy CEO."

"I'm just guessing like the rest of you, but I think boats like these are typical for the businessmen types. It's either boats or private planes." I went to step onto the dock, something I'd done hundreds of times over the years, but a piercing shout stopped my foot in midair.

"Hey! You can't go on this dock."

Val and I both turned to see some guy standing at the door of the yacht club, glaring at us. He wore cargo shorts with lots of pockets, a ripped T-shirt of Def Leppard's *Hysteria* album cover art, and a bandanna over what I guessed was thinning hair. Sunglasses covered his eyes, but from the downturn of his mouth, he wasn't happy.

He took a few steps closer. "I said, you can't be on this dock," he repeated, louder.

Never one to back down from a fight, I gave him my own steely gaze. "Why not? It's a public dock."

"Yeah, well, this boat is private property. Meaning the owner doesn't want people anywhere near it. Capeesh?"

I resisted an eye roll. Apparently our rich visitor had a bodyguard. A clichéd Italian one, at that.

"Who's the owner?" Damian asked eagerly.

The guy gave him a look.

Damian shrugged. "Had to ask."

"Get going," the *Sopranos* wannabe suggested.

I sent him an exaggerated salute and turned away. Val tried not to giggle. He watched to make sure we all went back to the SUV and even then, lingered on the dock in front of the boat. Guess he didn't want us to try to come back.

"What'd he say?" Adele asked, louder than necessary. She hadn't ventured forward with us, not wanting to look interested, but she was always looking for a fight.

"Nothing. Come on," I said, putting my arm around her shoulder and turning her back to the truck.

"What was that about?" Grandpa asked. He hadn't even bothered to get out of the passenger seat where he was doing something on this phone. Probably trying to get the story about the yacht from his police contacts. JJ wasn't impressed either. He sat on Grandpa's lap, more interested in watching the water than seeing the boat.

"Some uptight lackey protecting his paycheck. I have things to do anyway. Let's go home." It wasn't like we didn't have our fair share of rich and famous people who came to the island in the summer. We didn't need to know who this one was.

"You're not as impressed as I am," Damian said, a little pouty. I took pity on him. Guys from Ohio probably didn't see a lot of fancy yachts.

"I'm not," I admitted. "I mean, it's cool to look at, but I don't need the 'tude."

"True. Let's go. I'll take you home. Thanks for humoring me."

I climbed back into the third row of seats, leaving the middle for Adele and Val. As we drove back toward our house, my mind started to wander. I needed to put some makeup on, do one last sweep of the cat area to make sure everything was in place, and probably a bunch of other things I was forgetting right now. I was jolted out of my thoughts as Damian slammed on the brakes right before we got to our driveway. "What do you suppose is going on there?" he asked, pointing ahead.

I stuck my head out the window. There were two cars blocking the street, stopped on either side. I recognized one of them as Mish's Lexus. And she was engaged in some kind of shouting match with the driver of the other car—a BMW X5 with rental plates.

"No idea," I said. "But that's Mish. I thought she left a while ago?"

"She did," Adele said, sitting forward in her seat. "But looks like she didn't get far. Who the heck is she yelling at?"

Damian leaned on the horn. Mish didn't even glance at us. Still focused on whoever was in the other car, she leaned out of her driver's-side window and flipped Damian off without even looking at him. Then she said something else to the other driver, gunned the car, and took off down the street.

"Wow," Damian said. "She seems mad."

Grandpa shook his head. "People can't control their tempers."

"Probably a road-rage incident," I said. "Mish has the same, er, driving habits as me." Which meant aggressive and with little patience.

"That's why it's good I'm your grandfather," Grandpa said dryly. "I can fix all your tickets."

Damian waited for the other car to move, since it was on our side of the road. Finally it did, with a squeal of its fancy tires. But instead of taking off down the street, the car pulled a U-turn (referred to as "bangin' a u-ey" in

Bostonian) and parked haphazardly on the curb in front of our house.

I frowned. Why was the person Mish yelling at coming to our house? To register a complaint or something? Was it about the café? I hoped not. That was the last thing I needed.

Damian pulled into the driveway. I willed everyone to hurry up—I had to wait for Val and Adele to get out before I could fold over the seat and climb out of the back. Damian glanced back at me. "Who is that?"

"I have no idea," I said.

Val climbed out and moved her seat for me. I hopped out of the car as the BMW's driver's-side door opened.

A woman stepped out and beamed at us. She wore a red tank jumpsuit with five-inch snake-print stilettos—Jimmy Choo, by the looks of them—and her strawberry blond hair looked like it had been blown dry at a salon just prior to her arrival. It hung in long, relaxed waves over her shoulders. Silver earrings peeked out from behind it, catching the sun and sending off glints of light. I immediately recognized her from the photos I'd seen online and from her Instagram account.

She continued to smile at us, sparkling white teeth shining out of an oversized mouth that somehow still worked with the rest of her features. "Hi there. I'm looking for Maddie James," she said, walking over. "I'm Jillian Allen."

Chapter 4

Crap, was my first thought as Val, Adele, and Grandpa all turned to look at me. It was only 2:35! She was almost a half hour early. I hadn't even put my makeup on yet. But I had to make the best of it.

My second thought was, *Why was one of my volunteers shouting at our guest?* It was not the best way to make an impression. I'd have to talk to Mish. She probably had no idea who she'd been yelling at. Residents got cranky with tourists all the time, especially on the roads.

And my final thought was, *I love her outfit!* I stepped forward and pasted a huge smile on my face. "Jillian! Welcome. I'm Maddie James. This is my grandfather, Leo." I raised my eyebrows at Grandpa, who jumped into action.

"Ms. Allen. Leo Mancini. A pleasure," he said, offering his hand.

"Grandpa Leo is one of the co-owners of the café," I added. "You'll meet my other business partner, Ethan Birdsong, later."

Jillian enthusiastically clasped his hand between hers

and shook it hard. "I am *honored*. Truly. This is an incredible place you have here. With an amazing mission."

"Thank you," Grandpa said modestly. "We enjoy doing it. And it's all Maddie's doing. And this is my other granddaughter Val, and our shelter manager, Adele."

"Lovely to meet you all," Jillian said. Her smile was so wide I was afraid her face was going to crack. "And Jo will be just as delighted if she ever gets off the phone. Jo!" she shouted at the car.

I turned to see the passenger door open and a tiny Asian woman stepped out. In contrast to Jillian, she wore simple leggings and a tunic, and flat sandals. Giant sunglasses covered her eyes, and her bangs brushed the top of the glasses.

"Hi," she said, unsmiling. "I'm Jo."

"Jo Sabatini. My second-in-command," Jillian broke in, coming over to clasp Jo's arm. "She couldn't wait to see the place either."

"Well. We're delighted you're here," Val said.

"Delighted," Adele echoed, although she sounded anything but.

Jillian smiled at her, then her gaze fell on JJ, still in Adele's arms, and she gasped. "And—oh, my goodness— is that JJ?" She stepped forward, smooshing his face between her hands. He let out an unhappy squeak. "I've been dying to meet this little orange face! My day is truly made." She gave him a kiss on the top of his head.

Adele took a step away, moving JJ just out of reach. I poked her in the side.

"Well, let's get you inside. Right this way," Grandpa said heartily, bounding up the porch stairs with his keys in his hand.

Adele muttered something under her breath.

"If you don't have anything nice to say," I said in a

low voice, then marched past her, turning to look behind me. Damian still hovered half in and half out of the driveway, blocking traffic, intent on what was going on. I frowned at him and inclined my head in a *Go!* signal. He gave me another pouty face, then backed out of the driveway and sped up the street. I hurried up the stairs after Grandpa and Jillian, Val and Adele on my heels.

"Thank you for this tour," Jillian was exclaiming to Grandpa, also trying to look over her shoulder at me and not fall in her giant heels. "I'm a bit early, I confess, but I was so excited to get here I just couldn't help it. If you need a few minutes . . ."

Grandpa pushed the door open and held it for us.

"No, sorry, we had to run a quick errand," I said. "It's all good. Right this way." Without thinking, we'd let them in on the residence side of the house, which would prevent them from getting the full experience of walking into the café through the shop. Too late now. "Have a seat," I said, motioning toward the couch. "I'll be right with you."

Grandpa took that as his cue and sat down next to Jillian, engaging her in some kind of conversation about the weather and the island. Jo sat on the chair across from them and pulled out her phone. I hurried upstairs, checking my face in the bathroom mirror. I dabbed on some under-eye concealer and freshened up my eyeliner. It would have to do.

I turned to leave the bathroom and almost bumped into Val. "Why was Mish yelling at her?" she asked in a low voice.

"I have no idea. Maybe it was a traffic thing, like Grandpa said. I just hope she didn't connect the dots that Mish works here. Are you coming back down?"

"Yeah, in one second. I want to change. Adele is

checking to make sure there's no mess in the café," she added.

I smiled. "Of course she is. See you downstairs."

"I'm going to go help Ethan in the café. He's got a lot going on out there. You're gonna be impressed."

"I always am." I took the steps two at a time, skidding to a stop at the bottom. Grandpa and Jillian were laughing together on the couch. Grandpa really had a knack with people. It was why he'd been so good at his job. Aside from being a great detective, he also really could relate to other humans.

"Sorry about that," I said, joining them in the living area. "Are you ready to see the café?"

She clapped her hands. She certainly seemed exuberant about everything. "Ready? I can't wait! Right, Jo?"

"Coming," Jo said, standing.

Jillian jumped to her feet. "Are you coming, Leo?"

Her flirty tone made me glance at Grandpa, who reddened. "Right behind you," he said.

I led her down the hallway to the French doors separating the cat area from our living space. As I paused to open the door, I felt her breath on my neck, she was so close to me. She wasn't kidding about being excited about the cat café.

"So, I saw you were having . . . words with someone outside. Did something happen?" I asked casually as I pushed the door open. I was a second late to glance over my shoulder, so I missed her expression.

"Ah, you saw the conversation I was having when you pulled up." Jillian smiled apologetically. "I'm sorry about that. I hadn't expected to see Mish here. I'm afraid she isn't all that fond of me right now."

My mouth dropped. I'd expected her to say, *I accidentally cut that woman off when I was trying to find the*

house and she got upset, or something along those lines.
I hadn't expected her to *know* Mish.

"Wait. How do you know—" I began, but she squealed
with excitement and pushed past me into the café.

"Oh. My. Goodness. Would you look at this place?"
She turned in a slow circle, a huge smile on her face. She
reminded me a bit of Mary Tyler Moore in the opening
credits of her show. All she needed was a hat to throw
into the air.

Adele stood by the window, almost like she was standing guard. Harry was still there too. He was rolling around
on the floor with one of the kittens, which was kind of
adorable.

Jillian thought so too. Her squeal of delight sent a
couple of the cats running for their favorite hiding places.
"This is precious!" she cried, pulling out her cell phone
and snapping a photo before I even registered what she
was doing.

Harry turned, his face turning pink with embar-
rassment. As soon as Jillian turned away, I shrugged.
"Sorry."

Jillian didn't seem to notice his discomfort. "I am *in
love*." She walked slowly around, her head turning this
way and that, the overwhelming smell of her perfume
tickling my nose. "This is the most adorable place I've
ever seen! And this *house*. However did you find this phe-
nomenal location?"

"It's Grandpa Leo's house. It's been in our family for
generations." If she had done her research, which I'd assumed she had, she would've known that. Every piece that
had been written about my café clearly mentioned the fact
that it was part of my grandfather's house, which to me
was the better part of the story.

Grandpa didn't seem to mind explaining. In fact, he

loved talking about the house. "My great-grandfather built it," he said.

"Oh, that's right!" Jillian gave herself a gentle head smack. "I swear, I don't know where my brain is lately. I do remember reading that. Look at these little loves. How many cats live here?"

"Currently we have fifteen. I can introduce you to them."

"I'll do the honors." Grandpa winked at me and led them around the room, introducing each cat—the ones who weren't hiding, anyway—and told her their backstories, or at least as much as we knew of them. Sometimes we had little to no idea where these poor cats came from or what their lives had been like before they found Katrina and, ultimately, us.

I watched the tour, letting Grandpa do his thing. He really loved the café and in this role he really had gotten used to schmoozing people. It had resulted in a lot of adoptions and donations.

And he was doing a bang-up job today. Jillian certainly seemed impressed. Jo didn't have much of an affect, but at least she'd taken off those glasses and seemed to be paying attention. I watched her absentmindedly nuzzling kitty heads as she listened to Grandpa.

Jillian made all the appropriate commentary and *oohed* and *ahhed* over our residents, but I noticed she didn't touch any of the cats aside from JJ. It struck me as odd, but I chalked it up to a fellow rescuer recognizing that cats who had come from precarious situations could be skittish and she didn't want to stress them out. And, people were different. If it were me, I'd probably be picking them all up and snuggling with them.

Or, she might not want to get cat hair on that fancy outfit. I hated to think it was the latter.

If Grandpa noticed, he didn't blink. All those years of being a cop—that whole poker-face thing. Although he did seem quite curious about our guest. I caught him watching her a few times when he thought no one else was looking, and I couldn't figure out what he was thinking.

Once they'd met all the cats who weren't hiding, Grandpa led her into the store, where Jillian shrieked in delight over the JJ-branded clothing and promised to buy a few items to bring home to all her friends.

"She's . . . excited," Adele said under her breath as we watched from a bit of a distance.

"I'll say," I said. "But that's good, right?"

"Depends on how much of her you can take," Adele said. From her tone, it was obvious that she couldn't take much more. "That other one is quieter. I prefer her."

Once Grandpa finished his spiel, he turned back to me. "Did you want to show our guests the food part of the café?"

"Sure," I said, turning to them. "Ethan, my business partner, really wanted to have a separate café area where he could cook and bake and have more room for people to sit, either while they're waiting to visit with the cats or even if they just need a place to hang out. So we transformed the garage into his dream café. It's right outside here."

I started to lead them out the side door so I could take her to the garage, but Jillian stopped, turning in a slow circle, hands out like she was waiting for a vision to come to her.

I glanced at Grandpa. He shrugged.

"Is something wrong?" I asked.

"No! On the contrary." She dropped her hands and turned back to me. "This is an amazing place you've got here. I am *so* impressed. And you and your Grandpa." She turned to him and beamed. "Could you two be any cuter?"

Grandpa's face reddened a tiny bit. I, on the other hand, wasn't quite sure where this was going.

"Thanks," I said. "So, the café is this way—"

"In a minute." Jillian still had that giant smile on her face, looking from me and Val to Grandpa and back again. "How would you all feel about a fundraiser?"

Grandpa and I looked at each other. "A fundraiser?" I asked. "You mean, do we have any planned?"

"No. I mean, how would you like to have one? In partnership with our organization?"

I cocked my head at her, trying to keep up. "We're always looking to raise money."

She nodded vigorously. "Of course you are. I can help."

"But where would it be? In New Jersey?" I asked doubtfully. Why would people in Jersey want to support my little place?

Jillian's face suggested I was slow. "Of course not. Here on the island. As soon as we can put it together. And I have a great idea on how we can get people to really pay attention to this place, this event."

"Pay attention?" Grandpa asked.

"Yes, pay attention!" She swirled her hands in the air as if trying to conjure up some sort of special audience. "Get them here. Get them donating. Make sure they are in a *giving* frame of mind. I can't imagine a better place to invite my most generous donors to be part of."

I still wasn't really following. "So you want to have a

fundraiser and you'll back it? Meaning what, like you'll invite people here? It's kind of a long trip for your typical guests, right?"

"Oh, honey. That doesn't matter at all. We've got lots of secret weapons in our pocket." She winked at me. "So what do you say? You want to hear my proposal?"

Chapter 5

I was always open to hearing a proposal, and this meeting, while a bit odd, intrigued me. "I would love to," I said, glancing at Grandpa.

He nodded. "Fine by me."

"Excellent." Jillian glanced around. "Shall we have that coffee? I have a bit of time before my next appointment. And I'm *starving*." She patted her flat stomach. "And I can't wait to try some of the goodies you've been telling me you serve here."

"Right this way." I glanced at Adele, silently questioning if she was coming. She shook her head. I led the way out the side door and over to the garage/café, Grandpa and Val trailing behind us, Jo bringing up the rear. Before we even reached the door, I caught the whiff of something delicious. When I went inside, I had to do a double take. JJ sat on the counter, almost like Ethan had trained him to wait for us. He looked adorable. And of course, he gave his welcome squeak when we walked in.

The presentation Ethan had put together was even better. He had outdone himself for this visit. When we'd all left with Damian, Ethan had been barefoot and in his usual shorts and T-shirt. Not only had my tall, lanky, surfer-dude business partner changed into khakis and an actual button-down shirt—notable because it was all Val could do to get him to wear pants instead of Bermuda shorts in the middle of a Daybreak Island winter—but he had also taken steps to tame his unruly red hair by smoothing it back into a ponytail. He'd trimmed his beard too. I did catch a glimpse of flip-flops when I peeked behind the counter, but hey. Otherwise it wouldn't be Ethan.

He'd pulled together a couple of the café tables and laid out a spread of baked goods, as well as a cheese-and-cracker plate, a bowl of olives, and some fruit. He was quick. We hadn't even been gone that long.

Val, who was serving coffee, caught my eye and winked.

"Hey, Ethan. The place looks amazing," I said. "These are our guests from the League—Jillian Allen and Jo Sabatini."

Ethan turned solemnly from the counter where he was slicing into an obviously still-warm chocolate cake and stepped forward with his hand extended. "Ms. Allen. Ms. Sabatini. It is such a pleasure to meet you both. Ethan Birdsong."

Jillian, eyes wide as she took in the food, stepped forward and grabbed his hand. But instead of shaking it, she reached over and hugged him so hard I could see his eyes pop. She wasn't terribly tall, but her heels were so high she came up to Ethan's neck, an impossible feat for most people.

I watched Val's eyes narrow a bit.

"You are an angel from heaven," she declared, stepping back after a beat too long. "I may just have to hire you away as my personal chef."

Now my eyes narrowed, but I recovered before she turned back to me. "Ethan's wonderful," I said. "This is the second business we've owned together. And he's just as good at business as he is at baking. And you met my sister Val earlier."

Val lifted a hand in a quick wave.

"Of course. Do you work here too?" Jillian asked Val.

"Sometimes," Val said. "I have my own business, though. I'm an event planner."

"An event planner?" Jillian threw back her head and let out a delighted peal of laughter. "Another sign this was meant to be! That is wonderful. Well then, you need to sit down for this conversation too." She pulled out a chair and, without waiting for anyone to join her, began filling her plate with cheese and crackers.

Val looked at me, clearly wondering if Jillian was a little off her rocker. I honestly wasn't sure. I went to help Val with the coffee. "How do you take your coffee, ladies?"

"Just black, thank you. I can't afford the extra calories of the cream and sugar, as delightful as it is." She smiled ruefully. "I'd rather have one of these." She plucked a muffin from a plate piled high with them. "Is this berry?"

"Blackberry," Ethan said with a smile. "One of my specialties."

"Mmm." Jillian bit into it and nearly swooned.

Jo asked for black as well. I poured their coffees and set them down, then poured one for Grandpa and me. Ethan didn't drink caffeine, and Val was cutting back. She said coffee after two in the afternoon made her too wired.

We all sat. I was pretty hungry too and nibbled on some crackers and olives.

"So what do you think of the café?" Ethan asked.

Jillian swallowed her muffin. "I think it's absolutely the most delightful thing I've ever seen. The location, the mission, the people . . . I just can't get over it."

"That's wonderful," Ethan said, glancing at me.

"In fact, I love it so much that I had an absolute brainstorm while I was meeting all your residents," she explained to Ethan. "Which I was just about to elaborate on for your colleagues here."

"Really. Please, go ahead," he said.

She paused to take another bite. When she'd finished chewing, she said, "I want to formally propose partnering with you all on a fundraiser for the café. A *major* fundraiser." She sat back, triumphant, waiting for our response.

"Wow," Ethan said. "Really? You mean in New Jersey?"

"Oh, no, no, no, darling." Jillian laughed. "You two have the same brain," she said, winking at me. "No, right here on the island! I mean, the setting is half the charm, right? That's what I was saying to Maddie and Leo before we came out here. No, we can do big things here. *Big* things."

"How big?" Grandpa asked. "This is a small island."

"Of course, but it's summer. Which means it's, what, four or five times the typical residents?"

"At least," Grandpa said. "We have about twenty-thousand year-rounders. Over the summer, we get up to two hundred thousand plus."

"He used to be the police chief," I said.

For the first time since her arrival, Jo looked interested. She glanced at Grandpa from under those long bangs, her chin-length bob tilting with her head.

"That's impressive! And so is that number. The best part, they all have money." Jillian winked. "And I can get them to open their wallets. Trust me, the café and your rescue operations will be catapulted to the next level after one of our fundraisers. You'll be able to expand, think about a franchise, help more animals, whatever you want. Even think of dropping a JJ's in Boston, maybe?"

Ethan and I looked at each other. We did have the same brain, and I could tell we were running the same kinds of pros and cons. "In Boston," I said thoughtfully. "That would be something to think about. And a more straightforward model." I shook the thought off, focusing on the immediate matter. "But how does this fundraising idea work? Does your league typically run fundraisers for other places?"

"Sure we do," Jillian said. "We take a small percentage for our staff and expertise, of course, but the majority of the money is yours."

I could hear Adele's voice in my head: *Of course they take a percentage. All they care about is money.* I pushed it out. "What kind of an event do you have in mind?"

Jillian smiled. "Big. An auction. Silent, live. Celebrity guest. I actually have two in mind."

That made my ears perk up. "Celebrity? Like what kind of celebrity?"

"Like, an A-list actor. Maybe two." That wink again. It was starting to annoy me. I wanted to ask her if she had something in her eye.

It wasn't far-fetched; there were a lot of celebrities who summered on Daybreak Island. It was a coveted spot for sure. But I wanted to know exactly what I was getting. "Sweet. Who are they?" I asked.

She reached over and patted my hand. "I can't give away all my aces before we have an agreement, can I?"

"Agreement?" I repeated.

"Well, I want to know if you're in before we go any further. We need to agree that we're doing this, and have some ground rules for how we'll do it, don't you think?" She turned to Val. "And this is where you come in. You can plan the party! It will be a complete family affair—how great is that? The marketing materials will practically write themselves."

Val's eyes widened. "Me? Really?"

Jillian nodded vigorously. "Yes, you. You're exactly what we need. You know the island, the right venues, the best food, right?"

"Well, yeah, I suppose I do," Val said.

"Great. Then it's settled. I can bring staff over to help you. How many people on your team?"

Val was in the process of hiring her first full-time employee, although she hadn't yet found anyone who fit the bill. She'd been enlisting our youngest sister, Sam, when she needed someone. Sam was still "finding herself," and was currently doing so back at our parents' house, which meant she needed money. And Val's summer slate was booking out fast, to her delight, and she'd realized she couldn't do it all on her own.

"One full-timer and a couple part-timers," Val said breezily.

"Oh, you'll need an *army,*" Jillian assured her. "Which I can get you. Jo's team will come out. They are event pros. And it's just another way to support the local economy on this beautiful island! And who can resist so much family doing so many good things, working together, making a difference? I mean, really. The story is perfect."

I had to agree with her. As a creative and a business-woman at the same time, I was always looking for the best way to market ourselves. "I love it," I said.

"I had a feeling you would. So. We're settled, then?" Jillian asked.

"I'm good," I said. "I think it's a great idea." Katrina, for one, would be delighted to hear this. Especially given the budget cuts, which I knew were really bothering her. She already used a lot of her own money to help the animals, and she didn't even make that much. And she was currently dealing with a situation where a bunch of dogs had been rescued from a bad situation and needed foster care, which meant she'd need to give the foster parents funds to care for the dogs.

Yeah, she would be ecstatic.

I looked at my sister. I could tell she wasn't completely sold on her role in this venture, but she would take my lead.

She hesitated for a second, then smiled. "I'm in."

Jillian looked at Grandpa.

"How can I resist? I'm in too," Grandpa said.

"Wonderful! Ethan? Shall we make it unanimous?"

He looked at me and Val, then nodded. "Sure."

"Fantastic!" She clapped her hands. "You won't re-gret it!"

"Jillian, this is great. I don't know what to say," I said.

She plucked an olive out of the bowl and popped it into her mouth. "Say you're ready to get to work, because we're going to have a shindig! So how does two weeks from tomorrow sound?"

Val's eyes widened and she looked at me. "Two weeks?"

Two weeks from tomorrow. Today was Friday, so she wanted to have the event on a Saturday night, which made sense. Still, it was a heck of a short time. I'd put auctions together before, and we'd begun planning almost a year in advance.

Jillian nodded. "It would have to be. The name I have in mind has some other commitments as the summer goes on. Gotta grab the time while we can! You understand, I'm sure."

"Yes, but I'm not sure we can pull this together in two weeks," Val said. "We need a venue, which book out really fast this time of year. And you mentioned an auction—we need to find donors, and pick up items, and package them—"

"I told you, I'm bringing you a whole staff," Jillian assured her. "Don't worry. I just need you leading. I don't need you executing. We have people for that."

"We do have a lot of people who can help," Jo said reassuringly.

"But still," Val began, but I cut her off.

"We'll be fine. Val is just a perfectionist." I patted her hand. "This is an awesome opportunity. We get that. We'll get it done. I'm confident." I hoped I was doing a good job of convincing her. I wasn't sure I was totally convinced myself, but one thing I'd learned in all my years in business is that you never pass up an opportunity that could save you years of marketing efforts. And bring you a lot of extra funds. In our case, it meant helping more animals, and I wasn't about to say no to that.

Grandpa, smooth as usual, jumped in. "We have a big family. There's enough of us that we can get anything done when we put our minds to it," he said, seemingly to assure Jillian, but I think he was really assuring Val.

"Well, that's lovely. I mean, family is the most important thing, right?" Something crossed her face as she said it for a split second, a look that was so far from the bright, beaming smile and jubilation she'd displayed ever since she'd arrived. But just as quickly, it was gone.

"You bet," I chimed in, willing Val to stay quiet unless she had something positive to say. While her confidence had definitely been building since her divorce and her subsequent foray into an already-successful business venture—and of course, Ethan—she still had some doubts that reared their ugly head along the way. And Val was definitely not the fake-it-till-you-make-it type. She was the kind of girl who, in high school, had studied the lesson beyond whatever lesson she was getting tested on, just in case. She had to be one hundred and ten percent prepared for anything before she felt confident enough to try it. In a way, starting up this business on the heels of her divorce had been a huge step for her. I'd almost expected her to say she needed to go to project-management school or take event-planning courses or something that would make her feel like she had the ability to do the job. I'd been super proud of her for jumping in and figuring it out—and she was excelling and really making a name for herself.

This was another one of those tests. And I really needed her to be up for the challenge.

"You know I can always help," Ethan said. "I may not be the best waiter, but I can at least manage the catering."

Val was beginning to realize she was outnumbered. And I knew my sister. The last thing she would want would be to give off a vibe that said she wasn't sure of herself. I watched her make the mental decision, square her shoulders, and finally nod. "You're right. I'm being a worrier. We'll get this done and we'll rock it."

Jillian sprang to her feet so fast she almost toppled the tray of muffins in front of her and pulled Val into a hug with an eardrum-shattering squeal. JJ scrambled for cover under the table. "I am *thrilled*! You are going to have such a name for yourself after this. All of you. I just. Cannot. Wait!" She stepped back and nodded in satisfaction, looking at all of us. "This island is never going to forget this party. Trust me."

Chapter 6

With all that settled, Jillian left in a flurry of kisses and promises to call me later with "next steps," along with a lot of winking and vowing that we were going to be floored by what she had in store for us. "We must have a planning meeting *ASAP*," she pronounced, squeezing Val's hand. "I can't wait to meet your team!"

Jo followed her out, looking a little embarrassed by her colleague as they departed.

It took a few minutes for the dust to settle. I had a lot of energy, especially for my business and related activities, but the whirlwind that was Jillian Allen had left me kind of exhausted. I also felt like I had to keep Val motivated and enthused. Once I heard Jillian's car pull away, I turned back to my crew. They all still sat at the tables Ethan had pulled together. JJ was on the floor under Grandpa's feet, snoozing. Apparently he was the only one not fazed by the task ahead. Adele had come out, too, to see what the rest of the visit had been like, and was eating her way through what was left of the olive platter.

"Well," I said brightly. "She certainly is full of energy."

"A little overwhelming," Val said.

"I might call it intense," Grandpa mused, spearing an olive with a toothpick and popping it into his mouth. "And certainly oozing with self-confidence."

I got the sense he didn't exactly mean that as high praise. "She'll be fine. She wasn't *that* bad," I said, although my protest sounded weak even to my own ears. "And she has to be intense. She's got a huge job running the fundraising for that place."

"She didn't even pet the cats!" Adele protested. "What kind of cat lover doesn't even play with the cats?" She sounded so dumbfounded by the idea that I almost had to laugh. Adele would be perfectly happy in a world with more animals than people. Perhaps no people at all.

But of course she'd noticed that too. It had been odd. I mean, that's why people came to cat cafés, right? Granted, Jillian was here on other business, but she was still an animal person. "Look. If she's a bit hands off, well, that's fine. She's charged with the schmoozing to bring in the money and the big donors. Whatever works for the good of the animals, right?" It certainly wasn't my style, but in some of these bigger organizations, that was just how it was. And as long as they were doing good work, who was I to judge? "We have a huge opportunity here. To raise a ton of funds and get our place noticed all along the eastern seaboard. Can we all try to have a bit more enthusiasm about this?"

Val looked properly abashed. Adele did not. Grandpa kept eating. "You know I'll do whatever I can to help," he said finally, around a mouthful of cheese and crackers. "I think anything that benefits the animals is a good thing. Sometimes we have to put aside our own personal preferences."

Thank goodness for Grandpa Leo.

Val cut herself a piece of Ethan's yummy chocolate cake. Let the stress eating begin. "So I guess I should start planning something," she said. "Do you know where you want to have this thing?"

"It would be cool to have it at the café," I said thoughtfully.

"No. Sounds too fancy for that," Val said around a mouthful of chocolate. "Even if it is a good idea, I don't think she'll go for it. My guess? She'll want the fanciest venue on the island. Something waterfront."

"Will we be able to get something on such short notice?" I asked.

"See?" Val pointed her fork at me. "I'm not the only one who thinks we're jumping the gun here. These are the kinds of things we need to think about before we run off like fools counting our money."

"Relax," I said. "I'm sure she's got connections. She said she was here on other business, so she must be somewhat familiar with the island. She probably already has something in mind."

"She's staying at the Paradise," Grandpa said. "Why not have it there? It's fancy."

We both looked at him. "How do you know that?" I asked.

He shrugged. "I asked her when we were talking. While you were upstairs."

"Did you also ask her how she knows Mish? Because she totally avoided that question when I asked her."

Grandpa shook his head. "I didn't ask that."

"Well, I'd love to know why Mish was yelling at her," Adele said to me.

"The Paradise is a good idea," Val said thoughtfully. "And Dad knows them over there. Maybe he can pull some strings to get us a date." She looked at me. "You really think we can do this in such a short time? I don't want to get overwhelmed and mess everything up."

"You would never mess it up," Ethan and I said in unison, then both burst out laughing.

"I know we can do it," I said firmly. "Listen, there's times when you just gotta go big or go home. Think of it as our big break—both the café and your business. It could get us all national publicity. Definitely will raise our profiles on the island and beyond."

She ate her cake slowly. "Okay. I'll give it my all. I hope this Jo has got lots of staff to spare."

I tried to tamp down my impatience. I was nothing like either of my sisters. I was the typical oldest, driven and motivated and, yeah, a bit bossy. Val was the middle child, and she'd taken the middle-child syndrome to a bit of an extreme by becoming the stringent, rule-following, type-A personality in the family, next to my dad. If something went off plan, she lost her mind. And Sam was the woo woo, yoga-worshipping hippie who took my mom's personality a bit to the extreme. I often found myself impatient with both of them. "I'm sure she does. She's probably getting them ferry tickets as we speak."

"Okay. But if something goes horribly wrong, don't blame me." Val had to get that parting shot in.

"Oh, come on." I dismissed her concerns with a wave of my hand. "What could go wrong? It's gonna be great. By the way, who do you think the celebrity she has in mind is?" It was actually many small rescue organizations' dream to have a celebrity endorser. That was the kind of thing that brought you lots of recognition and funding.

"Maybe it's Chris Hemsworth." Val swooned a little. Ethan cocked his head at her. She pretended not to notice.

"Ooh, maybe. I think he likes animals. There was that magazine cover with the cute dog. But I would peg you for a Robert Pattinson fan, no?" I was teasing her; my sister had an unnatural obsession with the *Twilight* movies. Something she'd neglected to mention to Ethan, given the smirk he was trying to hide.

"You're a jerk," Val muttered, twin circles of pink standing high on her cheeks.

At least she'd stopped obsessing over the party. "Now"—I clapped my hands together and stood—"I need to go call Katrina and share the good news. She'll be over the moon. Don't you think, Adele?"

"I do, actually," Adele said. "She needs money."

Finally, a positive. And from Adele, too. Cheered, I put my arm around her and led her out of the café back toward the house. JJ, apparently also tired of the conversation, trotted along behind us. "I know she's been worried about funding. That's why I want to do this. Even if the money comes into the café and not the town directly, we can supplement her work."

Adele nodded. "I agree." She pushed the door open, letting JJ through first. He raced in with a squeak and made a beeline over to the kitten area. He loved kittens. Whenever we had babies, he spent most of his time with them. Like a surrogate dad or something. It was adorable.

She waited for me to step inside too. "Seriously, no one asked what that scene in the street with Mish was about?"

"I started to but she sidetracked me. She did say she knows Mish, though." Which troubled me a bit. If they knew each other, why hadn't Mish mentioned it when I told her about Jillian coming here? She had seemed a bit off after that. I thought of her stalking around out front on her phone, looking angry. Then she'd come back in, hadn't said two words, and left as soon as possible. But was back here half an hour later, when we came back from our marina outing with Damian.

"She *knows* her?" Adele asked. "And she didn't bother to mention it? How on earth would she know her?"

"I don't know." I needed to ask her. Whatever it was, I didn't want any problems that could get in the way of a successful event. I told Adele as much. "If she has a conflict or something with Jillian, we'll need to be mindful of that with the schedule."

Adele cocked her head at me. "You serious, boss? These cats need a lot of scooping. As you well know."

"I do know." I smiled. "And I'm still pretty good with a litter scoop. But that looked like a pretty intense conversation. And I was all the way in the back seat."

"Yeah. Something was going on out there, no doubt about it." Adele pursed her lips and shook her head. "But that's Mish. She's got a bit of a loud streak anyway."

"Mish?" I was surprised.

"Yes, Mish," Adele returned. "She's got a temper, that one."

"Really? You've seen it here?"

"Not with the cats or anything. But yeah, she got peeved at a delivery guy one day and almost took his head off when she realized we were missing part of our order. And her own people at the store?" Adele whistled. "They fall in line for sure."

"How do you know this?" I asked. "I've been friends with her since we were kids and I didn't know she had that kind of presence."

Adele smiled. "You forgot I have three jobs. Well, at least until you hired me on full time. Which reminds me, I need to quit something. But the kinds of jobs I have? You hear things. Can't really hide much on this island. Plus, she was a cheerleader. Aren't they usually pretty loud?"

Chapter 7

Adele and I called Katrina together to give her the good news about the fundraiser. She was over the moon as we predicted, despite how distracted I could tell she was. Apparently her new Lab charge wasn't the most well-behaved, which was probably why she had been running loose on the streets.

With the good news communicated, I left Adele to her new shelter-manager duties and headed up to my room, JJ on my heels. It was about time for his afternoon nap. Luckily, I'd cleared the afternoon of appointments so we didn't have to worry about time constraints, since I hadn't known what to expect with Jillian's visit. So now I had some free time to start thinking about our big plans.

But first, I wanted to call Lucas. Today had been such a whirlwind, I hadn't even had a chance to check my texts after I'd texted him earlier.

He had. I smiled a little. Things had been going so well with us I still had to pinch myself most days. I was *not* used to it. I'd never had a relationship like this. Before Lucas, I didn't have the best track record. I tended to pick long-haired musicians who had a lot going for them in the sexy department, but not a lot in the maturity department. As a bonus, Lucas was a semi-longhaired, mature musician. It was like I'd created him out of thin air. And ever since we'd gone through a bit of a rough patch a few months ago, our relationship had gotten even better.

Wish I was there too, he'd said. *I'll be home early tonight. Hey did you hear about the giant boat in the marina??*

Laughing, I called his cell. When Lucas answered I could tell I was on speakerphone, which meant he was grooming.

"Hey babe," he said.

"Hey. You have someone on the table?" Grooming speak for *Are you giving someone a haircut?*

"I do, but he's easy. I can talk. How did it go today?"

"It was . . . interesting." I filled him in on Jillian—the weird thing with Mish, Jillian's fascination with the café, and her offer. "Val is a little skeptical of our ability to pull it off, but it's too good of an opportunity to pass up. Katrina needs the funds."

"Wow. That's impressive. She really thinks she can get that many people, huh?"

"She does. She sounds pretty convincing, so I'm willing to give her the benefit of the doubt. This Mish thing is bothering me, though."

"Yeah, weird that she knows her. Are you going to ask her?"

"Of course. Oh, and about the boat? I saw it."

"You did?"

"Yeah. Damian came over and dragged us all there. It's impressive. They have bodyguards and everything. They chased Val and me right off the dock."

"You're kidding."

I laughed. "No. But it's fine. You coming home soon?"

"Probably an hour or so. What do you want to do for dinner?"

"We can cook something here unless you want to go out."

"Staying in sounds good to me. I'll call you when I'm on my way."

I tossed my phone onto the bed next to me. JJ, who was napping on my pillow, opened one eye and glanced at me with a look that said *Can you be any more disruptive? I'm sleeping here.* I gave JJ a pat on the head and headed downstairs to the living room. The house was quiet. Grandpa was on the sofa, his feet propped on his old black leather ottoman as he flicked through the news stations on the TV. The ottoman made me laugh. It had been around since I was a little kid, probably years before that. It had rips and tears, and the wooden legs were scratched up from years of use. My mom had told me Grandma had tried multiple times to get rid of it, even going so far as to buy him a fancy new one, but he'd sent it back to the store in that stubborn, Grandpa Leo way he had, insisting that this ottoman had character and was as much a part of the fabric of this house as he was.

Grandpa glanced up when I came in. "What's going on?"

"Nothing. Want to take a walk to Damian's with me? I want to get fish for dinner."

"Sure," Grandpa said. "I can do the grilling honors. But I get to pick the fish."

"Sounds good to me." I grabbed JJ's leash and harness from the hook next to the door and got him ready to go. "How come you're not downstairs?"

When Grandpa wasn't working in the café, out walking, or playing cards with his friends, he spent his time down in his basement office. He'd opened his own private investigation firm after he'd finally retired from the police chief role just a couple years ago. He hated not being part of the action, and this kept him busy. It had also helped me out on many occasions. He never seemed to have a shortage of things to investigate.

It was good for him. He'd been devastated at the thought of leaving police work behind. Now he had two fulfilling careers and a house full of family. In some ways, his life was fuller now than ever before, with the exception of Grandma not being around. I think at first he was just trying to fill the hole both she and his job had left behind, but now I liked to think he'd found happiness again.

"I have some work to do later, but I was taking a break." He held the door open for me, closing and locking it behind us.

"So what are you working on right now?" I asked as we headed down the street.

He glanced over with a small smile. "Why, you want to help out with some investigating?"

"If it's an interesting case," I said, only half joking. I did have a penchant for police work. I'd always been interested in Grandpa's job when I was younger. And since I'd been back, I'd been involved in more police investigations than I'd ever imagined.

"It's about a piece of property." Grandpa then muttered something about the traffic inching along our street. Summer on Daybreak. The weather was beautiful, the beaches were divine, the food was amazing, and the traffic was horrendous.

"Property?" I wrinkled my nose. "That sounds boring."

He didn't reply. We walked in silence for a bit, people hanging out their car windows pointing to JJ. It cracked me up—people thought cats on a leash were the funniest thing.

Just as we reached Damian's, Grandpa turned to me. "So how are you feeling about this woman, Doll?" he asked. That had been his nickname for me since I was a baby. Val had been so jealous when she was little that she'd insisted he give her one too. A better one, she'd said. So he'd started calling her Muffin and Pumpkin and other sweet-themed names. She'd gotten tired of them pretty quickly and decided she was happy to be just Val.

"Jillian?" I shrugged. "I'm excited. This is a great opportunity for the café. I'm going to take advantage of it."

"As you should. Just don't get in over your head. Or let your sister get in over hers. You know how she gets."

I wondered why he was asking, but Grandpa was probably just being Grandpa and trying to look out for me. "I do know," I said. "And we all promised we'd help her if she needed it. You too, right?"

He nodded. "Of course."

"Cool." I pulled open the door to the fish-market side of the Lobstah Shack. JJ squeaked with excitement. He knew he'd get a treat. Or perhaps an entire meal. One never knew with Damian.

While the restaurant part of the shack had a number of people enjoying dinner, the fish market had only one customer. And from the looks of it, a disgruntled one. Even from halfway across the room, I could tell the suit worn by the guy standing at the counter was pretty darn expensive. There wasn't a wrinkle to be seen on the back, and I wondered how he wasn't sweating. It was already pretty warm out for early in the season. And his tone of voice as he addressed the poor teenager behind the counter was not happy.

Grandpa and I glanced at each other and made a joint

telepathic decision to hang back so as not to embarrass the poor kid, who was already red-faced. He kept looking behind him as if he were waiting for someone to swoop in and save him.

"Sir, I'm sorry," he kept trying to interject, but the guy wasn't having it.

"I just don't understand," I heard him say, with exaggerated incredulousness, as if whatever the kid was saying was the most absurd thing he'd ever heard and he had to drive the point home. "How do you not have *fresh, wild-caught salmon*? This is a *fresh fish* store. On an *island.*"

The kid opened his mouth again to try to explain. I was about to go help him when Damian hurried out from the back, wiping his hands on a towel. He glanced over, saw me and Grandpa, and gave us a nod before he turned to the guy.

"Is there something I can help you with?" he asked. He made a *get out of here* motion with his head to the kid, who gratefully escaped to the back.

"I certainly hope so," the guy said. "I need fresh, wild caught salmon."

"I'm sorry, we don't have any at the moment—" Damian began the same explanation the kid had tried to make, but the guy cut him off too.

"I don't want to hear any lame excuses. Do I have to take my business elsewhere? I *need* that salmon!" His tone had taken on a wild desperation, as if the world as he knew it might end if he left this store without that particular fish.

Grandpa raised his eyebrows at me. I shrugged. Entitled tourist. The majority of people who summered on Daybreak Island were a completely different league of humans than the year-round residents. They had lots of cash to play with and they wanted a ritzy place where they could do so. They'd pretty much taken over, building giant homes that overshadowed the legacy, simpler homes out here. A lot of the mom-and-pop shops had gone away, to be replaced by high-end food and coffee shops and fancy boutiques. Part of me appreciated that, as Ethan and I were hoping to open our own higher-end business on the island—a juice bar—but I could sympathize with the feeling that this little island had become a playground for the rich to use and abuse any way they wanted, then leave the residents here in the winter months to clean up the mess.

"Sir." Damian spoke in a firm, even tone that I'd never heard before. It actually shut the guy up. I was impressed. "We don't have fresh, wild-caught Atlantic salmon because there's a shortage right now due to overfishing." He launched into a complicated diatribe about too many fishermen, dwindling populations, and climate change that also impressed me. Clearly he was taking this new part of his business extremely seriously.

The guy huffed and puffed a little but didn't seem to have any comeback to that. Instead, he muttered, "A fish market with no fish. That's the dumbest thing I've ever heard." And he turned and stalked out, not even glancing at me and Grandpa as he passed us.

I caught a glimpse of his perfectly tanned (and possibly Botoxed) face, slicked-back hair, and shiny blue tie and felt an instant dislike. Once the door had slammed shut behind him, we moved to the counter where Damian stood, shaking his head with a rueful smile.

"He was a sweetheart," I remarked.

"But you handled it well, son," Grandpa added.

Damian shrugged modestly. "Rich people," he said. "The world revolves around them, don't you know that?"

He came around the counter to give me a hug and shake Grandpa's hand, and rub JJ's ears. "So what can I get for you?"

"Fresh, wild-caught salmon?" I suggested.

He gave me a look. "You're funny."

Grandpa perused the selection in the case. "How about the swordfish?" he asked me.

I nodded. "Sounds good to me."

Damian gave JJ some fish in his special bowl and went to wrap our purchase. He handed us our bag. "There's more in there for JJ too. Good to see you guys," he said. "Maddie, we'll have to get together soon. I want to do a new marketing campaign for the fish market."

When Damian had first started his business, I'd offered to help him out a bit. Now I'd become his unofficial publicist. "Sure," I said. "Come by whenever. Hey, did you ever find out who owned that fancy boat?"

Damian shook his head. "No. Everyone's abuzz about it, though. And it's kind of making people mad. Cutting down on available space for other boats."

I laughed. "Rich-people problems. I wouldn't be surprised if it belonged to that guy who was in here."

"You know, neither would I," Damian said.

Chapter 8

"Mads. Have you seen Ollie?" Lucas stuck his head around the door where I was organizing shelves with my new JJ merchandise the next morning.

It was Saturday—exactly two weeks until the fund-raiser—and I'd woken up super early with thoughts of the event and all the associated tasks running through my head. Between marketing it and helping Val plan it, the next two weeks' activity would be fast and furious. Plus, I needed to make sure I had extra JJ merchandise on hand, if we were going to be getting more publicity and more traffic. I wondered if Jillian's team included a professional marketer or two and made a mental note to ask. It was only me and one of my volunteers, Clarissa, doing social right now for the café, using Instagram as our main marketing channel.

"Right here." I pointed to the floor where Ollie literally lay on my feet. He had become my second sidekick pretty much since day one when Lucas had brought him home, and he was less likely to forego hanging out with me for napping, unlike JJ. He was a sweet dog, a pit bull mix whom Lucas had rescued twice—once from a shelter, and most recently, last winter from his ex-girlfriend. Ollie was grateful to be here, and he loved everyone. He hung out with me when I worked, he went on walks with Grandpa, and he liked to be in the café when Ethan was cooking because Ethan always gave him snacks. He'd bonded with JJ so well it was like they'd grown up together. The two of them had become best buds. Ollie also liked to hang out with the cats in the café. As long as there were no cats that were terrified of dogs, I always let him. I'd wondered what it would be like introducing a dog into our house, but it had been seamless, like he'd always been here.

"I should have known." Lucas grinned ruefully and stepped into the room. "He barely cares about me anymore." Ollie wagged his tail, but didn't get up. I was getting a cramp in my foot, but didn't have the heart to move him. At least until I'd finished with these particular shelves. "I think he's more your dog these days."

"What can I say. Animals love me." I winked at him. "But that's not true. He adores you. Hey, what do you think of these?" I held up a new T-shirt I'd recently had made. JJ's face was on the front pocket, and the café sign with the name—JJ's House of Purrs—took up most of the back in sprawling script.

"Very cool." Lucas inspected it.

"I put a couple up online and they already sold. I'm going to get more made. I'm hoping when we start marketing the fundraiser, we'll get lots of orders." I folded it and placed it on the shelf. "We still hitting the beach later today?"

"You bet." Saturdays were super busy in the morning, and I had a full schedule with clients booked beginning at nine, which was awesome because it was still early June and we hadn't even hit full visitor/tourist capacity yet. Some of the sign-ups were my regulars, but there were other names I didn't recognize. But I was also making it a point to have some fun, and I planned to knock off early afternoon to take advantage of the weather. That's why I had a shelter manager, after all.

This was gonna be a good season. I could feel it. I was here with my family, I was helping cats, and best of all, I had Lucas. My heart was pretty full these days. And I wasn't taking it for granted for even one second.

"Cool. And then we can go out for dinner tonight since we cooked last night?" He cocked his head at me. "Why are you staring at me like that?"

I extracted my feet out from under Ollie and went over and threw my arms around his neck. "Because I'm happy."

I could feel him smile against my cheek. "Good, babe. I'm happy too." He hugged me a little tighter. Ollie came over to sniff around our feet. He never liked to feel he was missing out on something, especially hugs.

"I would love to get dinner tonight," I said when I'd finally let go. We hadn't had a date night lately because I'd been so busy getting the café ready, and his animal grooming business was really picking up the past few weeks. I ran a hand through my tangled hair. I hadn't even showered yet, but wanted to get some stuff done before we got busy. "You should get one of Ethan's muffins on your way out."

Before he could answer, the door to the café burst open, startling us all. Ollie stood up and barked. I usually didn't even unlock the door this early, but I'd gone outside for something and forgotten to lock it behind me when I'd returned. Lucas grabbed Ollie's collar before he could bound to the door.

I went over to see who was there. "I'm sorry, we're not—Oh! Jillian. What are you doing here?"

Jillian Allen stood in the doorway, grinning like the cat who'd eaten a canary. I hated that saying, but it was completely appropriate at the moment. She brandished a bag full of pastries and a giant box of coffee from one of the fancy island bakeries. Which immediately made me cringe, given that Ethan had been baking and making coffee all morning.

She shoved the bag at me. "Those are Danish. The special ones that your grandfather likes," she said with a wink. "Now. Do I have a surprise for you!"

The special ones my grandfather likes? How on earth would she know that? I glanced self-consciously at my ratty T-shirt and shorts and frantically tried to remember if I'd even brushed my teeth. I was not prepared for company, especially company like this.

"A surprise?" I managed, glancing behind me at Lucas, who looked equally as surprised at the way she'd barged in. "What kind of surprise?" I could hear a ruckus behind her, but couldn't see past her to figure out what it was.

She stepped aside and bent at the waist, sweeping her hand forward as if she were introducing the Queen of England. "Peyton Chandler!"

My mouth dropped open as my eyes traveled past her to the woman standing slightly out of sight, waiting for her introduction. At first I thought I had to have misheard her. Peyton Chandler was one of the renowned actresses in the business, known for playing cheeky roles depicting badass women, including a superhero in a popular series. She'd been around for a long time and had reinvented herself over the years until she'd reached her current peak—she'd been starring in the Catwoman franchise for the past five years. It wasn't an accident—Peyton's career had taken a turn toward roles with strong animal connections after she'd made headlines for her animal rescue efforts after a major hurricane blasted its way along the East Coast nine or ten years back. She'd been part of major efforts in New Jersey and New York, and had been commended for her hands-on work that had saved many cats and dogs—and even a ferret family.

She had bonded with one of her rescues, a rare flame point Siamese female who had been found drenched and bedraggled, floating on a piece of someone's house. No one had ever claimed the cat, so Peyton kept her, naming her Rhiannon in a nod to her obsession with rock legend Stevie Nicks and showering her with the best kinds of things money could buy for a feline, as well as constant companionship. Word was, Peyton and Rhiannon went everywhere together, and the cat had even starred alongside her human in a number of movies because Peyton had refused to have a stand-in. I'd also heard Rhiannon had her own dressing room on every movie set, as well as a personal chef and a part-time "petter"—someone who would sit and pet her during the scenes when Peyton was busy.

Needless to say, Peyton's doting on her feline friend had earned her a cult following in the rescue world, a whole other fan base than her typical Hollywood followers. Rhiannon had even gotten her own magazine covers a few times. And Stevie Nicks herself had paid tribute to the pair at a gala in Los Angeles a few years ago, where Rhiannon was invited to be the guest of honor.

And now Peyton stood on the threshold of my cat café, with the famous feline in her arms, smiling at me. I blinked, wondering if I just needed more coffee. But despite my disheveled appearance, I was excited about Rhiannon. I loved flame points.

Rhiannon hid her face in the crook of Peyton's elbow. She was a cool-looking cat, with big blue eyes and orange markings throughout her face, ears, and tail. Her paws were also orange. The rest of her body was white with a tiny glimmer of rust color showing through, especially when the sunlight through the window hit her fur. She wore a sparkly pink leather collar topped off by a little dangly paw-print charm. It fastened with a rhinestone buckle and was attached to a matching leash, which also had multiple matching paw-print charms dangling from the handle. I'd heard Rhiannon had her own clothing and accessory line. This must be part of it.

I did wonder why Peyton had chosen pink as her color. It seemed to clash with the orange. Personally, I would've gone for green. That was usually what I put on JJ. I liked to call him an Irish cat.

I'd met only one flame point Siamese before—a friend of mine in California had one. You barely ever saw them in shelters or rescue places. That was a fact for most Siamese breeds. They were fancy cats, and unless you had a bad breeder who was dumping cats they considered "defective," you usually didn't stumble across them in a rescue capacity.

Peyton swept past Jillian like the Hollywood royalty she was, stopping with a dramatic tilt of her head, sending her cascade of thick, blond hair tumbling down her back. She wore a simple black skirt and red silk tank top with a pair of open-toed Louboutins that literally made me drool. "Hello," she said, in that breathy voice that had caused many men to swoon, at least in her younger days. I wasn't exactly sure how old she was—she looked darn good for whatever age she happened to be—probably late forties, certainly past the typical Hollywood prime age. "I'm Peyton. It's lovely to meet you, Maddie. I've heard so much about this wonderful place. And this is Rhiannon."

I forced myself to stop gaping at her. "I-I'm honored to meet you both," I managed, feeling completely inadequate. "And this is, um. This is Lucas. My boyfriend," I added, jerking my thumb behind me at where Lucas still stood.

"Hello, Lucas." She smiled at him, that open, welcoming smile that sent her followers swooning.

"Great to meet you," Lucas said.

An impatient face loomed over her shoulder, nudging her forward. She sent a quick frown his way before turning back to me. "This is Chad Novak. My agent."

She stepped aside to reveal a man in an expensive suit with slicked back hair and what looked like a perpetual frown darkening his face. My eyes widened. It was the guy from Damian's fish shop. The one who'd been a complete jerk to Damian and his employee. He recognized me too. It took him a second, then I saw the recognition hit. He gave me a curt nod.

Her agent. Yikes. Nice guy. I wondered if he'd been acting that way on his own, or if it was an extension of her.

Another woman stepped in behind them. She was older, probably late sixties, judging by the lines carved around her eyes and mouth. Her silvery blond hair fell in waves to her shoulders, which were wrapped in a violet silk scarf.

"And this is Esther. My assistant. She comes with me everywhere," Peyton said with a little laugh.

"Hello. So nice to meet you all," I said, awkwardly reaching out to shake hands with Esther, who was closest to me.

"Someone needs to keep an eye on you," Esther said, and I got the sense she was only partly teasing. "Maddie. Lovely home." Esther shook my hand, thankfully, so it wasn't dangling in midair. Chad didn't bother.

"Thank you. And this is my sister Val," I said, as Val appeared, clearly curious about the crowd..

Peyton turned to her. "Wonderful to meet you. Peyton Chandler. I'm so excited to be here."

"We are too," I began, but Val's excited voice cut me off.

"Holy crap. It's Catwoman!" She stepped forward, clearly in awe, glancing at me as if to say *What the heck is going on here?*

Peyton laughed. "That's quite an introduction."

"Wow. This is . . . wow," Val said, a dopey smile on her face.

I'd never seen her starstruck before. I poked her.

Peyton pretended not to notice. "Jillian's told me about your family business and the great things you're doing. If you could show me around a bit, then we can do some photos?" She waved vaguely behind her.

I took a better look outside the door and my eyes widened. There were at least twenty people with cameras standing outside, ranging from video cameras to regular cameras. They were already snapping pictures, and as a flash went off it knocked me back to reality. I offered Peyton a weak smile, but she didn't even notice as she moved past me, her head turning from side to side as she took in the café. Chad followed, avoiding my eyes.

Lucas, thankfully, stepped in. "Right this way," he said graciously, and led her into the café.

I waited until she was out of earshot, then shut the door and turned to Jillian. "What's going on? Did I miss a memo?"

Jillian laughed. "You're so cute. No, you didn't. It's all me, I'm afraid. I had an absolute brainstorm this morning—and luckily Peyton was up for it. I asked her if she'd do a photo shoot at the café in anticipation of the event. And that's my other surprise." She paused for dramatic effect. "Peyton is our celebrity guest!"

My jaw dropped again. "For the fundraiser? You're kidding!"

"Nope." She grinned. "How much do you love me right now?"

I shoved at my hair. "That's amazing. Really. But I wish I'd had a heads-up. I'm not exactly ready for a photo session." I indicated my outfit. "Plus I have a full schedule of clients booked today, starting at nine."

She arched her perfectly shaped eyebrows at me. "Oh, please, Maddie," she said, waving me off as if I were a pesky fly. "You look fine. And your clients will get a glimpse of one of *the* biggest Hollywood names in history! This is a once in a lifetime! Peyton Chandler! I told you I had a surprise for you."

I wasn't really sure how to feel at that moment. I mean, of course it was supercool to say Peyton Chandler had showed up at my café and posed with my rescue animals. But I would've liked to be ready for it. The place, luckily, was clean, but I wasn't. Grandpa wasn't here, and I just felt unprepared.

"It's awesome, for sure. Did you know about this when we were talking yesterday?" I asked.

Jillian's smile faded. For the first time since I'd met

her yesterday, the bubbly, enthusiastic, sunshiny persona faded. "Really, Maddie. You have to be more flexible in this business," she said. "I'm offering you a shot at a lot of press and a lot of money. A thank-you would be nice. Now, if you want to get changed, I suggest you hurry up. Peyton has limited time, and we need to huddle for a planning meeting after the photo shoot. Jo is on her way over too."

I bristled, but luckily Lucas appeared next to me. "We'll be right back," he said smoothly, then tugged me out of the room and upstairs.

Chapter 9

Once we'd reached my room, Lucas pushed me firmly inside and shut the door. "What's that all about?" he asked. "I take it you didn't know they were coming? And . . . Peyton Chandler? Did you forget to mention that part?"

"Of course I didn't know they were coming! You think I'd be greeting a Hollywood actress looking like this?" I glanced down with some disgust at my T-shirt and shorts. "I haven't gone that far into crazy-cat-lady status. And no, I had no idea Peyton Chandler was the celebrity she had in mind. OMG. If I wasn't so flustered right now, I'd be over the moon about this."

"So . . . they want to do a photo shoot? Like now?"

"Apparently. And a planning meeting for the event. Jillian said yesterday she had a plan for the fundraiser and a celebrity endorsement, remember I told you? But I figured she'd tell us who she had in mind. And I definitely thought she'd tell me about something like this first! God. It's barely eight a.m.!"

"A photo shoot without telling you?" Lucas asked doubtfully.

"Yeah. I guess she likes to surprise people." I scrubbed my hands over my face. "I have to get ready. I have to find Grandpa. And Ethan. Can you help me track them down? Crap! I need to text Adele and tell her not to come until later. I don't even want to hear what she'll say about this." I shuddered at the thought. That would be a tirade about rich people to remember.

"Of course I'll help you," Lucas said. "Ethan will be right back. He went out to get some flour or something before I came in to the café to see you."

"Jeez. How do you know all this stuff? I never know where my family is. Okay. Grandpa may have gone for his walk. Hopefully he took his phone. I need something to wear." I felt quite frazzled right now. "And Becky! We need to call Becky. She needs to cover this for the paper!"

"Babe. Relax. I'll call your grandfather and Becky. You text Adele and get ready." He gave me a quick kiss. "Also, you look beautiful already."

"Aww. You're lying but thank you."

Lucas went off to try to get everyone together. I texted Adele and gave her the morning off, insisting when she tried to protest, and made her promise to come in at one. Then I went to my closet and started racking hangers, looking for something presentable yet not too formal for a casual morning at my cat café. After tossing half a dozen outfits out of the way, I settled on a sundress that I'd recently found in one of the new boutiques on the island and was saving for a date with Lucas. He'd promised to take me into Boston for a fancy dinner. I headed into the bathroom and cleaned up as quickly as I could, pulling my hair back in a ponytail and putting on the minimum amount of makeup I needed to look presentable. People would be looking at Peyton in the photos anyway—I wasn't naive enough to think otherwise—but I had to make the effort.

Fifteen minutes later Ethan was back, Grandpa was on his way, Becky was sending a reporter, and I had fixed myself up enough that I didn't feel awful about getting pictures taken. I gave myself one last critical glance in the mirror then headed back downstairs. Lucas had begged off from being in the photos despite my peer pressure to get him to join me. I saw him sneaking out the back door with Ollie once he knew that I was set.

When I got back to the café, Jillian was nowhere in sight. Peyton, Chad, and Esther were alone in there. Chad leaned against the wall right inside the doorway, texting someone. His jacket, much too heavy for the already-warm summer day, was tossed on the couch. Peyton sat on one of the floor cushions, snuggling with one of the cats. Rhiannon was still in her lap, and she didn't look too excited about her surroundings. Esther walked slowly around, admiring everything. Chad glanced up when he saw me come in. He must have done some mental strategizing and decided to ignore the fact that I'd seen him act like a jerk at the fish market and prove to me what a great guy he was. He turned on a thousand-watt smile that I could see right through.

"Maddie. So great to meet you and get to spend some time here. This place is incredible," he said, waving a hand around.

"Thanks," I said. "Are you a cat fan?"

"Of course," he said. "Love them. Wish I could have one, but there's allergies in my family. My oldest kid."

"That's too bad," I said.

We stood in awkward silence for a moment until his phone buzzed again. He turned his attention to the text. I grabbed the opportunity to wander over to Peyton.

She looked up and smiled. "This cat is so sweet," she said, and for a minute I forgot she was a celebrity. She just looked like someone who loved cats and relished spending time with them. "Esther, did you see this one?" she called to her assistant. "What's her name?" she asked me.

"Ashley," I said. "She is super sweet." I crouched down next to them to rub the cat's ears. "Does Rhiannon like other cats?"

Peyton smiled. "Sometimes." She rubbed Rhiannon's cheek with her finger. JJ, sensing a new cat, came over to sniff around her. Her ears went back.

Esther came over and knelt down, holding out a finger to Ashley, who sniffed it with interest.

"She likes the laser toy," I said, pulling one off a hook on the wall and handing it to Esther. I had laser toys hanging all over the café, an invitation for people to play with the cats.

"How do you use it?" Esther asked.

I showed her. Ashley shot out of Peyton's lap to chase the red dot. Esther laughed with delight. "This toy is amazing," she said to Peyton. "We must get one for Rhiannon."

Peyton nodded. "Where did Ashley come from?"

"She was an owner surrender," I said.

Peyton wrinkled that perfect, perky nose. I wondered if she'd had work done on it. "That makes me so mad," she said, but really she sounded sad.

"I know. But sometimes it's not because they're bad people," I said. "That's actually the case with Ashley. Her owner was old and had Alzheimer's. She had to go to assisted living. Which makes me sad that they aren't allowed to take their pets. I've always wanted to find a way to do something about that."

Peyton's eyes widened. "Me too!" She sat up straighter. "When I was little, my grandmother had a cat that she loved so much. It was a street cat she'd rescued who was all beat up. For years it was just the two of them. Then she got really sick and had to go to a nursing home because my mom and my uncle didn't want to take her on. And she wasn't able to take Marley. I know it's why she died so fast. She missed him so much."

"What happened to Marley?" I asked.

"My uncle ended up taking him. I basically threatened both him and my mother that if one of them didn't take the cat, I would never speak to them again." She grinned. "I was ten. And I also told them Gram would haunt them both forever. Guess it worked. And I guess it was easier to keep the cat than to take care of Gram. He ended up really liking Marley."

I laughed. "That's awesome. But yeah, sometimes it's because the person truly can't take care of the cat anymore. That's a sad story for everyone."

"You're right. It's the people who give up their pet because they're moving, or some other bad excuse. They don't do that to their kids. Why should it be any different for cats?"

She was passionate. I liked that. I grinned at her. "You're singing my song, sister."

Peyton looked like she was about to say something else when Jillian barged in.

"Let's go, everyone," she said in a singsong voice. "Your paparazzi awaits." She eyed me from head to toe. I couldn't help but feel she was judging my appearance now versus a few minutes ago and decided it really hadn't been worth the wait.

"We can start, but my grandfather is on his way back," I said. "He should be part of this."

"Of course he should!" Jillian exclaimed. "We'll make sure to get a number of shots of Leo. We're waiting for Marco anyway, right, Peyton?" She turned that intense gaze toward Peyton.

My ears perked up. "Marco? Like, Marco Moore?" I asked, looking from Jillian to Peyton, eyes wide. Marco was another A-list actor, and Peyton had been linked to him for years. He was hot. And another animal lover, which made him even more sexy. Marco Moore was coming to my café too? Suddenly this didn't seem like such a terrible idea.

"He will be here shortly," Esther answered Jillian. "Yes, Marco Moore," she said to me.

Peyton got to her feet. "I'd like to take a picture with her." She still held on to Ashley. "We should tell her story so she gets a home quickly."

"Love it," I said. "Yes, we can do that first."

"And we need photos of you and JJ. Where did he go?" We both looked around. He'd been there a moment ago.

"I'll find him," I promised. JJ was the real story. And very photogenic. He'd probably decided it was time for a nap.

I went to find him while Jillian went outside to herd the photographers in. He'd made his way into the kitchen, where he was on the counter eating what was left of someone's eggs. "Bad cat," I scolded halfheartedly. He squeaked at me.

I picked him up and returned to the café, where they were checking lighting and angles and all that camera-type stuff. JJ squirmed to be let down so he could investigate all the action.

"Just make sure they're careful not to let the cats out," I told Jillian. "How many photographers are there, anyway?"

"Well, there's one from our staff at the League, then Peyton's photographers. And a couple of media outlets that Chad promised exclusives to."

"Oh. Well, the local newspaper is coming," I said.

"They are?" She pursed her lips. "We'll have to see if that's allowed."

Before I could ask her what that meant, she'd moved away, calling out directions for different shots. It looked like we'd be doing this for a while since the crews had to work in shifts, given the size of the room. "I do have customers coming," I said, after what seemed like a hundred different shots with only the first crew. It was just about nine, and I was worried about keeping people waiting.

"Invite them in," Peyton suggested. "It's fine with me."

"Not part of the agreement," Chad muttered to her under his breath. He'd been sticking to her like glue the whole time, barely getting out of the shots. But I could hear him loud and clear, and once he realized it, he tried to backpedal. "They might not want their pictures taken. And they'd need to sign a release."

"Then you can ask Jillian to take care of that," Peyton said.

"I'll help," Esther said, shooting Chad a dirty look. This guy didn't seem very popular.

As if on cue, the door opened and a young guy with giant glasses stuck his head in. "Hey there. I'm Chip, with the *Daybreak Island Chronicle*."

Chad looked like his head was about to explode. "We only invited certain outlets," he said. "This one is not on the list. Jillian?" He spun around looking for her.

"This is the island paper," I said. "My best friend is the editor."

"It's fine, Chad," Peyton said with a barely suppressed

sigh. "We can't exclude the local photographers. That would be disingenuous."

Chad looked anything but happy, but he spun on his expensive Italian heel and strode over to Jillian to discuss all of this.

"Come on in, Chip," I said. "Meet Peyton Chandler."

Chip's eyes bugged wide. "Wow," he said, shoving his glasses back up his nose. "Becky didn't mention this part." He began scribbling furiously in his notebook while trying to fumble with his camera at the same time. I felt kind of sorry for him.

Grandpa Leo arrived. He scoped out the situation and slipped right into the fray. He was made for this. I, however, was already kind of tired. I didn't know how Peyton did it. I also didn't want the cats to get fatigued. And I was trying to keep an eye to make sure no one let any of them slip out the door as the photographers were switching off.

Jillian returned with a release form, and I went outside to talk to my first client about what was going on and to offer them a spot in the photo shoot. It was a local, an older woman named Avis, and she couldn't get inside fast enough to meet Peyton. Problem apparently solved. I anticipated it would be that way for most of my clients today.

While we were taking a quick break so Peyton's makeup person could powder her nose, Grandpa came over to me. "Isn't that the guy from the fish store?" he asked in a low voice, nodding to Chad.

I nodded. "Sure is."

"So who is he? He famous too?"

"Her agent," I said with an eye roll.

Grandpa raised his bushy white eyebrows. "Really."

"Yep. But her boyfriend is coming. He's . . . nice."

"Hmm," Grandpa said with a knowing look. "Nice, eh?"

"Nice," I said, a tad defensively. "He's another big actor. He's cute."

"I figured as much," Grandpa said.

Peyton wandered over while two new camera guys had an argument about who got the side-window lighting. "Mr. Mancini. This is just so wonderful, what you're doing here," she said. "I hope we get a chance to talk a bit more today after all . . . this." She waved at the cameras. I wondered if she actually liked the publicity part of her job. She struck me as low-key for as big of a name as she was.

Grandpa Leo blushed. "Why thank you, but it was all my granddaughter's idea," he said. "Maddie has been helping animals ever since she was a little girl."

Peyton smiled at me. "She definitely seems like the type."

"I hope you're enjoying your stay," Grandpa said.

"Oh, my goodness. It's so lovely here," she said.

"How did you get to the island?" Grandpa asked. "Did you fly?"

Peyton shook her head. "I have a boat. It's docked at the Daybreak Island Marina."

Grandpa and I slowly looked at each other, then back at her.

"The, uh, big black boat?" I asked, trying to sound casual.

Peyton nodded sheepishly. "I know, it seems like it's a bit big for this marina," she said with a laugh. "But I love it. I live on it when I'm not filming. I only have a small apartment out in Los Angeles otherwise. I love being on the water."

"That's a classy way to travel," Grandpa said with a nod.

"It's very nice. By the way, do you know where I might find some wild-caught salmon? Chad has been trying to find me some, but we've been striking out."

I had a sudden, hysterical urge to laugh. This whole scene was surreal. Peyton owned that insanely ginormous boat. And apparently Chad had been trying to find the salmon for her.

Before we could answer her, Jillian appeared in the doorway again, dragging someone behind her. "Here he is!" she announced. "The man of the hour!"

Marco Moore stepped into the room and smiled a thousand-watt smile directly at me. "Hi there," he said.

Chapter 10

Marco Moore was even hotter in person than he was on-screen. Up close, his sleepy brown eyes, shadow stubble, and messy brown hair seemed even more appealing. He wasn't very tall, but his wide chest and bulging biceps more than made up for it. I was kind of glad Lucas had left because I didn't want him to see me drooling.

Grandpa dug his not-so-subtle elbow into my ribs to jolt me out of my trance. I'd been starstruck for a few minutes with Peyton, but this was different. This was *Marco Moore*. In my opinion, way hotter than Chris Hemsworth or the vampire guy—who I actually thought wasn't hot at all. I don't know why Marco hadn't even crossed my mind when I'd been debating the celebrity's identity with Val. It made total sense. He loved animals too. He didn't star in movies with them like Peyton did, but he was well known for donating to a lot of animal charities and speaking out for animal rights. He'd even done a series of commercials for the ASPCA. He was a lot younger than Peyton, but they looked good together.

I shook off the stupid look I was sure was on my face

and stepped forward to shake his hand, hoping I sounded like the cool, savvy businesswoman I wanted to portray. "Mr. Moore. It is a true pleasure to meet you."

"Likewise," he said. His hand was soft and warm.

I could feel Grandpa staring at me out of the corner of my eye. He was going to totally make fun of me later but I didn't care. It wasn't every day not one, but two celebrities showed up at my café to take pictures with my cats.

"This is a great place you have here," Marco said, looking around. "I apologize for being late, but I had a quick call this morning I needed to take."

"Dude," Chip the reporter breathed. "Are you Marco Moore? From, like, *Flames of Eternity*?"

Ugh. Of all Marco's movies, that was my least favorite, a sci-fi flick that hadn't done all that well at the box office. I stifled a laugh. I needed to tell Becky she should assign a more seasoned reporter next time for something like this.

"I am," Marco said with a smile.

"Marco! Darling, over here!" Jillian called. "We need to get you powdered and ready to go. Peyton has been stealing the show."

"As she should." He smiled at Peyton, a quick, warm gesture, but he let Jillian lead him to the makeup artists stationed over at my front counter.

I needed to go outside and alert my next client. We were having them wait in the café, where Ethan had permitted the photographers to take pictures as long as our clients assented. When I peered inside, I could see the photographer in the café relentlessly shooting. A bunch of people were in there eating and drinking. I wasn't sure if they were clients, or passersby who had seen all the action and stopped in for a snack. Either way, it made me happy to see. I popped my head in and called for my next appointment, a young couple who was thrilled to be part of the shoot. Especially the wife, when she heard Marco Moore was there. I joined Ethan behind the counter so the photographer could get a shot of the two of us, then led the guest inside where Jillian waited not so patiently.

"There you are." She strode over and grabbed my wrist. "Let's get moving, shall we? The natives are getting restless." She indicated the waiting photographers, who were crowding closer to the door, impatient to get the show on the road. Maybe they were heading out on the next ferry. "Leo, JJ, come on!"

We let Jillian drag us into position. Then everything was a blur for the next couple of hours. I wondered how models did it for hours and days on end, with people moving them around, posing them, barking orders. In this case, they even started shoving different cats into our arms until I stopped that pretty quickly. Most of the cats had gone into hiding anyway from all the lights, the people, the activity. Rhiannon had been quietly going along with everything this whole time. I got the sense she was used to it. You barely even knew she was there.

Finally Chad sent the wrap-it-up signal to the crew. Once the bevy of photographers and poor Chip had cleared out, Grandpa came over and put an arm around my shoulder. "Well, that was fun," he said.

I studied his face to see if he was teasing. He certainly looked serious. "Yeah, it was good. A whirlwind, but good." I took a breath and looked around. Jillian and Chad were in the corner, heads together, having what looked to be a serious conversation. Peyton and Esther sat on the couch with JJ and a couple of the kittens, laughing at their antics. They seemed to be the only ones not exhausted from the whole ordeal. And Marco was coming my way.

I felt a rush of nerves and braced myself.

"Here comes your boyfriend," Grandpa teased in a stage whisper. I elbowed him.

Marco stopped in front of us. "Mr. Mancini. This house is gorgeous," he said. "I'm a huge fan of old houses and I know most of this is your private residence, but would you care to show me around? I'd love to see the whole house."

"Of course we can show you around!" I blurted.

Grandpa looked at me with an amused smile. "Absolutely," he confirmed. "This way." We led Marco through the French doors into the house. Grandpa launched into the whole story about his great-great-grandfather building the original, and how over the years each generation had expanded or remodeled to get it to where it was today. I was pleased that he especially loved the book nook on the third floor that Grandpa had built just for me when our family lived here when I was a kid.

"This is just awesome," he kept saying. "And the location. You guys are so blessed."

It struck me as a little odd that a major celebrity who was probably the co-owner of the giant yacht parked in the marina sounded wistful about our house, but hey, it was nice to hear, whether it was true or not.

"Have you guys ever thought about making this a bed-and-breakfast?" he asked. "Now *that* would be a draw. Cats, ocean, hospitality, and by the looks of your café outside"—he jerked a thumb in the direction of the garage—"an amazing chef. You guys would be booked solid all year long."

I cringed inwardly at the thought, but I could see Grandpa's wheels turning in his head at the suggestion.

"I think we have a full enough house at the moment," I said. "Right, Grandpa?"

He looked a little disappointed but nodded. "For now. I mean, you two couples will eventually get married and move out—I hope—and maybe then I can do it." He winked at me, but I still wasn't sure if he was kidding or not. Who knew Grandpa had such a secret entrepreneurial spirit? Then again, maybe it's where I'd gotten mine. I guess it was what kept him young.

But his comment seemed to please Marco. "I'd come stay here," he said.

This made me laugh. "Over that fancy boat you guys have? Seriously?"

Marco smiled. "The boat is nice. This place is homey."

"It sure is," Grandpa said, glancing at me. "We've made sure of it, even with my wife being gone."

"I'm so sorry," Marco said, his eyes clouding over. He didn't just sound like a guy offering trite sympathy—he sounded like he really felt bad for Grandpa. It made me like him even more.

"Thank you." Grandpa cleared his throat. "Well, we'd better get back. I'm sure people are looking for you."

Marco followed us as we trooped back down to the café. He went right over to Peyton. "You should see this house. I told them they should open a B&B," he said to her. "It's amazing. And the view is to die for."

"Is that right? Well, I'd come stay here," Peyton said, stroking the cat between her eyes. I could hear her purring even from where I stood.

"I already told him that."

"Then I'll make sure you two get the best room in the house," Grandpa declared.

Chad came over and paused in front of us. It seemed he was now trying to charm Grandpa. He reached out a hand to him. "Mr. Mancini. I didn't get a chance to meet you earlier. Lovely place you have here. Thank you for sharing it with us."

Grandpa shook his hand. "Thanks," he said.

Chad seemed to be expecting more. When he didn't get it, he mumbled something about a phone call and went back to the corner with his phone. I noticed Jo had also arrived and slipped in unannounced. She was busy on her phone, too.

Jillian, meanwhile, hovered in the wings watching everyone socialize. She seemed impatient now that the festivities were over. Finally she came over with that bright smile pasted on. "I'm so sorry to bother," she said, not looking sorry at all. "Peyton, Marco, may I have a word? Outside?" She inclined her head toward the window in case they needed a reminder of where outside actually was.

Peyton looked less than enthused. "Can it wait?"

"I'm afraid not," Jillian said, her smile trending more toward a grimace.

Peyton handed the kitten in her lap to Esther, who looked on disapprovingly as she got up and walked to the door. Marco didn't say anything, but followed suit. When he reached the door he glanced back at me. "It was a pleasure to meet you both, Maddie and Leo. I hope to see you again." He left, letting the door slam behind them.

Chad pushed himself off the wall from where he'd been texting again and went out after them.

Grandpa glanced at me. I shrugged. He turned to Esther, who still sat with the two kittens in silence. "So how long have you been working with Peyton?" he asked her.

"My goodness, I've almost lost track," she said. But the way she said it told me she knew exactly how long, down probably to the hour. "About seventeen and a half years. But I've known her since she was a little thing." She smiled. "She's family."

I rose, curious about what was going on outside, pretending to straighten cat beds and tidy up while I stole glances outside my window. None of them looked happy. Peyton wasn't saying much at all, just staring off into the distance as Jillian spoke. The window was open, but I couldn't catch much of the conversation. Whatever Jillian was saying, she was very passionate about it. She kept jabbing the air with her finger. Chad interjected every now and then. Finally Marco cut him off, said something and walked away. He got on a bike, fastened a helmet on his head and fixed sunglasses over his eyes, then pedaled furiously down the street.

A bike? Marco Moore was riding a bike around the island? It would be a mob scene if people caught wind it was him. I heard Jillian call after him, sounding frustrated, but he ignored her and vanished from sight.

I turned my attention hurriedly back to my tasks when I saw Jillian and Peyton coming back toward the house. Peyton trailed slightly behind. Chad went to a big black car and climbed into the driver's side. When Jillian and Peyton came in, they were both all smiles, though.

"Well," Jillian said brightly. "Are we ready to get down to business? We have a planning meeting to do and Peyton doesn't have much time. And when these photos drop on our site later today, we're going to have an outpouring of interest in people coming here for the fundraiser, so we better have a good plan!"

"Sure. Let's go into the kitchen," I said, motioning them to follow me.

"Jo, come on," Jillian called.

"Esther? You coming?" Peyton asked.

Esther and Grandpa had been chatting this whole time. They looked like they were enjoying each other's company. It was nice to see. Grandpa worked too much. He missed Grandma a lot.

"Of course," she said, and stood.

Grandpa looked a little disappointed, I thought, but he rose too.

"You're coming too," I said, looping my arm through his. "You're part of the event planning team, after all."

Chapter 11

I excused myself to go get Val out of the café to join us. She'd retreated out there during the photo shoot to help Ethan, although I imagined she would rather have stuck around to see Catwoman in action.

I stuck my head into the café. "I need you," I said when Val looked up from the table she was wiping. "We're going to start talking about the event."

She finished what she was doing, then tossed the rag behind the counter. "I'll be back," she told Ethan.

He saluted her with his mug. "Have fun."

"I can't believe they showed up without telling you first," Val said as we crossed the driveway back to the house.

"Tell me about it," I started to say, then paused when I heard a voice. An angry one.

"No, I won't reconsider. Peyton, we discussed this. You are going to do it, period. Over. End of story." Jillian.

I put a hand on Val's arm to tell her to stay quiet, then crept to the side of the house and peeked around. Jillian and Peyton were on the back porch and Jillian was right up in her grill.

I ducked my head back around before they could see me in time to hear Peyton respond, just as furiously but with a lot more composure. "This idea that I'm here to do your bidding? It's going to stop. Mark my words."

I heard the back door slam and hurried back over to Val. "Come on," I said, pulling her inside after me.

"What was that about?" she asked.

"I have no idea." But it sounded like Jillian and Peyton weren't the best of friends. Was this a continuation of whatever they'd been talking about with Chad and Marco?

But by the time we walked through the house to the kitchen, Peyton and Jillian were back at the table with Grandpa, Jo, and Esther. Jillian's thousand-watt smile was back in place and Peyton was laughing at something, and I wondered if I'd imagined the whole conversation.

"There you girls are!" Jillian turned to us, beaming. "I can't wait to start planning!" She pulled out an iPad. "So, what do you have for us so far?"

Val pulled out a chair, glancing at me as if to say *What am I supposed to have??*

"She's got a planning team," I said, sliding into the seat next to Grandpa. "She's already pulled them together. Right, Val?"

"Yes. I have a three-person planning team, and some other people available to help on the ground, if needed. And of course, Maddie will advise."

Jillian tapped on her screen, making notes. "Okay. Jo, how many people are we bringing out?"

"I have about twelve people who will work the event," Jo said. "The first shift of five arrive today to help with planning, the rest will be here next Thursday. They will be your on-the-ground team. They'll help with soliciting and collecting the auction items, get everything packaged and looking good, help with the decorations, hire the people, work the event itself."

"And they are all *fabulous*," Jillian added helpfully.

"Great," Val said. "My sister and my mom, who are on my planning team, will also help with the auction items."

"Lovely. We need an auctioneer too. Jo, can you look into that?" Jillian asked.

"Hold on," Val said before Jo could respond. "I already have someone for that role."

"Great!" Jillian looked up. "Who?"

Val glanced at me with a smile. "Leopard Man."

Grandpa laughed and high-fived her. "Atta girl," he said.

"How fun!" I clapped my hands. "He'll be great at that. And people will come just to see his tail!"

"Who?" Jillian asked, looking perplexed. "What tail?"

"This guy who lives on the island. He's . . . very well known. And he loves cats," Val said.

"Well, that's wonderful," Jillian said. "How much experience does he have? And what do you mean, *his tail*?" She looked from Grandpa to me, a small smile on her lips, waiting to be clued in to the joke.

"Oh, he doesn't have *any* experience," Val said. "He's always wanted to do it, he said. And he's a character. He'll be great at it. He wears a tail with his best outfits," she added, not even trying to hide her grin.

Jillian stared at her, the smile fading. "No experience? My dear, that's a *skill*. It requires *expertise*. You can't just have someone try it because they think it will be fun. Especially not for an event like this one!" Her eyes were as wide as saucers. She looked like Val had just told her they were going to have severed heads as a main course.

I covered my laugh behind a cough.

Val shrugged. "I want him. He's going to be great."

They stared at each other. A showdown. I had to admit I was proud of Val for standing up to her and taking the lead on this.

"I'm sure it will be great," Jo broke in smoothly. "Local color and all. We can give him some tips."

I wanted to high-five her. She might not have much affect, but she seemed reasonable.

"I agree," Peyton said. "He sounds delightful. I can't wait to meet him."

Jillian did not look happy at all, but she apparently decided to not make a big stink in front of the whole group. She pursed her lips and turned back to her tablet. "We'll discuss it later. Have we made any progress with a venue? How about hotel accommodations for out-of-town guests? I would expect that I can get about two hundred here. Maybe more, but it is short notice." She took a sip of her coffee, tapping on her phone with her free hand to check something. "Yes, two hundred, maybe two fifty." She swiped the screen clear, then looked expectantly at Val. "What are our options?"

"We were talking about the Paradise," Grandpa said. "Where you're staying. At least for the event. We can figure out the accommodations once we settle on the event location."

"The Paradise would be perfect," Jo agreed.

"Yes. They have a lovely outdoor area with a gazebo," Jillian said. "It would be an excellent location."

"The space can hold a lot of people too," Val said. "I can see if they can fit us in." She hesitated. "It's pricey, though. What's our budget?"

That was a great question. I didn't have the funds in my tiny little cat café budget to spend forty thousand on a venue. And I still wasn't sure what kind of money Jillian thought she could raise for us. Not that I wanted to use it all on a venue.

But Jillian swatted away the question with a flick of her hand as if she were batting away a pesky mosquito. "Not to worry. We have a fund specifically for backing events like this one, for smaller outfits with potential. After all, it's when we help each other that we all make the most difference, right?"

"Right," Val agreed. "So that means . . ."

"The pricier the better. That means we can charge more per ticket," Jillian said. "A fancy location, an A-list celebrity . . . and her person." She winked at Peyton, who smiled a bit at the reference to Rhiannon being the real draw.

"How much exactly will the tickets be?" I asked.

Jillian smiled at me. "I'm still debating, but I'm thinking a thousand a head," she said, so casually that I almost thought I'd misheard her. "So if we did two hundred people minimum, that would be two hundred thousand dollars. Of course we'd recoup the fees for the venue in our twenty-five-percent cut, but with Peyton's endorsement I think we could even work out a better deal than that. What do you think?" She looked at me as if for approval.

Val stared at her, eyes wide, before turning to me. "Wow," she said.

I ignored her. "Sure," I said, trying for the same breezy attitude to show her that fundraisers that pulled in a grand a ticket were something I was definitely used to. I could see Val's mouth literally hanging open in my peripheral vision.

"Good," Jillian said. "Then we're on the same page. Oh, and I almost forgot!" She jumped up and went to where Rhiannon still lay cuddled in Peyton's lap. I thought she was going to take the cat or at least pet her, but instead she grabbed the leash attached to her collar and held it up triumphantly. "See this? This is what we'll be giving away at the event. People are going to go *crazy* for them."

"Careful," Esther said, removing Jillian's hand from the leash. "You're jerking her neck."

Jillian, for once, looked properly chastised. "Sorry," she muttered.

"Yes, we'll be giving away a version of this leash-and-collar combo." Peyton looked at Jillian. "You're getting the color adjusted, right? And we're doing something about this." She touched the little charms that hung from the leash. "It's not an ideal design."

"They fall off quite easily," Esther added. "I lost one just this morning."

"Yes," Jillian said. Her tone had a touch of frost to it now. "I'm expecting the new shipment today. I had them overnighted, just to make sure. This is one of the prototypes they sent us," she explained, turning to me. "The color is a bit off. We asked for them to make it less of a rose pink, and more of a bright pink. Peyton likes to make a statement. Also, the glitter is a mix of gold, silver, and rose gold. Peyton likes only silver glitter."

"I see," I said. It looked fine to me, but I guess Peyton could afford to be picky if she was endorsing something.

"It's fine, but it's not the shade I want," Peyton said. She turned to me with an apologetic smile. "I'm picky about Rhiannon's brand. It's been fine-tuned over the years."

"You don't need to explain to me," I said. "I get it. JJ has a brand too."

Jillian ignored our sidebar. "So, should we have a

formal meeting with the venue, then?" she asked Val. "We'll need to get it held quickly."

"I can see if we can meet them tomorrow," Val said.

"Great," Jillian said. "Now. Let's talk decorations. Peyton, I'm assuming you want to stick with the brand colors?"

"Yes. The *right* ones," Peyton added.

"Understood. I'll let you know as soon as I have the leashes and collars. I'm glad we ordered the different prototypes to make sure we understood the colors in person. Now we know." Jillian made a note. "I think we need to plan one more pre-event," she said thoughtfully. "Something to really get people jazzed. Peyton." She turned to her. "What do you think of doing a meet and greet here at the café? You and Marco?"

Peyton tilted her head to one side, thinking about that. The rest of us waited with bated breath. That actually sounded like an awesome idea. We could sell tickets at the meet and greet. My marketing wheels were already turning. And if Rhiannon was there . . . cat lovers from all over would rejoice.

"I would do that," Peyton said finally. "Marco would too. On one condition." She looked at me, her face serious.

"Sure." I leaned forward, trying to anticipate her ask.

"Can I go play with the cats for a bit longer while you all finish here?"

I grinned. "By all means," I said. "That was easy."

Chapter 12

Twenty minutes later, Grandpa dispersed the meeting. I think Jillian was giving him a headache. Val went back to the café. Esther and Grandpa went back to see what Peyton and the cats were doing, and I walked Jillian and Jo outside to Jillian's car. I noticed as I stepped out onto the porch that my litter delivery had arrived. All four hundred pounds of it. I had to order my supplies in bulk since we were, well, an island and even Amazon couldn't just appear at the click of a button. So once every quarter I got a ton of cat litter—the forty-pound bags—so I didn't have to worry about it for a while. The only problem was, I needed to store it once I got it, which meant Grandpa's man cave would be full of litter. And lugging around all those bags was never fun.

"What a productive day," Jillian proclaimed, when we got to her car. "This event is going to be *fabulous*. I can feel it. Right, Jo?"

"Absolutely," Jo said, still unsmiling. I wondered if she was this serious all the time, or just at work.

"I'm looking so forward to this," Jillian said, and opened her door as Jo got in on the passenger side.

Another car pulled up to the curb. I recognized the bright yellow Subaru Crosstrek because it was the only one of that color on the island. And it belonged to Stevie Warner, Mish's husband.

Jillian recognized it too. I knew because I felt her whole demeanor change—she went completely stiff. Which meant she knew Stevie too, not just Mish. Now I was dying to know how.

At that same moment, Adele pulled up into the driveway in her beat-up Prius and our one-o'clock appointment pulled up right behind her.

"Well, okay then," Jillian said hurriedly. "See you at the meeting." She got into the car. It wasn't until she'd rocketed off down the street that Stevie got out of his car. I watched his eyes linger on her vanishing brake lights until she turned the corner, then he waved at me. "Hey, Maddie."

"Hey, Stevie. Mish isn't here."

"I know. I'm actually here to see your grandfather."

"Grandpa Leo? Why?" I couldn't help it; I was nosy.

But Adele came over, interrupting. "What was that stunt all about this morning?" she demanded, not even acknowledging Stevie.

"What stunt?" I asked with a sigh. "Giving you the morning off?"

"I didn't want the morning off," Adele huffed. "I had things to do. And I bet the place is a mess. Mish called to tell me she wasn't coming in either." She glanced at Stevie accusingly, finally acknowledging his presence.

"She did?"

"She didn't call you?" Adele looked like she was about to blow a gasket.

"She's not feeling well," Stevie said apologetically. "It's been kind of a rough couple weeks for us. My grandmother passed away a few weeks ago. Lots of family stress and it's taking its toll on Mish."

"Oh, I'm so sorry," I said. "But it's no problem." I shot Adele a warning look. "It's fine. It was kind of a . . . busy morning anyway. Can you help our guest?" I waved at the elderly lady who waited patiently at the door. "Oh, and Peyton Chandler is inside. With Rhiannon."

Adele stared at me. I thought her eyes were about to pop out of her head. "You're kidding."

"No. Can you give the customer a heads-up? And don't act too starstruck." I winked at her.

Adele nearly ran over to the woman to lead her inside. I glanced at Stevie, who looked uncomfortable. "Grandpa's inside," I said, taking pity on him. "Come on, I'll take you in." I figured I'd just get the scoop from Grandpa later about why he was here.

Stevie followed me, his shoulders hunched like he was trying to hide. Probably from Adele, but it was still weird to see him so subdued. Stevie always had a lot of energy. He was constantly cheerful, overflowing with a kind of nerdy excitement about life that made him endearing. I think that's why Mish had fallen for him way back when. She had been a popular kid in the traditional sense of the word—cheerleader, pep rallies, the whole deal. When she'd started dating Stevie, I had to admit I'd been surprised. Stevie was the president of the chess club—yes, we had one—and really kind of a geek, albeit super sweet. It had seemed like an odd match at the time.

But it wasn't. Despite the fact that every guy on the football team tried to date her, Mish only had eyes for Stevie since junior year. They'd both gone to community college on the mainland and gotten married right after graduation.

"Hey, you need this brought in?" he asked when we got to the porch, pointing at the boxes of litter stacked up.

"Oh, yeah, but don't worry about it. I'll grab them later, I just haven't had a chance yet."

"No worries." He effortlessly hoisted two of them. I held the door open for him. He was stronger than he looked despite being so skinny. "Where do you want these?"

"Would you mind bringing them down to the basement? Grandpa needs to share his man cave with our supplies, to his great chagrin. I'll get Grandpa. He's in the café."

"No problem."

"Hey," I said as I showed him the door to the basement. "Do you know that woman who was leaving when you drove up?"

"What woman?" he asked.

"The woman in the BMW?"

"I didn't see anyone," he said. "But I guess I wasn't really paying attention."

I frowned, but didn't push it. I showed him where to stack the boxes, then headed back up to find Grandpa.

He was in the café as I suspected, still chatting with Esther while Peyton sat on the floor surrounded by cats. I had to smile. It was nice to see Grandpa seemingly interested in a lady.

"Hey," I said. "Stevie Warner is here to see you." I raised my eyebrows at Grandpa, a silent question.

He ignored it. "Tell him I'll be right down," he said.

"He's moving the litter for me. I told you'd meet him in your office."

Grandpa straightened his shirt a bit, as if preparing for an important meeting. I caught Esther watching him too.

I wondered what Stevie wanted with him. Various scenarios were running through my head. Of course at the top of the list was something to do with Mish. But husbands retaining PIs were never a good thing for a marriage. I always liked to think of PI work as daring and exciting, kind of like the heroes and heroines of books, like Carlotta Carlyle and Stephanie Plum. Although Grandpa assured me that most of his jobs were pretty benign, for which on some level I was grateful. I didn't actually want him running around chasing bad people, or his car getting blown up like Stephanie Plum.

"It was lovely chatting with you," he said to Esther. "I do have some business to attend to. I'll see you again, though."

"I hope so," Esther said. "Nice to meet you, Leo."

She watched him leave the room. A cat climbed up into Esther's lap. She glanced down and smiled, stroking his fur.

I sat down in the spot Grandpa had vacated. "That's Charlie," I said, motioning to the kitten.

She focused on me, almost as if she was startled I'd appeared. "He's darling," she said.

"So you've worked with Peyton for a long time. That must be exciting."

"I keep a low profile," Esther said with a smile. "I leave the exciting stuff to her. But it's fun to be on the water a lot, and she's lovely. She's like a daughter to me."

"That's nice." I remembered reading somewhere that Peyton's real mother had died when she was a teenager. "So do you think she'll adopt Ashley?" I asked, nodding at them.

"I have no idea," Esther said. "I'm sure she's a lovely cat, but Peyton sometimes takes on too much. And she's got her hands full these days."

Chapter 13

"A thousand bucks a ticket? Really?" Val plowed through one of Ethan's muffins, talking around a mouthful. "Did you know she was going to drop that number?"

I was out in the café after they left, looking for food too. There was plenty—all yummy and, truth be told, fattening. Ethan's muffins were to die for, and today he had cupcakes and croissants as well. He had dumped Jillian's Danish right into the trash after she left—he hated when people brought competing pastries into our house.

"I had no idea," I said. "But that's a lot of money." I glanced around to make sure there were no customers. The coast was clear for the moment.

"You really think she'll get it? I mean, no offense, but you're a little guy."

"Gee, thanks. And yes, I think she'll get it." I selected one of Ethan's pre-made Buddha bowls and grabbed a fork. "She has the connections. That's why I'm willing to deal with her . . . random demands." I *was* a little surprised at the amount of money they were ready to just throw at this. I mean, forty thousand was not nothing, especially for a rescue organization. And out of all the rescue places on the eastern seaboard, why me? I mean, it was flattering and all—and as Cass would say, *Why* not *you, Maddie?*—but still.

It could be part of a new marketing strategy for the league, I supposed. Cat cafés were all the rage nowadays, and we were an unusual version of one. Typically, places like ours were found in urban settings and catered to busy professionals who either had no time, space, or pet allowances in their apartment leases. But we were different. Our base was smaller, just given our location, and we depended a lot on the summer months, like everyone else on the island. And while most cat cafés worked directly with rescues, ours had become a lifeline for Katrina. The town ACO was the only help for animals in need, which put a heck of a lot of stress on Katrina.

It was also true that we'd gotten that message out, even beyond the island. I had to give Becky credit for that. She'd done some great stories not only on the café itself opening up, but on the direct support our efforts provided to the town, animal control, and by extension, taxpayers. She'd also had one of her reporters do a series on cat rescue throughout the state of Massachusetts. It had covered feral cats, poverty and its impact on people caring for their animals, crowded shelters, and rescue-worker burnout and had highlighted some of our volunteers. In addition, Best Friends Animal Society in Utah had even mentioned us in their tribute to a famous artist who had benefited their efforts as well as the island's. So for a little place, we'd gotten some big traction. Maybe it wasn't all that odd that we'd come onto Jillian's radar.

"Anyway, I hope the Paradise ends up coming through. Do you think they'll meet with us?"

"Already done," Val said. "I called and told them who I was. And reminded them who Dad was. And I called Mom. She's going to join us for the meeting."

"Smart move," I said with a grin. People were usually more than happy to accommodate the Daybreak Hospital CEO's wife.

"Yeah, they said they would be happy to accommodate whatever we needed."

"Who?" Grandpa asked, walking in. "I need a coffee."

"Coming right up," Ethan said.

"The Paradise," Val said. "We have a meeting tomorrow morning."

"I need to text Jillian," I said, pulling out my phone to do so. "And hey, Grandpa. Why was Stevie here?"

Ethan handed Grandpa his coffee. He accepted it, eyes on me. I wondered if he was even going to answer my question.

But he did. "He wanted to talk about a job."

"A job?" I leaned forward. "What's going on?"

"Madalyn. Obviously that's confidential."

"Oh, come on, Grandpa! They're my friends. Mish works here." It was weak, but I had to try. "Does it involve Mish?"

He stared me down until I sighed and gave up, glancing at my phone. Jillian had texted me back with about a thousand exclamation points about how excited she was to meet with the hotel in the morning.

"Fine. But seriously, are they okay?"

"You'll have to ask Stevie if you need to know that badly, Doll," he said. He leaned over and patted my head like he used to do when I was a little kid, then headed out.

Val smothered a chuckle.

"It's not funny," I said. "I need to know."

"Why? You're just being nosy."

"I am not! What if it has something to do with Jillian?"

"Why on earth would it?" Val asked.

"She definitely knows Mish. She said it the other day before she avoided telling me why they were yelling at each other. And I know she recognized Stevie's car. She couldn't wait to get out of here when she saw him drive up. You think they're having an affair or something?"

Val and Ethan were both staring at me as I spun the story in my head. It was the only thing that made sense, though. But it also made me mad to think about. I'd personally punch Stevie in the nose if it were true.

I knew I could be nosy, but I got it from Grandpa. And if whatever was wrong was affecting Mish and her work here, then I should know about it. Shouldn't I?

Of course I should. With the fundraiser coming and all, it was going to be even more important. And Stevie was my friend too.

I finished my Buddha bowl and grabbed a vegan cookie. And decided that yes, of course I should. And there was no time like the present, especially while everyone else was occupied. "I've gotta run," I said. "See you guys in a bit." And I hurried out before they could ask.

Chapter 14

I checked back inside before I left. Peyton seemed in no hurry to leave the café. I told Adele to give her whatever she needed, then I put JJ's harness on and, under the guise of needing snacks for Lucas's and my afternoon at the beach, we slipped out. I really did need snacks. I hated being on the beach with nothing to eat, and we didn't have any real beach-appropriate snacks in the house. This reminded me that I hadn't heard from Lucas yet. Once I was on the road I called his cell.

He answered on the fourth ring, sounding distracted.

"Hey," I said. "You almost done?"

"I'm sorry, babe. I'm running a little long here," he said. "I have a difficult client who's not enjoying her bath."

"No worries. I actually have to run an errand anyway. I should be back in an hour or so."

"Perfect. I'll see you then."

I hung up, relieved that I had a little time to kill, and pulled up in front of the co-op. I was trying to be on a healthy kick. Plus, JJ loved to visit the co-op. The people who worked there adored him and always gave

him treats and catnip toys. Today was no different. After
the staff had fawned over him and he'd been appropri-
ately spoiled, I loaded up on plantain chips, organic
dark chocolate, and some trail mix. At the last minute I
grabbed a bunch of colorful mixed flowers—a summer
bouquet—as an excuse to go to Stevie and Mish's, then
hopped back into Grandma's car and headed toward the
east side of town.

Stevie and Mish lived out on the Duck Cove line, in
a house that had been in Stevie's family forever. I had
only vague memories of them. His dad had died when he
was young, and his mother had moved off-island before
I'd left for California. I knew Stevie's grandmother had
lived here until her recent passing. I didn't know if he
had anyone else. Mish's family still lived somewhere on
the island as far as I knew, but I didn't think they were
close.

It took me less than ten minutes to get there, since I
was going against all the downtown traffic. I drove from
memory even though I hadn't been out here in years,
thanks to many of the landmarks, like the sign for the
Daybreak Wildlife Refuge bordering Stevie's property,
that I remembered as a kid coming out here for birthday
parties.

I almost missed the street but caught the sign at the
last minute, yanking the wheel of Grandma's car to catch
the turn. The tires screeched in protest. This poor car
was getting old. I really needed to get myself a car, but
none of us had been able to part with Grandma's old Ford
Taurus. Not my style—I was more of an SUV gal—but
it made me feel close to her. But it was twenty-something
years old now and had a lot of miles on it.

I slowed in front of the entrance. I'd kind of forgotten
this place was so big and imposing. There were a few

houses on the property, which spanned a large swath of the street. On one side was the wildlife refuge, and on the other the ocean. Perfect location. The only neighbors were across the street, and the houses were all large and spaced out enough that privacy wasn't an issue.

I pulled through the wrought-iron gate that stood halfway open and cruised slowly down the long driveway. I remembered Grandpa telling me once that Stevie's family had what they called "old island money," so this amount of property wasn't surprising. Also, they'd probably built this up back when the land cost maybe one-tenth of what it did now.

I couldn't remember which part of the estate was actually Stevie's, though. I drove past the first house, which looked like a little guesthouse. It seemed empty. The big house was next. *Big house* was an understatement—it looked more like a mansion. There were a few cars parked in the circular driveway, so someone other than his grandmother must live there. Beyond the big house, there was a small cottage with more cars parked out front—one of them was Stevie's yellow Subaru. You couldn't miss that. The other car was a black BMW. With rental plates. An X5. I pulled up a little closer. Yes, I'd seen this car before. Out in front of my house when Jillian came over.

I rolled to a stop and tapped my fingers on the steering wheel, thinking about this and trying not to jump to conclusions. I glanced over at JJ, who stood on his hind legs, paws on the dashboard, staring intently at a squirrel nibbling on something in the middle of the lawn. The squirrel stared defiantly at JJ as it ate its treat. JJ's tail swished in anticipation of a good chase.

"Not happening, bud," I said. "We like squirrels. So what do you think? Do we go to the door and see if we can find out what's up here? Or leave it alone?"

He glanced at me and squeaked. I think he meant *Let me out of this car NOW.*

My phone vibrated. Lucas. I picked up, my eyes still on the door. "Hey. What's going on?"

"Hi babe. I'm done. Heading home. Where are you?"

I paused. "Still running an errand. I'll fill you in later."

He groaned. "What does that mean, Maddie? Are we still going to the beach?"

Lucas knew me well enough to know that when I was kind of evasive, I was usually meddling in something. I really wasn't trying to be evasive, though. It was just too long of a story to get into right now. Plus, the front door had opened and Jillian stepped into the doorway, turning around to speak to someone behind her. She held a big box and used her knee to keep the door open.

"We are. Definitely. But I have to go. I'll see you at home in like half an hour. I got beach snacks!" I disconnected before he could probe any further. I thought about taking off, but they would totally see me if I did. So I shut the car off, grabbed JJ and the flowers, and got out, striding over to the front walkway. Jillian turned and stared at me as I walked up. For once, she seemed to be speechless.

"Hey!" I exclaimed, trying to sound surprised. "Fancy meeting you here!"

"It certainly is," she said with forced enthusiasm, shifting the box to her other arm. "What are you doing here?"

I brandished the flowers. "For Mish. Because she wasn't feeling well. We never actually got to talk about how you know each other. This is such a coincidence!"

"Certainly is. Let me get out of your way. But first, look!" She shifted the box toward me. "The new batch

of cat leashes just arrived. They are *gorgeous*. I can't wait
to show Peyton. I think they'll pass muster this time."

Still avoiding the whole Mish thing. I peered into
the box and pulled one out. It honestly didn't look much
different than the one Rhiannon had been wearing, but
they were still pretty. The pure silver glitter was the only
change I could pick up at first glance—it gave them a
sheen that had been missing with the multicolored glitter.

"You must take one for JJ," she said.

I looked at it doubtfully. "It's not really his color."

"He'll love it," she said, thrusting one into my hand.

Stevie stepped out onto the porch behind her, also
staring at me like he'd never seen me before. "Maddie?"

"Hi. I, uh. Is Mish home? I wanted to see how she was
feeling. I brought flowers," I said, waving my little bouquet. "And JJ. I felt bad that she was sick."

"Oh. That's very sweet," Stevie said. "Hi, JJ." He
reached over and awkwardly patted JJ's head, then
looked back at me. "She's actually better today and she
went over to the shop for a bit."

"I'm leaving," Jillian said over her shoulder to Stevie. "We'll talk more later. I'll be back for the rest of
the boxes." She flashed another sweet smile at me. "Bye,
Maddie! See you tomorrow."

"Yes, see you tomorrow," I said as she hurried to her
car. She opened the hatchback, threw the box in with a
bit more force than necessary, then jumped in the driver's side. She did a rushed three-point turn and took off,
kicking up sand in the wake of her tires.

Stevie crossed and uncrossed his arms awkwardly
and leaned against the door jamb. "So. Want me to give
those to Mish?"

I nodded and handed him the bouquet. "Thanks. So

how do *you* know Jillian?" I asked. "Because I know your wife knows her."

Stevie looked down at the ground, shuffling his feet. I had a flashback to when we were kids—probably first or second grade—and I used to see him during gym class, wistfully waiting his turn at bat during softball days, looking very much the way he did now. He'd never been sporty, although I think he'd wanted to be.

But the answer he gave me wasn't what I was expecting. "She's my cousin," he said.

"Your . . . cousin?" My brain worked to process that.

He half smiled. "Yeah. What, did you think I was cheating on Mish?"

I felt my face redden. "Of course not," I lied. "But why didn't you tell me? Why didn't *Mish* tell me? And why don't I remember her?"

"You don't remember her because she never lived here. My aunt left the island at eighteen and rarely visited. Jillian's only been here a few times, and even then, it hadn't been for years." Stevie sighed and looked away. "It's complicated, Maddie. I'd rather not get into it. If we could keep your café stuff separate from our family stuff, that would probably be better."

"Especially since Mish doesn't get along with her," I said.

He cocked his head at me. "Why do you say that?"

"Because they were out in front of my place yelling at each other when Jillian came over the other day."

Stevie cringed. "You're kidding."

I shook my head slowly. "Nope."

"I'm sorry."

"Not your fault. Family feud or something?" I asked with a small smile.

He didn't answer. Clearly it was none of my business.

"Look. I'm not trying to pry. I just don't want whatever is going on here to affect what she's trying to do for the café," I said. "I don't know if you know, but she's doing a fundraiser for us. There's a lot of money at stake for the animals."

Stevie's gaze held mine, his face unreadable. "Yeah. Her good deed of the week," he said. His tone reeked of sarcasm. "Don't worry, Maddie. I'll keep Mish away so it doesn't screw anything up for you. Thanks for the flowers." And he went back inside, closing the door in my face.

Chapter 15

My alarm woke me the next morning from a sound sleep. For a minute I was confused about why it was going off on a Sunday, then remembered. The meeting at the Paradise Hotel with Val and Jillian. I sat up, grabbing for the phone to turn it off. Lucas slept next to me, unfazed by the alarm. JJ too. His one upright ear twitched, the only sign that he was awake and annoyed at the noise I was making.

But too bad for him, because I was taking him with me. He had a knack for charming people.

I focused on the clock on my phone—eight thirty—and tossed it aside with a sigh. Val and I had to be there at ten. Really, all I wanted to do was snuggle in bed with Lucas, then hit the beach for a real beach day. We'd made it there for a measly hour yesterday, by the time I'd gotten home from my afternoon of running around being nosy. Luckily Lucas was a good sport about it. I'd used the time on the sand to bring Lucas up to speed on everything that was going on with the fundraiser and the Mish, Jillian, and Stevie dynamic. But I hadn't been able to reconcile the information I'd learned yesterday that Jillian and Stevie Warner were cousins. They were about as alike as the sun and the moon, from what I could see. Of all the possibilities floating through my head, that hadn't been one of them.

This made the whole Mish dynamic even more interesting, at least to me. I wasn't sure about Lucas, but I'd talked his ear off about Stevie's previous comment about family stuff going on that was "taking its toll" on Mish with his grandmother's passing. I knew family stuff could be rough, but I wasn't sure why Stevie went straight to keeping her away from the café. Was her relationship with Jillian so strained that she really needed to be banned from the café until the fundraiser was over? And if so, why?

But really, it was none of my business, as Lucas had reminded me until the sun started to set and we needed to leave the beach. Grandpa would strongly echo that sentiment. So I should just leave it alone. It was hard, for a number of reasons. One, I was curious. I probably should've been a reporter when I'd decided not to be a cop. Both required extreme nosiness and a desire for the truth, both of which I had in spades. And two, I'd known Mish and Stevie since we were like five years old. Granted, that didn't automatically make it my business, but when you lived on an island like this year round, people seemed more like family than they would in any other setting. I cared about them. If they were having a hard time and I could help, I wanted to. I just wasn't sure how yet.

Now I leaned over and gave him a kiss on the forehead. He didn't wake. I threw my covers off and headed downstairs to get coffee before I got in the shower. Val and Ethan were already up. Ethan had the coffee brewing and Val sat at the kitchen table with her computer.

"The Paradise is gonna be an awesome place to have this event," she announced when I entered the room.

I grunted and headed for the coffee pot. Ethan handed me a cup before I could even get there. He knew me so well. After a few sips, I focused on Val. "You think?"

She nodded. "The view is amazing. Look at this." She spun the laptop around and showed me the outdoor function area. It looked dreamy, I had to admit, with all the twinkling lights, the fire pit, and the ocean glittering in the background.

"Beautiful. You're sure they're not booked?"

Val shook her head. "I called yesterday after Mom left to confirm. Made sure to tell them that Peyton Chandler was the guest of honor. She winked. "They didn't say it, but they cleared their schedule for us. And since I talked up the whole helping the police department and animal control function, they're going to actually reduce the cost. So we're good."

"Wow." I was impressed.

"She's good," Ethan said, setting a plate of eggs in front of her and leaning over to kiss the top of her head.

"I know. That's what I was trying to tell her all along." I drank the rest of my coffee. "Any eggs for me?"

"Coming right up."

"Are you going to be ready to go?" Val asked.

I shot her a dirty look. She knew I hated to be rushed in the morning. "Yes," I said through gritted teeth.

She ate more eggs, still smiling. "Jillian will be impressed, you think?"

"Absolutely," I said, amused. I drained my cup and went over to refill it, then filled JJ's food bowl. He appeared as if out of nowhere at the sound of the spoon hitting the bowl. I put his bowl down, added some of his favorite Temptations treats next to it, then stood. "I'm going to shower."

I poked my head into the café on my way upstairs. Clarissa was there cleaning, feeding, and taking Instagram photos of our residents. I thought about Mish and how indignant she'd gotten at Stevie's suggestion that she should stay away and wondered if she'd been in touch with Adele about the schedule. I waved to Clarissa, shut the door, and headed upstairs.

After I'd showered and gotten ready, I got JJ into his harness, poured a to-go cup of coffee despite Ethan's incredulous look at my need for a third cup, and grabbed my keys. "Ready?" I asked Val, who was still hard at work on her laptop.

"Yeah, I'm good." She closed the computer then went over to Ethan and gave him a kiss. "I'll see you soon. Are you going to the nursing home?"

"Not today," he said. "Taking a few days off."

She squeezed his hand. "I understand. I'll see you in a bit."

I picked up JJ and we headed out. "What's wrong with Ethan? He doesn't like the nursing home anymore?"

"He does like it. But one of his favorite residents died recently." Val sighed and climbed into the car. "I feel bad for him. She was the first one he's been super attached to."

JJ climbed onto Val's lap. He liked the passenger seat, and if someone else was along for the ride, they just had to deal with him sitting on them. Also, he liked when there were people there because it boosted him up higher than if he just had the seat to sit on.

"That's sad." I knew Ethan had been closer to his

grandparents than his own parents and that seniors had a special place in his heart. It had only been since we came to Daybreak that he'd found the time to actually volunteer at a nursing home, something he told me he'd wanted to do for ages and just never got around to back in California.

"He'll bounce back. But he took it hard." Val was back on her phone. "So you think we'll have to get Peyton's approval on the decorations?"

"I do. She seems kind of . . . picky. But the new leashes came in. Jillian had them yesterday."

"She did? When?"

"There's actually one in the back seat," I said. "She gave me one for JJ." I realized I hadn't told Val about my trip out to Stevie's, or any of that story. I filled her in quickly.

"Cousins? You're kidding."

"I'm not," I said. "But there's definitely some issues there."

"Wow. Hopefully she and Mish won't cross paths too much." Val glanced at her watch. "Grandpa said Jillian's staying there, so hopefully she'll get the meeting started if we're late?"

"I'm sure she will," I said. But despite her worry, we made it to the hotel five minutes early. I pulled into a parking spot near the lobby door and we hurried inside. I hadn't been in here in years, and it was gorgeous. Already one of the more modern hotels on the island, the new owner had done a lot of renovations since he'd bought the property last year. It looked more like a waterfront mansion than a hotel, with a wraparound front porch, private balconies for every room, and the pool and garden areas out back facing the ocean.

Val went right up to the front desk, where a woman

with short blond hair dyed purple greeted her with a smile. "Hello. We're meeting Marianna at ten to discuss an event? Someone from our party may already be here."

The woman skimmed a list in front of her. "It doesn't look like she's been called yet. I'll buzz her. She'll be right down."

"Thank you." Val turned to me. "Want to see the patio while we wait?"

"Right through there." Purple Hair pointed out the back door. "We closed it off to guests for your walk-through." She leaned forward a bit, her face eager. "Is Peyton coming?" she asked in a stage whisper.

"I'm afraid not today," Val said apologetically.

"Oh." She looked crestfallen. "Well, enjoy." She lost interest in us pretty quickly after that, even when JJ squeaked at her for attention. I never trusted people who could ignore an adorable furry friend.

I put JJ down to walk. I probably should have put the new leash Jillian had given me on him, just for appearances' sake, but it hadn't occurred to me until just now. We followed Val to the back door leading outside. I had to admit it was pretty breathtaking. The hotel sat slightly above the ocean, which made the views even better. And the way they'd set up the area made it feel more like a tropical paradise getaway than an island in New England. JJ's nose and ears were on alert. He loved the ocean, so I assumed he was doing his usual sniffing routine. He tugged on the leash as he paced around, his nose going a mile a minute. I wrapped the leash around my hand a couple extra times so he didn't try to bolt, and took a minute to enjoy the surroundings.

Tiny white lights were strung up above the expansive patio, and they crawled up the partitions that were also set up for privacy reasons, or to separate parties, I assumed. There was a large fire pit for the main area, and I could see a couple of smaller ones set up around the perimeter as well. Their patio designer had positioned the furniture for maximum ocean view, and there was a gazebo out on the lawn that also had lights and flowery-looking decorations set up to make it inviting.

There was also someone sitting in it. I squinted, trying to see through the morning sun glinting off the ocean. Val wasn't paying attention—she was still looking around, probably imagining how many people she could fit out here, where the tables would go, what they would do if it rained. All those things that made me happy I wasn't an event planner because I knew I'd miss a giant detail and screw the whole thing up.

"I thought they said they closed this off from guests so we could do the walk-through," I said to Val.

"Hmm?" She didn't even look at me as she furiously typed notes into her phone.

"Over there." I nudged her and pointed. "In the gazebo."

She finally glanced up. "I don't know. Probably someone snuck out to enjoy their morning coffee. They'll need to get out of the way, though."

My sister was funny when she got really focused. I walked over toward the gazebo. The figure sitting inside it was facing the water, head slightly tilted to the side. It was a woman, given the long hair. She must not have heard us out here, because she didn't turn. Understandable, given the ocean waves crashing in the background. As I stepped closer, I recognized the strawberry blond hair. Jillian's hair. She must've come out on her own to scope the place out.

"Jillian?" I called out.

No answer.

Val joined me. "She's here already? I thought they said she hadn't come out yet?"

"They said she hadn't called Marianna. Maybe she came out just to get a feel for it." We headed over to the gazebo, JJ tugging on his leash, straining against the harness to get there faster.

Jillian hadn't moved, despite Val's and my conversation. I felt a tiny sense of misgiving starting in my belly and pushed it aside. "Jillian?" I called, stepping up to the gazebo, then stopped short.

Val, still focused on her phone, bumped into me and looked up in annoyance. "What are you doing?" She peered around me, then gasped. The phone fell out of her hand. We both stared at Jillian, whose unseeing eyes stared out to sea, head tilted slightly to the right. A pink, glittery cat leash still hung from around her neck. It had loosened, making it easy to see the deep, red indentation left behind.

Chapter 16

I reacted first, shaking myself into action at the sound of JJ squeaking urgently. I knelt in front of Jillian, shaking her arm. "Jillian?"

No response.

"Jillian!" I shook harder. Her head tipped even more to the right, and her body slumped even farther. She had on yoga pants and a tank top. I noticed her feet were bare. That was so odd. Why was she here for a meeting in bare feet? And not wearing her usual fancy outfit?

I risked a look at her face but had to look away when I saw how . . . dead she looked. A flash of silver caught my eye. I looked down and saw a tiny silver paw print charm on the bench next to her.

And then Val started screaming.

I stumbled away from the body, falling back on my hands. JJ's leash slipped off my wrist. Before I could reach for it, he bolted into the gazebo and stopped at Jillian's feet, sniffing, his tail swishing back and forth.

I grabbed the leash and pulled him back to me, then took Val's arm and dragged her away toward the patio area. I could see people starting to pour out of the building, pointing and staring. "Val. Be quiet," I hissed at her, fumbling in my bag for my phone. My hands were shaking so bad I kept dropping it. I finally managed to grab it and press the emergency call button to report the body.

The dispatcher tried to get me to stay on the phone, but I gave her the address and disconnected to focus on Val. She'd stopped screaming, thank goodness, but was now staring at the gazebo, her face completely devoid of color. More and more people were coming out of the building now to see what the ruckus was about. They shouldn't be traipsing around. It was a crime scene.

I called Craig Tomlin. Craig was my ex-boyfriend from high school. He was also a cop in Daybreak Harbor and had worked with Grandpa before he retired.

He answered after three rings, sounding distracted. "Hey Maddie. What's up?"

"I'm at the Paradise Hotel. I need you."

"Um. Excuse me?" He sounded genuinely taken aback.

I felt a hysterical giggle bubble up in my throat as I realized what that had sounded like, but choked it back. "Not like that. Someone's dead."

I could feel him tense even over the phone. "What? Not funny, Maddie."

"I know it's not funny," I snapped. "I need you here. There's a body. And not just any body. It's Jillian Allen."

"I don't know who that is. Did you call nine-one-one?"

"I did. Now I'm calling you. Please come." I thought of the leash hanging around Jillian's neck, the angry red gash it had left on her perfect skin, and shivered.

"I'm on my way."

I stuck the phone back in my pocket as Purple Hair from the front desk ran over to us. "What happened?"

"You need to keep everyone inside. That woman is dead. The cops are on their way," I said, trying to keep my voice steady.

She gasped and stepped back, her hand flying to her mouth. "Dead?"

This conversation could get redundant pretty quickly. Luckily the sound of sirens wailing snapped our attention away. JJ's ears went flat. He hated sirens.

I tapped Val's arm. "I'm going to meet them," I said.

She nodded, not even looking at me. I figured she was in shock. Finding a body—especially this body—was shocking at best. Terrifying at worst.

I turned back to Purple Hair. "Get everyone inside."

She snapped into action and climbed onto one of the couches, putting two fingers into her mouth in a piercing whistle. "Everyone inside please!" she shouted.

I stepped into the lobby, then stopped and leaned against the wall. I felt like I couldn't breathe and slid down to a sitting position, trying to suck air into my lungs. What had happened here? Who could have done this? Had it been a random act? Someone who tried to rob her, perhaps? Sometimes these fancy hotels were targets, because people knew the rich tourists stayed here.

I finally caught my breath and rose unsteadily to my feet. I got to the front door just as three police cars and one ambulance pulled up to it, lights flashing. They killed the sirens but left the lights on as cops piled out of all the cars and headed inside. The paramedics were in less of a hurry, climbing out of the ambulance and moving to the back to unload a gurney, their movements almost relaxed as if they did this too often to be bothered by it.

In the midst of all the activity, a bright yellow blur

caught my attention. The car roared around the corner from the side of the hotel and raced toward the road, taking the turn on two wheels. It was hardly noticeable despite all the other chaos going on, but the yellow Subaru was hard to miss.

It was Stevie Warner's car.

I froze, my gaze following his car. Why was Stevie here? What business could he possibly have at the Paradise—aside from Jillian?

A shout distracted me. The cops were trying to keep people from coming into the hotel and called directions to one another about where to station themselves. I didn't see Craig, but I saw Sergeant Mick Ellory get out of the second car. Ellory was fairly new to the island and we'd gotten off to a rocky start when I'd first moved back to the island. We'd since gotten to a good place. It helped that he'd started seeing Katrina—after a rough divorce, I'd recently found out—and she demanded peace between us.

He saw me right away and headed over. "Maddie. What's going on? Someone's deceased?"

I nodded, swallowing hard. "Jillian Allen. The woman who came here from the rescue league in New Jersey." Katrina would've told him about her for sure. "We came here for a meeting with her—"

"Who's we?" he interrupted.

"Me and Val. We had a walk-through with the hotel. This is . . . where we were planning to have the event." I trailed off.

"And?"

"She was in the gazebo. It looks like someone . . . strangled her."

"Did you touch anything?"

"I touched her . . . wrist. To see if she . . ." I could feel my chest getting heavy with the weight of my discovery as it really started to sink in. "She was dead."

"Anyone else around?"

I shook my head. "People started to come out, but I told the clerk to keep them inside."

"Good. Show me," he said, nudging me in front of him.

I went back inside, clutching JJ tightly. Ellory ushered me ahead of him through the lobby. I was aware that crowds were starting to gather—guests of the hotel, the staff, whoever happened to be around on this beautiful Sunday morning. It seemed so odd that such a beautiful day could bring such a terrible event.

As we reached the door leading out back, Ellory paused and pulled out his radio. He placed his hand on my arm, asking me to wait. I did, letting my eyes roam the lobby area. There were a few small groups clustered, and one bigger crowd trying to get near the door and see what was going on. One of the cops had positioned himself there to keep everyone back. There were also people on the giant staircase in the middle of the hotel—a cool staircase that broke apart halfway up to wind around the elevator, which was in the center of the lobby, and rejoined at the top. There was one lone figure at the top that my eyes landed on. I did a double take.

It looked a lot like Chad Novak, Peyton's agent. I squinted for a better look. Like Jillian, he looked different dressed in casual clothes, but the hair was the same. It was definitely him. Ellory pulled me aside as the other cop cleared the way for the paramedics to come through with the gurney. The cop on the other side of the door opened it for them. They maneuvered the gurney through, the clanging sounds of metal send-ing a pall over the chattering group. This made every-thing real.

"Ready?" Ellory put his hand on my elbow and led me outside into the fray. It was a totally different environ-ment out here than when I'd left. I saw Val sitting on one of the patio couches. A cop sat with her but they weren't talking. The other cops were over by the gazebo. The paramedics made their way across the grass.

Ellory looked at me. "I called the coroner."

Great. I felt my stomach lurch at those words and looked away, sucking in the ocean air to try to combat the nausea. "I called Craig."

"I know. He's on his way. Go sit with Val. I'll be over in a second."

He headed toward the gazebo.

I went over to Val. The cop with her nodded at me, then moved away, giving us some privacy. I sat down and put my arm around her. "How you holding up?"

She looked at me, her eyes red and watery. "She's dead. How can she be dead?"

I shook my head. "I don't know, Val. I have no idea."

"My phone," Val said suddenly. "I dropped it over there. At the gazebo."

"One of the officers will get it," I said. I felt sorry for her. She looked positively beside herself. I couldn't imagine the effect this would have on her. I had, unfor-tunately, had some experience with dead bodies myself.

"I want to call Ethan," she said, and the tears started again.

"I'll call him." I wanted to call Grandpa and Lucas too. I handed JJ to her, hoping he would distract her. She buried her face in his orange fur. He was such a good comforter.

I called Grandpa. Thankfully, he answered. "Morning, Doll," he said. "I missed you this morning."

"I know. Are you home?"

"I am. Just got out of the shower."

So he hadn't heard anything on his scanner. "We have a problem."

I felt him snap to attention. "What's wrong?"

"Val and I are at the Paradise. We came for our meeting and found Jillian Allen dead."

Silence. "What happened to her?"

I closed my eyes against the image of Jillian, head skewed to the side, that red indent in her neck. "It looks like she was strangled. The cops just got here." I lowered my voice and turned away. "Can you come? And bring Ethan if he's around?"

"Yes. On my way."

"Is Lucas there?"

"He took the dog out for a walk."

"Okay. I'll call him."

We disconnected just as my phone started ringing. My mother.

"Maddie? Where are you?" She sounded frantic.

"At the hotel," I said. "Where are you?"

"At the hotel! I just got here but I can't get in. There's all kinds of commotion. What's going on?"

Shoot. I'd completely forgotten my mother had been coming for the meeting. "There was an . . . incident. You may want to just go home, Mom. I can catch up with you later."

"I will most certainly not go home," she said indignantly. "What's going on in there? Are you girls alright?"

"Val and I are fine. Let me see if I can come get you."

"Actually, Craig just pulled up. I'll come in with him." She hung up on me.

There was no changing my mother's mind when she got like this—especially when she knew her girls were in some way involved in whatever was occurring. I let it go, figuring Craig would handle it, and was just about to call Lucas when Ellory appeared in front of me.

He nodded at the cop, who jumped to his feet. "I'll take them from here."

Chapter 17

Ellory sat down across from us. "Val. Are you okay?" he asked.

Val hiccuped back a sob, but nodded.

"I'm sorry you had to see this," he said. "Can you answer a few questions for me?" He looked at both of us.

"Yes," I said. Val managed another nod.

"Tell me about this woman. Jillian . . ." Ellory trailed off, waiting for me to fill in the blank.

"Allen," I supplied, pausing as a waiter came up to the table with a tray. Someone must've asked them to bring us something to drink. The wide-eyed guy with shaking hands deposited a glass of iced tea with lemon for each of us then backed away. It struck me as so odd—we were sitting on this beautiful furniture drinking tea, overlooking the ocean. If there wasn't a dead body currently being removed from the adorable gazebo, it would have been the perfect summer morning.

"Jillian Allen." Ellory noted that in his little book. "Who is she again?"

"She's with the Shoreline Animal Rescue League

in New Jersey," I said. "She is—was—the executive director."

Ellory glanced up. "New Jersey?"

I nodded. "They work with shelters and rescue places all along the East Coast, though. She called me a couple weeks ago and said she wanted to come see the café."

"That's a long way to come to visit your café. They don't have any in New Jersey?"

I glanced up as Craig strode onto the patio, my mother in tow. She saw us and made a beeline. Ellory sighed but didn't say anything. Most of the cops knew they didn't have chance when it came to former chief Mancini's family.

"Girls! There you are. What on earth is going on?" My mother had clearly chosen her clothes with care for this meeting. She wore a dress that I would expect to see on her for one of my dad's hospital functions, a slim black maxi that she'd enhanced with a colorful scarf of teals and purples. Her usually unruly curls were smoothed back into a neat bun, with just a few errant ones escaping around her face.

"Mom." Val looked relieved. She jumped up from her chair and let my mother hug her tight. "Jillian is dead. It was awful," she said, and started to cry, burying her face in my mother's shoulder. My mother glanced at me over Val's head, the horror apparent on her face. *Dead?* She mouthed to me while she patted Val's back. "Oh, honey," she said into her hair. "I'm so, so sorry."

Ellory looked at me. "You still able to talk?"

I nodded. I kind of wanted my mommy too, but I had the reputation of being more of the "steady Eddie" in a crisis, like my grandfather. I'd learned from him how to tune out the chaos and tune into the next right action, and that usually got me through—even when I was freaking out inside.

I wished Lucas was here.

"So you were about to tell me why a Jersey girl was up here doing animal rescue stuff."

I shifted uncomfortably in my chair and refocused. "She heard of us and wanted to help." An image of Stevie's yellow Subaru speeding through the parking lot flashed through my mind. There was no getting around it. They'd find out sooner or later. "She was also here because of a family situation. She's related to Stevie Warner."

Ellory frowned. "Really? How?"

"She and Stevie are—were—cousins." I didn't add any additional commentary. The fight with Mish would come up eventually. Especially since I wasn't the only one who had witnessed it.

Ellory wrote that down. "Is Stevie her next of kin?"

"I have no idea," I said. I didn't know if Jillian was married, or had a partner, or even children. Oh God. What if she had children? This was terrible.

"When did she get here?"

"I'm not sure. I met her for the first time on Thursday." It seemed so long ago already. "She came over to see the café." I ran him through the past few days, starting with Jillian's fundraising proposal, her introduction of Peyton Chandler and Marco Moore, her ask of Val to be the lead on the party planning, right up to today's meeting. "We were here to do the walk-through with the staff, get the lay of the land for the event, figure out what we needed. Val and I showed up a few minutes early. Jillian was already out here."

Ellory tapped his pen on his notebook. "I noticed she had casual clothes on. And no shoes."

"Yeah. That tells me she wasn't here for the meeting yet."

"Was she staying here?"

"She told my grandfather she was, and she must have been. Not sure where her shoes would be otherwise."

We both fell silent for a moment. My mother was still comforting Val. I wondered if Ellory was going to want to talk to her again.

"What's up with the leash?" Ellory asked finally. "She have a dog?"

I shook my head. "They're cat leashes. I guess you could use them on a small dog too. Anyway, they're the favors for the event. They showed up yesterday. She had the box with her when I saw her at Stevie's."

"So who would have access to them, besides her?"

"I don't know. She said she had staff coming out here. Not sure if they'd already arrived. I guess she could've brought them here, but I'm not sure why she would have done that already. We were here to finalize the venue today." I hesitated, remembering. The leashes had been delivered to Stevie's house. That meant he and Mish had access to them too. *Which doesn't mean anything at all*, the good half of my brain argued. Your friends are not killers.

Ellory caught my pause. "What?"

"Nothing."

He knew I was holding something back, but sudden activity caught both of our attention. "ME's office is here," I heard the door cop call out.

Medical examiner. If that didn't make it official.

"There she is. The ME will tell us for sure." He nodded at the woman who had just emerged from the hotel onto the patio. "She wanted to see the body before it was moved. So you didn't see anyone else out here when you got here?"

I shook my head. "The staff said they had closed off the patio for guests so we could take our time and have the whole space to look at."

"Then she must have been out there before they closed it off."

I nodded. "She definitely wasn't dressed for a meeting."

"What time did you say you got here?"

"About five minutes before ten. Do you think . . ." I trailed off.

"What?"

"That whoever killed her was still out here some-where?"

"I don't know. We have teams combing the neigh-borhood. We figured if someone took off on foot that way"—he pointed to the side of the grounds, where a large white fence separated the property from its neighbor—"maybe they were hiding and watching the action. There's an opening over there. It's pretty easy to get onto the property. But it's highly likely whoever it was just walked back into the hotel and out the front door." He eyed me, and I knew he was going to circle back to our previous conversation.

I spoke quickly. "By the way, Val dropped her phone over there." I indicated the gazebo, keeping my eyes averted from the scene unfolding. "Can she get it back?"

"I'll talk to the crime scene techs. They probably bagged it. Your grandfather is here," he said, nodding over my shoulder.

I turned and saw Grandpa talking to the cop at the door, then he came through onto the patio. He came straight over to us, stopping to say something to Val and my mother, then sat down with me and Ellory.

"What's happened?" he asked, his face grim, looking from Ellory to me.

"Someone strangled Jillian," I said without preamble. I was tired of saying it at this point.

"Any suspects?" Grandpa asked.

Ellory shook his head slowly. "Not yet. I was just getting to that part of the conversation with Maddie."

"I told you we didn't see anyone," I said.

"Right, but I'm also interested to know who she's interacted with while she's been here, any conflicts she may have had, that sort of thing."

I tried to keep my face as stoic as possible. "I just met her a couple of days ago."

"Okay. Did she mention any trouble? Was she interacting with anyone while she was here that looked tumultuous?"

I could feel Grandpa's eyes boring into my brain from the side. Ellory noticed it too, because he leaned forward.

"Maddie. I don't have to tell you how important this is, do I?"

I sighed. "Of course not. She was a . . . big personality. Kind of bossy, but I think that's just how she was. But I did see her arguing with someone."

"Who?"

I met Ellory's eyes. "Mish Warner."

He frowned. "Her cousin's wife?"

I nodded.

"So a family issue?"

"I don't really know what the argument was about. They were in their cars on our street and you could just tell they weren't happy with each other." It wasn't exactly a lie. I'd asked Mish about the argument, not Jillian. And as Grandpa Leo always said, there were three sides to every story—yours, mine, and the truth. And Mish hadn't really given me much to go on there either. She'd just said she wasn't happy about Jillian "weaseling her way" into the café. Jillian could've had a completely different perception of the whole conversation.

"Sergeant Ellory."

We all turned to the man towering over us. Chief McAuliffe. The Daybreak chief who had taken over after Grandpa Leo retired.

Ellory stood. "Chief. Did anyone brief you? I'm getting a statement from one of the witnesses."

"Not yet. I'll wait for you to brief me." The chief regarded me curiously, then glanced at Grandpa. "Leo. No rest for the retired, eh?" His tone was teasing but his eyes were flinty. It was no secret that the new chief didn't like that Grandpa ended up in the middle of police investigations more often than not. I figured it was insecurity on his part. Grandpa had been here for his entire career, worked his way up from patrol, and had an impeccable reputation and standing in the community. He had left big shoes to fill, and McAuliffe was still trying to prove himself almost four years in.

Grandpa stood and shook his hand. "Small island," he said. "Sometimes it just can't be helped."

"And this is your granddaughter, right?"

I stood too. "Maddie James." I didn't hold out my hand. I didn't love this guy. He was condescending to my grandfather, and he didn't care much about animals. I'd watched him give Katrina's budget the shaft, and he hadn't stood by her last year when she'd been in trouble. To me, that said a lot about his character.

Grandpa, sensing my mood, turned to Ellory. "Do you need anything else from Maddie? If not, I'd like to get my girls home." He glanced at the chief. "And let you all do your jobs."

Chapter 18

After a quick side conversation with Ellory, Grandpa ushered us back into the lobby.

"Why is the chief here?" I asked. "You usually don't visit crime scenes at that level. Is it because he's friends with the owner?"

"That's right," Grandpa said. "It doesn't look great that he recommended this venture to his buddy and now someone was killed here on his watch."

So the chief was there for damage control. Closing this case would be a huge priority for him, since he clearly had a personal stake in it. I wondered if any of it was going to become a backlash on Katrina, if he found out that Jillian's presence here was even indirectly benefiting the ACO efforts. I sincerely hoped not. He already had an eye on her, and not in a good way.

Grandpa looked back at Val, still subdued but a bit steadier. "You okay? Ethan's outside."

That brightened her spirits. "I just want to get out of here. I'll be outside," she said as she headed for the door.

"Lucas too," he added. "I picked him up on the way."

"You're the best, Grandpa." Then I remembered Val

dropping her phone at the gazebo. "Shoot, her phone. She never got it back."

"They'll bring it over later. Mick already let me know. He wants to talk to her again. I asked him to give her a couple hours."

"Ah, that's right. You know all the tricks of the trade." I pushed open the front door and stepped outside, stopping to take a breath. Even though I'd been outside all morning, being on that patio had been suffocating. Out here, the air seemed lighter. Like I could breathe easier. At the front of the crowd of onlookers I could see Ethan, Lucas, and Ollie. Val had already made her way over to Ethan, who immediately stepped forward to offer her shelter from the crowd.

"Maddie." Lucas and Ollie rushed over. Lucas enveloped me in a huge hug, capturing JJ between us. He let out a muffled squeak of disapproval. "What happened? Are you okay?"

I took a minute to breathe him in. He smelled like the outdoors—sea salt and sunscreen, the scents of summer. "I don't know," I admitted, my voice muffled by his shirt. "It still feels surreal."

"Your grandfather said it was that woman? The one planning the party?"

I nodded, lifting my head from his chest. Grandpa had his phone out and was speaking to someone, walking in small circles around the parking lot. I wondered who it was. Ethan, my mother, and Val were walking toward my mother's car, Val in the middle of them. I felt sorry for her. No one should have to see what we'd seen this morning. And Val wasn't great at crises in general, and the ones she usually handled were a heck of a lot more benign than this one. Like, someone who ordered chicken got beef instead at a party. Although when it came to her business, she was really chill. It was the personal types of crises that threw her.

Lucas was still waiting for me to tell him. I could tell he was getting antsy. "So, what happened to her?" he prompted.

I reached down to pet Ollie, who was climbing my leg desperately looking for attention. "Someone strangled her. With one of the cat leashes we were going to give away as party favors." Just saying the words made my stomach flip again. I pressed my hand to it. "But you're not supposed to know that. The leash part."

His face had turned white, though. I don't think he even registered the leash bit. He was still trying to process the strangled part. "You're kidding, Maddie. That's . . . horrible. Who would've done that?"

I shook my head slowly. It had been a really long day already and it was barely noon. I was only upright because of the adrenaline rush that was still pumping through my blood, but I was in for a crash soon. And then I would need to really process this whole thing. Jillian was dead. One minute she'd been planning a fundraiser for our little cat café, and the next, someone had killed her. "No clue. Can we go home now?"

He took my hand. "Of course. Let's go. You have your grandmother's car, right?"

I nodded, pointing vaguely in the direction I think I'd parked it. It seemed so long ago now. As we were walking over, my phone rang. I glanced at it. Craig.

"Sorry," I said to Lucas. "I have to get this." Lucas and Craig didn't really care for each other. Mostly because when I'd returned to the island, Craig had wanted to get back together. I'd entertained the idea for a bit, but then things with Lucas happened and ultimately I decided to move forward, not backward. And Craig was happily in a relationship with Jade Bennett, who owned Jade Moon, a popular bar on the island. Still, the two of them had never quite gotten past their differences.

"Craig. Hey." I pressed the phone to my ear. Lucas opened the car door for me and I slid inside with JJ, grateful to shut the noise of the scene out.

"I have Val's phone. Ellory and I will bring it by around two. Let her know, please?"

"I will," I said. "What's going on in there? Find anything out?"

Silence. Which meant he couldn't talk. "We'll be over after we finish up here."

"Yeah." I disconnected and tossed the phone into the cupholder, leaned back, and closed my eyes as Lucas loaded Ollie in the back seat and climbed into the driver's side. JJ curled up in a ball on my lap and closed his eyes. It had been a long morning for him too.

"What's up?" Lucas asked.

"The cops are coming over to talk to Val. She was kind of in shock in there. And she dropped her phone near the body."

Lucas winced. "I don't blame her. So you don't have any idea . . ."

I shook my head. "No." I wondered if Ellory had sent a team right out to Stevie's house. They would probably start there if Jillian didn't have any information on her to identify an emergency contact. I also wondered how many people knew about their family ties, or if Stevie would know immediately that I was the one who had told them. I mean, it wasn't a secret, right?

I wondered if I should call Mish and give her a heads-up. Would she be happy at the news? I immediately felt bad at the thought. No matter what she thought of her husband's cousin, she wouldn't want her dead. Would she?

I thought of Stevie's car speeding out of the lot earlier and realized that I had no idea what to think. Mish had clearly hated Jillian. Stevie hadn't seemed all that fond of her either. But that couldn't mean one of them had hurt her. I'd known these people my whole life. Stevie was a nerd, for goodness' sake. A lovable, gentle nerd. And Mish was, well, just Mish. Apparently she could be loud and opinionated, but deep down she wouldn't hurt a fly. Would she?

But then why did my stomach feel so sick when I thought about the possibility that I was wrong?

"I need to talk to Mish," I said to Lucas. "Can you take me to her store?"

"I can, but she won't be there," he said. "She's at the café. She arrived just as I was leaving to walk Ollie, just after ten."

Chapter 19

"She did?" I tried to process that. Mish showed up around ten at our house. We found Jillian right around ten at the hotel, already dead. But for how long? Did that clear Mish, or implicate her?

"She did. Why?"

"How did she look?"

Lucas frowned. "What do you mean? She looked like Mish."

"Did she look . . . ill? She's been sick." I didn't want to ask *Did she look like she'd just killed somebody?* I was horrified I was even having that thought in the first place.

"I'm not sure. I just saw her running in, we didn't talk. Why do you need to talk to her? Is it about . . . what happened?"

I nodded.

He stopped at a red light and glanced over at me. "I'm not sure that's the best idea, Mads. What are you going to say to her? Do you really think you should be preempting the cops? I'm sure she's on their list."

"I'm sure too, but I have to ask her what happened

with Jillian. Why she was yelling at her out in the street. I feel like I need to get to her before they do. She's going to find out soon enough. Unless they already got to Stevie." I rubbed my temples. I had a headache and I desperately wanted to go lie down for a bit and reconcile these paranoid thoughts that were running through my head. What was wrong with me? Normal people didn't automatically suspect their childhood friends were murderers.

Lucas didn't look convinced, but he didn't say anything else. We were silent the rest of the short drive home. As we passed the marina, I caught a glimpse of Peyton's giant boat. I thought of Chad Novak on the steps of the hotel, watching everything, and wondered who knew what at this point. Had the word leaked to the guests? Had he figured out it was someone he knew, and if so, had he gotten to Peyton yet? And why was *he* there? Although he could've been staying there too—maybe they had coordinated their stays. It made sense, since Jillian probably had to work through Chad for access to Peyton. Also I got the sense that Chad and Peyton weren't besties, despite their professional relationship, so it made sense he might not be invited to stay on her yacht despite the size of it.

Grandpa's truck and my mom's car were already in the driveway when we pulled up. But Mish's car wasn't. I sat up straight in my seat. "Shoot! Did she leave?"

"She didn't drive," he said. "At least, her car wasn't here earlier either. I assumed Stevie dropped her off?"

I thought about that. If Stevie had dropped her off, he must've been alone when I saw his car this morning. It was also after ten when I'd seen him. Had he dropped her off and gone straight to the hotel? Why? He couldn't have had a planned meeting with Jillian, since she had a planned meeting with us. Unless he was supposed to meet with her after she finished with us.

"I have no idea," I murmured. But maybe that was a good thing. If she'd been with someone, she would've had an alibi. I pushed the door open and slid out of the car. "I'll be right in. I'm going to the café and talk to her. Can you bring JJ in?" I closed the door and hurried away before he tried to stop me.

When I entered the café, it was quiet. Mish was alone, save for one guest, who sat on one of the floor pillows with three kittens flopped around her in various stages of ecstasy while she rubbed all their tummies.

Mish glanced up from fluffing cat beds and straightened when she saw me. "Maddie. Hey. I hope it's okay I came in. I know I wasn't on the schedule, but I texted Adele. She said it was fine."

"It's perfectly fine," I said. "Where is Adele?"

"She went out to get some baby food for the kittens. She'll be right back."

Good, because she was going to need to take over the café after I broke the news to Mish. "How are you feeling? I was worried."

"Yeah. Migraine." Mish touched her head briefly. "I'm sorry. And the flowers. I should've called to thank you. They are beautiful."

This was awkward. And it was going to get worse pretty quickly. There was no way I couldn't tell her, and it appeared the news hadn't yet traveled.

"No need to be sorry. I wanted to make sure you were okay, that's all." I clasped and unclasped my hands.

She peered at me. "Are you okay?"

I sighed. "No, Mish." I grabbed her arm and pulled her out of earshot of our guest. "What's the deal with Jillian Allen?"

Her gaze locked on mine. "What do you mean?"

"I mean, you two are related. Did you forget to mention that?"

She sighed and picked up Charlie, nuzzling her cheek against his fur. "We aren't related. Stevie is related. There's a difference."

"Well, whatever the difference is, you should've mentioned it. Along with the fact that you kind of hate her."

"You noticed?"

"Noticed you yelling at her in the street? Hard to miss. Stevie told me they're cousins. How come you didn't tell me?"

Mish closed her eyes and rubbed her temples. "You caught me off guard when you mentioned she was coming. Honestly, the last place I expected her to pop up was at your café. I didn't really know what to do. I wanted to ask Stevie if I should mention it. And I guess . . ." she dropped her gaze. "I didn't want you to know I was associated with her."

"You know this island, Mish. Better than me, actually. I had a break for ten years. It's hard to hide things. Why would you want to keep it a secret?"

"It's complicated."

She had no idea. "Is it really that bad? She offered to do a lot for the café—"

Mish cut me off. "She wants to *look* like she's doing a lot for the café. Don't let her fool you."

Stevie had made a similar comment. Something about Mish's good deed of the week. "So what were you two arguing about the other day?"

I could see her weighing the *none of your business* response, but in the end she decided against it. "I was mad that she was trying to weasel her way into the café. Why are you asking so many questions about this, Maddie?

I promise I won't ruin things for you." Her voice held a touch of sarcasm, and I wasn't in the mood.

"Mish. Did you see her today?"

"No. I haven't seen her since yesterday. She came by to pick up her packages. And talk to Stevie. I didn't want to be there so I left. Again, why are you asking?"

I took a breath, then looked her in the eye. "Jillian's dead." I probably should feel bad about blurting it out like that, but I didn't see the point in beating around the bush.

She stared at me for a second, then blinked slowly. "What?"

"She's dead. Val and I just went to meet her at the venue for the event, and she was dead." I watched her closely, looking for some sort of sign that this was not a surprise, then immediately felt horrible for the thought. Mish wasn't a killer.

Mish sank down onto the floor, releasing Charlie. He hopped down and went to his bed, where he proceeded to clean his tail.

"Mish." I sank down on the floor next to her. "This is important. Where's your car? I didn't see it outside."

She looked up at me, apparently still processing what I was saying. "In the shop. Stevie dropped me off. He had a few things to do this morning and I didn't want to sit at home."

"What time did you get here?"

"Around ten."

She's lying. The thought flitted through my mind before I even realized it, but it was true. I'd seen Stevie around ten, maybe a little later. But with the traffic around here, there was no way he could've dropped her off then made it to the hotel that quickly. Unless my timing was off, but I didn't think it was.

I didn't say any of that. Instead, I rested my head against the wall.

"Does Stevie know?" she asked finally.

Good question. Because I was also curious about why he'd been at the hotel. "I don't know. Do you want me to drive you home?"

She shook her head slowly. "I'll call him. What's going to happen now, Maddie?"

I sighed. "I have no idea, Mish. Who would have wanted her dead?"

"My guess? There's a lot of options," Mish said.

Chapter 20

Mish wanted to be alone while she waited for Stevie. She went outside to sit on the steps. I debated going after her, but figured it was best to let her be. Since we still had a guest, I waited for Adele to show up. Luckily she came back within five minutes.

"What's going on? Where's Mish?" she asked, dropping a bag full of baby food jars on the counter. "A treat for the kittens," she said, motioning toward the bag.

"Mish was outside a few minutes ago. She's leaving early."

Adele rolled her eyes. "That girl. Shows up when she feels like it, leaves when she feels like it. I have a schedule for a reason."

"Adele," I interrupted. "She has a good reason today. Jillian is dead."

Adele stared at me. "Come again?"

"Jillian. She's dead. Val and I found her at the hotel when we went for the meeting. Someone killed her."

Adele whistled. "Your fancy friend got herself killed? How about that."

Nothing like sympathy for the victim. "Were you here when Mish arrived?"

She nodded. "Yeah. It was just after ten. I noticed because our ten o'clock appointment was a few minutes late and they showed up at exactly the same time."

"Did you see who dropped her off?"

"No. I was inside." She cocked her head, observing me curiously. "Why? She kill her or something? I saw them yelling at each other but didn't realize it was that serious."

"No! God, no. Don't say that, please." I was mortified that either she'd read my mind or my horrible thoughts weren't that far-fetched.

Adele shrugged. "Just asking."

"Can you cover the guests?"

"I was planning to anyway. 'Til people came in messing with my schedule," she grumbled.

"Okay. Don't mention this to anyone yet, please."

"Who am I gonna tell? The cats?"

I left her to it and went into the house. Val was nowhere in sight. Grandpa and my mother were on the couch.

"I sent Val upstairs to take a shower," my mother said. "She's not feeling so great."

"I get that," I said, sitting down opposite them.

"How are *you* doing?" My mother focused on me. "Are you okay? Lucas and Ethan are getting some food ready for you."

"Fine," I said.

"I doubt that." She squeezed my hand, then leaned back and closed her eyes. "That poor woman," she said after a moment. "She was so happy yesterday. So excited to plan this event." She opened her eyes and looked at me. "What will happen with the event?"

"I have no idea." It didn't seem like the best time to

be thinking about that, which must have occurred to my mother too because she covered her mouth with her hand as if she could take the words back.

"That was terribly insensitive. I have no idea what's wrong with me," she said, looking mortified.

"Mom. Don't worry. You're shaken up. We all are." I reached over and patted her hand.

"Do you think Peyton knows?"

I wished people would stop asking me questions like I was an expert on this whole thing, or any of these people. I'd just met them all this week, for crying out loud. "I have no idea."

Lucas returned with a glass of water with lemon and a little mini quiche, which he set down on the table in front of me. "Eat," he said. "You need some fuel. You've had a rough morning. Leo, Sophie, would you like one? Ethan made them fresh this morning."

My mother declined. Grandpa accepted. He rarely turned food down. Lucas went to fetch their plates and I picked up my fork, taking a tentative bite. My stomach still felt upset, but the food was so good and soothing that I found myself eating like I hadn't eaten in a week.

After a few bites, I looked at Grandpa. "Is there something you aren't telling me?"

By the look on his face, I could tell I'd caught him completely off guard, which was my intention. A cop who expected something to happen was of no use to me. Grandpa was still good on his feet, but I figured bringing this up out of the blue I'd have some kind of advantage.

Grandpa returned my stare. "There's probably plenty of things I'm not telling you, Doll—but maybe you never asked." He leaned back in his chair, folding his hands over his belly. "Which particular thing are you referring to?"

"Stevie Warner. Why was he here looking for you the other day? And why didn't you tell me he's Jillian's cousin?"

"What?" My mother glanced sideways at Grandpa. "That woman is—I mean was—related to Stevie Warner?"

"Did she tell you that, or did Stevie?" Grandpa asked.

"I went to Stevie's yesterday and she was there. He told me. I think he didn't want me to think he was cheating on Mish or something. Which I was starting to worry about. How come you didn't tell me?"

"Because Stevie is my client, and it really wasn't up to me to share."

"What did he hire you for?"

"Madalyn. You know I can't discuss my clients' cases."

"Grandpa." I matched his tone. "You know this is affecting me and the café now. And clearly Val"—I waved my hand in the direction of the stairs—"who's a mess after what happened today."

"Whoa," Grandpa held up a hand. "Hold your horses. This woman's death could be totally unrelated. You're jumping way ahead of yourself."

"Unrelated to what?" my mother asked, exasperated. "I have no idea what's going on here. Can someone please enlighten me?"

"It's a property dispute," Grandpa said.

I narrowed my eyes at him. "The one you mentioned the other day? But you made it sound so boring. And you didn't mention that Stevie was part of that!"

He ignored me and turned back to my mother. "Marcella Cox's two daughters. Diane and Deidre. You remember them, Soph. You went to school with Diane."

My mother nodded. "Stevie's mother."

"And Deidre is Jillian's mother," Grandpa said.

"Wow." My mother sat back. "I'd forgotten all about Deidre. She was older than Diane. She left the island before we graduated, didn't she? And she hasn't been out here in probably more than twenty years, from what I remember. Didn't Marcella disown her or something?"

"I think they had a falling out and hadn't spoken in years. Anyway, Marcella died recently and there's a bit of a . . . kerfuffle with her estate. She left some instructions that weren't very popular with her living relatives."

"But wouldn't that be between the daughters?" I asked.

He shook his head. "Aside from her not speaking to one of them, neither of them live out here. Or want to. And Stevie has lived on the property his whole life. So she decided to bypass her daughters."

"Jillian doesn't"—I winced—"didn't live here either, though. Did she suddenly change her mind?"

Grandpa said nothing, which I took to mean he was done with this conversation. I couldn't blame him. He did have a duty to his clients to keep their secrets. It was just frustrating. Or maybe he didn't actually know. "Grandpa. Did you know who Jillian was when she came here?"

Grandpa regarded me with that stare that probably took down hundreds of criminals in his day, all the way from petty thieves to murderers. "I knew there was an issue with Stevie's extended family. I didn't know it was her until after she came here the first time to meet with you. Mish went to Stevie and told him she was coming here. That prompted his visit to me."

"What did he hire you to do, exactly?"

"Stevie was worried about Jillian undermining the terms of the will. I'm not getting into that part," he said, holding up a hand when I opened my mouth to interject.

"He wanted me to see what she was doing while she was here, who she was speaking to, anything that might give him an indication of how she was going to try to get around the terms of the will. She felt entitled to the property, but he felt more so. He's lived there forever, as you know. And he's . . . dependent on the money they're bringing in."

"Money?"

Grandpa nodded. "They're using the house as an Airbnb."

So that was why there were so many cars out in front of the big house the other day. I shoved my plate away and leaned back against the couch. "I just told Mish she was dead."

"You did?"

"I did. I couldn't really pretend like nothing had happened, could I?"

Grandpa's lips were pressed tightly together, a sure sign that he disapproved. I didn't much care at the moment. I really had wanted to see Mish's reaction, which had been surprised enough, unless she was a good actor, with one caveat.

She hadn't asked me how Jillian had died.

Chapter 21

I had more questions, but my phone rang. I glanced down at the caller ID. Becky. I closed my eyes briefly. That meant one thing—the news was out and my involvement had leaked.

Resigned, I pressed the green button to accept her call. "Hey."

"What is going on?" she shrieked in my ear.

I held the phone away, cringing, until I was sure she was done. "With?" I asked wearily.

"Um. Are you serious? With the woman who was murdered today at the Paradise!"

"Yeah. That."

"Yeah. That," Becky repeated. "My reporter got your name from the log as the person who gave a statement?"

"Yep. Val and I were there to meet with her."

"You're kidding. So this was . . ." I heard her flipping pages in a notebook. "The rescue league person?"

"Yes."

"The one who was coming to see your café, right?"

"The very same."

"So what happened?"

"No idea," I said, remembering Ellory's words about the leash. *Not for public consumption.* I wondered when the press conference would be held. Her identity must be out, if Becky knew. Although she did have a good relationship with the cops, and they might have told her on the condition she didn't print it until they gave the go-ahead.

"This is crazy. So I also got an anonymous tip that she's related to Stevie Warner. And there's some kind of family dispute over property."

I hadn't expected that news to break so quickly, although I guessed it must be common enough knowledge for people who've lived here forever. That was the thing about an island like this, and one of the reasons I'd left in the first place. Everyone knew everything about everyone. And didn't hesitate to tell anyone who may have missed it. But an anonymous tip? Seemed so . . . clandestine. "Really," I said. "Any idea who the tipster was?"

"Nope. But that's what anonymous means, right?" A pause. "Sounds like you knew they were related?"

"Yes, I did."

"How?"

"Stevie told me. She was at his house when I went there yesterday."

"So what do you know about the situation?"

"Not much. Just that they didn't seem to get along. I was more focused on what she wanted to do for the café. That's why I was there today when . . . she was found. We were there to look at the venue."

I could hear Becky scribbling furiously. "You know I need to put this in the story, right? That you guys were working together?"

"I figured."

"It's more press for the café," Becky pointed out.

"Am I supposed to feel good about that?"

"I don't know. Any press is good press, right?" Becky sighed. "I'm sorry, Maddie. I hate that you're involved in this."

"Me too."

"But since you are, can I send my reporter over to get the deets on the event and how you all were working together?"

"Today? Beck—"

"I know, it's a crazy day, but yes. I need to print the longer version of this story tomorrow. I'm holding on her name right now until they notify next of kin, but then it will be online. This is going to be big news once it gets out that Peyton Chandler was involved in this fundraiser."

I frowned. "How do you know Peyton Chandler was involved?"

"The hotel people."

I thought of the purple-haired woman at the front desk this morning, so disappointed that Peyton wasn't coming to the walk-through. "Send the reporter," I said with a sigh. "I'll do it."

"Great. It's Jenna. You remember her, right?"

"How could I forget." Jenna had written about a huge murder and scandal that had happened right after I'd gotten back to Daybreak, in which I'd had the misfortune of becoming involved. It was the sort of thing that stuck with a person.

My other line beeped. I glanced at the caller ID. I didn't recognize it. My finger hovered over the decline button, but at the last minute I decided to answer. "I have to run. I'll see Jenna later." I clicked over. "Maddie James."

"Maddie, hello." I didn't recognize the subdued female

voice on the other end. "This is Jo Sabatini. With the Shoreline Animal Rescue League?"

Oh jeez. I'd completely forgotten about Jillian's staff. "Jo, yes, hello. I'm so sorry about Jillian. I can't even imagine what you and your team must be feeling." As I said it, it suddenly struck me that I hadn't seen Jo anywhere this morning. I'd assumed she was coming to the meeting too, and that perhaps she and Jillian would have met beforehand.

So where had she been?

"Thank you. This event meant everything to Jillian. She was so excited about it." Jo paused as her voice wobbled a bit. She took a moment then continued. "I want to assure you we'll continue with the event. Jillian would want it that way."

I frowned. They still wanted to throw this party? At the same place where Jillian had been murdered? "Um. Well, that's very kind of you, but are you sure? It seems so . . . unimportant right now."

"Our mission at the League is to help animals, in any way we can. This is definitely a priority for us. As I said, Jillian believed so strongly in our mission." She paused, as if collecting herself. I could tell she was trying desperately to keep her tone even and calm despite the circumstances, much unlike the highly excitable Jillian. "I promise you, we'll keep our word and get this fundraiser done. I know how much you and the shelter were counting on this money."

"Listen, Jo, I totally appreciate that but I understand how hard this must be for you and your team," I said. "I completely understand if we should postpone."

"No, not at all. Like I said, Jillian would have wanted it this way. So, if your sister is still in, I'll be in touch?"

Good question. And one I certainly wasn't going to bring up to Val right now. "She's . . . still digesting all this," I said. "I'll talk to her once she's feeling a bit better, okay?"

"Sounds great. You have my number now. We'll talk soon." Jo disconnected.

"What was that all about?" Grandpa asked.

"The rescue league. They still want to do the fundraiser."

"You've got to be kidding me."

We all swiveled around at Ethan's voice coming from the kitchen doorway. He was staring at us like he'd never seen us before. "They still want to do the event? Who was that?"

"It was someone who works with Jillian," I said. "Keep it down, okay? I don't want to talk to Val about it today."

"You're not seriously still thinking of doing it, are you?"

"I don't know," I said. "I can't really focus on that now. Why?"

He shook his head. "I just think it's a bad idea. I mean, look at everything that's happened once you got involved with that woman?"

I stared at him. This was not like Ethan at all. "What happened to her was awful, but it has nothing to do with us," I said.

"Look. Why don't we talk about this tomorrow?" Grandpa suggested. "Nobody's feeling great today so we probably shouldn't be making decisions."

The doorbell rang.

"I'll get it," I said, anxious to get out of the room that had suddenly become full of tension.

But when I got to the door, I regretted it. It was Jenna. Man, she was quick. She'd probably been waiting outside my house until Becky had given her the okay.

Jenna turned on her five-hundred-watt smile when she saw me. "Maddie. Hi," she said. "Thanks for speaking with us. I have a photographer, okay?"

"Sure, come on in," I said, holding the door open.

"Great. Kevin, this way." She turned and motioned to the photographer behind her. He slipped past me with a look of apology. Jenna could be a bit like a bull in a china shop.

When I turned back to the living room, it was empty. Grandpa and Ethan had disappeared. Nothing like throwing me to the wolves. I motioned to the now-empty couches. "Sit," I said. "Can I get you anything?"

Jenna shook her head, still smiling. "Just the scoop," she said with a wink. "So, this dead woman. Let's start with the family scandal."

I stared at her. "Sorry. What family scandal?"

"The Warner family scandal." She leaned forward in her chair. "I've learned that the victim was related to the Warners, and that there's a battle going on for a pricey piece of property here on the island." Her eyes glinted with the promise of a big story. "And with the passing of the rightful owner—the grandmother—all bets are off. Do you think that's why she was killed?"

Chapter 22

Leave it to Jenna to pounce on the family scandal angle. "I'm sorry, I don't know what you're talking about," I said.

Jenna leaned forward, legs crossed, pen tapping impatiently against her reporter's notebook. "I thought you knew. Let me fill you in. The victim was a cousin to one of our residents. Stevie Warner. I believe his wife volunteers here." She smiled sweetly. "Jogging your mind yet?"

I excused myself to use the bathroom. Once I'd locked myself in, I called Becky back. "Are you serious?" I said when she answered.

"I usually am. About what?" She sounded unfazed. I could hear a lot of noise behind her, like she was out of her office and in the middle of the newsroom where all the buzzing about the murder was happening. She loved this stuff. I adored my best friend, but she was a little twisted in that regard. Becky Walsh might look like the sweet girl next door—petite, blond curls, angelic face—until she opened her mouth or picked up a writing instrument. Her sarcasm could bring down the mightiest of men, and when she put pen to paper, well, she could take down an army. She was the absolute definition of *little but fierce.*

"Your reporter is here trying to find out if Jillian died because of her family issues! You said you were sending Jenna here to talk about the café."

"She'll cover both. Hey, the family rift is definitely a possible motive," Becky said. "Don't you think? Property disputes, especially with a lot of money in the balance?"

That now-familiar image of Stevie's car speeding away from the Paradise this morning ran through my brain again. I closed my eyes. "I don't know what to think. What do you know about the property dispute?"

"Nothing, yet. We need to get our hands on the grandmother's will, now that we know the story. We'll be checking it out first thing tomorrow. But the anonymous tip suggested she appointed an executor to make the final decision on who gets the estate. Sounds weird, but rich people can be a little eccentric, right?"

I had no room to pace in this tiny bathroom. Pacing helped me think. Instead, I went to the window and peered out. The day was still as beautiful as it had been this morning, if not better. There wasn't a cloud in the sky and I could just catch a glimpse of the ocean from here. Upstairs, I had the full view. I turned away. "Did you know she was going to go down this path with me?"

"No, but I don't ask for my reporters' strategies every time they go on an interview. I figured she'd wait to see the details of the will, but I guess she wanted to get a jump start. Did Stevie tell you about the property dispute?"

"No. Grandpa did, a few minutes ago."

"How did *he* know?" Becky asked.

"Seriously? Grandpa Leo knows everything," I said, evading the question. "So you don't know who the executor is that she appointed?"

"I don't, but I will tomorrow. I have no idea where the other family members come in."

"Their mothers are sisters," I murmured, remembering Grandpa's words. "But they don't live out here either."

"It's all crazy town. But at least now we know where Stevie gets his money."

"No one ever thought Stevie had money," I protested. "Did they?"

Becky snorted. "They have that expensive lease on Mish's store, they both have nice cars, Mish is always dressed to the nines, and their kid is in that fancy boarding school. How many people do you know who live like that on a teacher's salary? He tutors for a living. And coaches chess. Last I checked, those weren't the most lucrative careers, especially on a small island. And Mish's family—well, they were less well off, if you remember."

She had a point. Funny, I'd never really thought about Stevie and Mish's financial status. They didn't seem particularly flashy to me. I knew Mish poured a lot of effort and time into her store. I guess I'd assumed it made them plenty of money. Mish's family had been what most people might think of as low-to-moderate income. On the island, that translated to poor, especially among the upper class. But it hadn't affected Mish's status. In school, she'd worked hard to make up in personality what she lacked in money.

"This is messed up," I said. "How the heck did I end up in the middle of this thing?"

"Good question, girlfriend. But you always do," Becky said. "And we need to get a jump on this thing. By tonight—if not sooner—we're going to have all the Boston channels, plus the major tabloids here. The cops owe us a press conference. Or at the very least, a press release confirming the details. And the victim. As for Jenna, she'll write about the café too. She's just . . . exploring a different angle."

"Why the tabloids?" I asked.

"Peyton Chandler."

"But she had nothing to do with it!" I protested. "She wasn't even there."

"Doesn't matter. She's linked to the rescue league and the fundraiser. She's here on the island. You think these guys care about being literal?"

Ugh. This was going to get ugly. And since she was already going down this path, I needed to tell her. "Listen," I said. "This is totally off the record. Do *not* tell Jenna."

She waited. "What?"

"I saw Stevie's car today. At the Paradise after we found Jillian. When I went outside to meet the cops."

Becky sucked in a breath. "You're kidding."

"I wish I was."

"You're sure it was him?"

"How many bright yellow Subarus are there on the island?" I asked.

"Good point. But did you see *him*?" she pressed.

I thought about that. I'd been too far away to see who was driving and just assumed it was Stevie. "No. I guess I didn't. Either way, you can *not* repeat this," I reminded her.

"I won't. But it's good to have in my back pocket depending on how things go. Maddie, I have to go. I think our first tabloid is on the case. I'll be right there!"

she shouted to someone in the background. "Go talk to Jenna and keep me posted, okay?"

I told her I would and hung up, tapping my phone against the palm of my hand. How deep did this family angst really go? I was kind of afraid to find out. But I knew one thing for sure. I was going to be first in line to view that will tomorrow. Well, maybe second, knowing Becky. She would probably make her reporter sleep on the courthouse steps tonight to be the first to get the scoop.

When I returned to the living room, Jenna was tapping her foot impatiently on the floor while she scrolled through her phone. When she saw me, she turned the smile back on. "There you are. Ready?"

"Sorry about that," I said, sliding into the chair across from her. "Let's get some ground rules straight, though. The only thing I'll comment on is the café and the planned fundraiser. I don't know anything about the victim aside from the fact that she was running this event with me and my sister. Okay?"

Jenna tilted her head, studying me intently. "Okay," she finally said.

It seemed too easy. "Okay, then," I said, motioning for her to start.

"One caveat," Jenna said.

I should have known. "What?"

"Can you help us get access to Peyton Chandler?"

Oh, for Pete's sake. I really needed to talk to Becky about this woman. "I don't see how I can do that," I said. "I've only met her twice, and it was through Jillian. I'm hardly in a position to convince her to do anything." I didn't mention the meet and greet we had discussed.

"Well," Jenna said, "I know Becky would be thrilled

if we could do an exclusive with her. So if there's any way." She flashed me a thousand-watt smile.

In that instant, she kind of reminded me of Jillian. "Yeah, sure. If I talk to her again I'll ask." I hated that she threw Becky in my face, but it always worked. "Let's do this, because I only have a few minutes."

Apparently feeling like she'd gotten what she wanted, Jenna focused on the café and our hopes for the fundraiser. We actually had a decent conversation, and I barely noticed the photographer getting some shots of me talking.

Until my doorbell rang.

Shoot. It had to be Ellory. He was due any minute to talk to Val.

Grandpa appeared as if out of nowhere. He nodded at us. "I'll get it."

Sure enough, he returned with Craig and Ellory. Ellory scoped out the room. He didn't look thrilled to see Jenna, but he greeted us both with the same polite tone.

Jenna's eyes, meanwhile, had brightened with that glint of a breaking news story.

"Well," I said brightly, rising. "Shall we go get those photos?"

"In a minute," Jenna said. "Nice to see you, Sergeant. Any word on the case?"

"No," Ellory said shortly.

"When do you expect the press conference?" she asked.

"I'm not sure. Our spokesperson will let everyone on our list know. Leo, a word?"

Grandpa led them to the kitchen.

I glanced at my watch, feigning impatience. "Do you want photos? I'm going to need to get going soon."

Jenna weighed her options. She finally seemed to

decide photos were her best bet, so I led her to the café and delivered her into my mother's care. Mom would make sure she kept her eye on Jenna and saw her out when she was done.

With that off my plate, I headed back inside to the kitchen, where Grandpa had taken Ellory and Craig.

"Ethan went to get Val," Grandpa told me.

"Where's Lucas?"

"I think he went upstairs," Grandpa said. "He was hiding from the cameras."

I turned to Ellory. "Any news?"

"Not much to report," Ellory said. "Still gathering evidence and trying to understand who this woman was." He looked tired already. I knew that the cops hated when non-locals came to their island and got themselves killed. It had happened a couple of times, and it brought a lot of headaches. Not to mention a media circus. Especially when the person was tied to famous people like Peyton and Marco. Like Becky, images of private media jets and helicopters already en route to get on-the-ground coverage would put Ellory and his team over the edge. As far as Becky was concerned, this was her story, as the lone newspaper on the island. And the cops resisted the media even more when it wasn't our local paper or station.

So basically, until this case was solved we were going to have cranky cops and cranky journalists.

"Do you want to talk to Maddie again while I talk to Val?" Craig asked Ellory.

I looked at Ellory. "You need me again?"

"I just have a couple more questions for you," Ellory said. "You mind?"

Chapter 23

Val came down a minute later. Craig took her out to the living room to talk in private. I wasn't sure what else they thought they were going to get out of her, but she'd been on the scene so they had to check the box.

Apparently I, on the other hand, was a different story. "I don't know what else I can tell you," I said to Ellory, pulling out the chair next to Grandpa.

He patted my knee and start to rise. "I'm going to get out of your way," he said.

"Actually," Ellory said. "I was hoping to talk to both of you."

"Me too? Well, sure." Grandpa lowered himself back down and clasped his hands together. "How can I help?"

Ellory's stoic gaze traveled from me to Grandpa and back. "What do you know about Jillian's relationship to the Warners?" he asked.

Since he was still looking at me, I figured that meant I needed to take this one. "Like I told you earlier, they were cousins."

"I know that, but what was their relationship like?"

"I honestly don't know. I didn't even know they were

cousins until yesterday. I saw her and Mish . . . having words in the street the other day, then I saw her at Stevie's yesterday. That's when he told me."

"Leo, I take it you knew that before yesterday," Ellory said. It didn't sound like a question.

Grandpa lifted his shoulders in a shrug. "I know a lot about the people on this island."

"What else do you know about their relationship?" Ellory asked Grandpa.

"I'd heard a bit," Grandpa said. "But Jillian didn't spend much time here, as you've probably learned."

Ellory waited.

Grandpa did too.

"Was it good? Bad? Indifferent?" Ellory asked through gritted teeth.

"There were some issues relating to Marcella's death," Grandpa said. "And her will. The estate is worth quite a bit of money. I don't know much else, though. Have you spoken to Stevie Warner?"

"Not yet," Ellory said. "I just found out from Maddie earlier today about their relationship. I asked him to come in and speak to us this afternoon."

"Why do you think Grandpa would know anything?" I asked.

"How well do you know the family?" Ellory asked Grandpa, ignoring me.

"I knew Marcella fairly well. She and my wife had been friendly," Grandpa said.

I hid a smile. Ellory had probably forgotten Grandpa was a master at interviews—or interrogations.

Ellory waited a beat. When it became clear that Grandpa wasn't going to offer anything else up, he sighed. "Did Stevie Warner express any animosity toward his cousin in your presence? I understand she was working with Maddie and Val on an event and had been spending time here."

"Animosity is a subjective term, isn't it?" Grandpa said. "Honestly, I never saw them together. Stevie had . . . alerted me to the family issue. Then Jillian contacted my granddaughter and they decided to work together, and I didn't want to put her in the middle of whatever was going on." He glanced at me. "I guess that didn't work out so well. I'm sorry, Doll."

"Not your fault, Grandpa," I said.

Ellory turned to me. "So Jillian never mentioned any of this family drama to you."

"No. We'd only met a couple times and we were focused on the event."

"Did she say why she was here in the first place?"

"When she first called me, she said she would be here on other business but wanted to see the café."

"When was this?"

I thought back. "About two weeks ago, maybe a little less?"

Ellory wrote that down.

"Who else was involved in this fundraiser?" he asked.

"Jillian had gotten Peyton Chandler and Marco Moore to be guests of honor. Peyton is a big animal person. They both are."

"So she had a relationship with them."

"I guess," I said. "I don't really know how connected they are, but she seemed to know them pretty well. She probably worked mostly through their agent." I thought of the four of them outside of the café the other day, having that serious conversation. None of them had looked happy then either. Not to mention the Peyton/Jillian argument I'd heard on the back porch.

"Who is that?"

"Chad Novak. I think he was at the hotel this morning." I suddenly remembered I hadn't told Ellory that. "I saw him on the stairs inside."

"Was he staying there?"

"No idea. Jillian was."

He cocked his head. "How do you know that?"

"She told me," Grandpa said.

Ellory drummed his fingertips on the table. "Interesting. You're sure?"

"That's what she said. Why?"

"Because she wasn't registered as a guest," Ellory said.

I looked at Grandpa. "That's weird. She was dressed like she'd just gotten out of bed. Bare feet and everything. You think she was under a different name?"

"Could be." Ellory made a note.

"Check Jo Sabatini. They work together at the League. Maybe she reserved rooms for everyone?"

"I will. Any other names come to mind?"

I shook my head. "She didn't mention anyone else by name. But . . ." I had to tell him. He'd find out anyway. "She got her packages delivered to Stevie's house. The boxes of . . ." I winced a little bit. "The leashes and collars. She was picking them up from Stevie's when I went there yesterday. I did wonder why she didn't get them delivered to the hotel if she was staying there."

"I have no idea." He closed his notebook and offered me a small smile. "See? And you thought you had nothing new to tell me." He stood.

Grandpa and I stood with him.

"I'm going to see how Craig's doing," he said, an unspoken order to wait here.

I sank back down into my seat. Grandpa went to pour us more coffee. My phone buzzed on the table. I glanced at it. Another number I didn't recognize. I almost let it go to voice mail, then decided this really wasn't the day to do that and wearily picked it up. "This is Maddie."

"Maddie, hello." I recognized that breathy voice immediately, but she still introduced herself. "This is Peyton Chandler."

I sat up straighter in my chair, as if she could see me. "Peyton. How . . . how are you?" I assumed she'd heard, but couldn't be sure.

"Well, I wish I could say I was fine, but how can we be fine after what happened? How are you holding up? I hope it's okay that I called. I asked Chad to get me your number."

I wondered where he had gotten it. "It's perfectly fine. Thank you for calling." I paused, not sure what else to say.

There was an awkward silence—apparently Peyton didn't know what to say either—then she said, "Would you and Val like to come out to my boat and talk today? We have a lot of loose ends to discuss."

I wasn't entirely sure what she meant by that. Maybe Jo and the rest of the League's team had already reached out to her about keeping the fundraiser on the books? Now I was intrigued. "Sure. I mean, I'll have to ask Val, but I'm sure it will be fine."

"Okay. That would be great. Say four o'clock?"

I agreed, then hung up and looked at Grandpa, who was patiently waiting for me to tell him what that call was about. "Peyton Chandler," I said.

He nodded. "I gathered."

"She wants me and Val to go over to her boat later."

At this, he arched an eyebrow. "For what?"

"To discuss the 'loose ends.'" I took the coffee cup he handed me. "You think Val will be up for it?"

"Up for what?" Val asked, walking into the kitchen.

"There she is," Grandpa said, going over to give her a hug. "How did that go?"

"It went fine. I didn't have anything different to tell them than Maddie. But I got my phone back." She held it up with a weak smile. "So, what will I be up for?"

"A visit to the marina. Peyton Chandler called and asked us to come over later," I said.

"She did? Why?"

"No clue." I spread my hands wide. "But I think we should go see."

"Do you really think that's a good idea?" Ethan, who had come in right behind her, chimed in. "This whole thing is kind of a mess."

"She's probably just going to tell us she's leaving and wants to say goodbye. She was really kind to offer to help, so I think we should go. It will be fine." I looked at my sister.

"I agree. I'll go," she said. She reached over and patted Ethan's hand. "Don't worry about me. Besides, I need a distraction. I don't want to go upstairs and pretend to take a nap and keep seeing . . . Jillian's body." She shivered a bit. "Come get me when it's time to leave."

Chapter 24

I went upstairs to find Lucas. My head was kind of spinning and I needed to sit down for five minutes. He was in my room with Ollie and JJ, sitting on the bed. He looked relieved when I came in and reached for my hand. "Hey. All okay?"

I nodded, flopping down next to him and closing my eyes. "As okay as I guess it can be."

"The cops find out anything else?"

"No. I told them about the agent being at the hotel. It's weird." I sat up. "Jillian told Grandpa she was staying there, and she was dressed this morning like she was. But she's not registered as a guest."

"You think she was staying with someone?"

"I have no idea. Peyton Chandler just called and invited me and Val to her boat later."

"You're kidding."

"Nope."

"For what?"

"I don't know. I guess we'll find out when we get there. She mentioned 'loose ends.' And Jillian's other person from the League called earlier. She wants to still try to have the event. I wonder if that's why Peyton is calling."

"They want to have it still? Jeez, nothing like mourning their colleague, huh?"

"I know, right? I can't figure out why this is so important to them."

"Well, it's a good story, right? Soldiering on in the face of a tragedy and all that?"

I dropped my arm over my eyes. "You've been hanging around with Becky too much."

That afternoon, we took Val's car to the marina. As she drove, I rested my head against the back of the seat. "How are you doing?" I asked finally.

She stared straight ahead. I could see how tense her jaw was from the side. "I don't think I'll ever get that vision out of my mind."

"I get it." I sighed and turned to look out my window. The island looked . . . normal. People were going about their business, laughing, dragging beach chairs and kids around, eating ice cream. A perfect island Sunday. Even if the news had broken already, the tourists were going to be too busy having fun to worry about it—if they even tuned in long enough to hear. "I'm sorry."

"Why are you sorry?" In a very uncharacteristically Val gesture, she reached over and squeezed my hand. "It's not your fault. And you actually got close enough to . . . well." She cleared her throat. "I'm sorry for you too."

Wow. Val was not the touchy-feely, talk-about-emotions type. This event had had some effect on her. I squeezed her hand back. "Thanks. Hey, is Ethan okay?"

"I think he's more shaken up than I am," she said with a little laugh. "And that's saying something. But he's fine."

"Understandable. But he seemed pretty serious about you not coming out here today and distancing yourself from this."

"I know. He's just being protective. I was really rattled this morning, Maddie. I know you have a thicker skin than me, so you probably don't get it." She slowed as we came to a cluster of cop cars at the top of the street leading to the marina. Apparently it was true—no one was getting in unless you had specific business. Apparently the whole island was coming to gawk at Peyton Chandler's boat. And probably at Peyton Chandler.

"I don't know why people think that. I am not ever going to be okay with finding a dead body. And what's going on?" I craned my neck to try to see around the flashing lights, a feeling of dread starting to build in my stomach. Had something happened here too?

Val must've been thinking the same thing. Her hands were clenched on the steering wheel, knuckles white. A cop came over to the car, leaning close to the window.

"Help you?" he asked in a bored tone.

"We have an appointment at the marina," Val said.

"With who?"

I resisted the urge to correct his English and leaned over. "Peyton Chandler."

He barked out a laugh. "Sure thing. You and the rest of the island. The marina's closed to anyone without a boat."

Val looked at me, raising her eyebrows.

I stood my ground. "She invited us. Is she okay? Did something happen?"

Now he was looking at me like I was an escaped mental patient. "She invited you," he said. Skepticism dripped from the words.

"She did. Maddie James."

"Mm-hmm. And she invited me to sleep over later too," he said. He stood, rapping the hood of the car with his knuckles. "You can turn around right here."

"We're not leaving," I said. "I'll call her."

The cop pulled out his radio as I pulled out my cell phone. Good. I hoped he called Ellory. Ellory might not like it that we were there, but he would know we weren't just celebrity stalkers. I hoped the number Peyton had called me on was her direct line and not some diverted number that would go to a call center. I hit REDIAL and waited for someone to pick up. As I did, I glanced in the sideview mirror at the car behind me. Then sat up straight. "You have got to be kidding me."

"Maddie?" Peyton had picked up. "Are you here?"

"Peyton. Hi. Yes, sorry. We are at the top of the street but the police won't let us through."

She sighed. "I'm very sorry about that. We were getting a lot of people coming to the docks to gawk at us. Someone tried to get on the boat earlier this morning. It was quite upsetting. Let me call down there. Give me a moment." She disconnected.

"She calling them?" Val asked.

"Yeah." I threw open my car door.

"Where are you going?" I heard Val asking, but I ignored her and marched to the car behind me, knocking on the passenger-side window.

Kevin the *Chronicle* photographer hit the button and the window slid down. He looked sheepish. His driver, Jenna, did not. "What are you doing?" I demanded, leaning into the car.

Jenna shrugged. "I was in the area still and saw you pull in here. So I figured we'd see where you were going."

"You have to leave. This is the reason why this"—I waved my hand at the blockade—"is occurring."

The cop's radio crackled. I heard a garbled voice, but couldn't make out what it was saying. The cop glanced at me, leaned in and said something to Val, then motioned for me to hurry up.

I looked back at Jenna. "You have to leave."

She smiled. "We'll see."

I got back into the car. As we passed the cop I leaned over and said, "The car behind is media."

He sighed, muttered something under his breath, then waved us on. As we drove down the street, he moved in front of Jenna's car.

"What was that about?" Val asked as we pulled up to the marina gate, where we were stopped again to confirm our visit.

I waited until they waved us through before responding as we cruised through the empty parking lot and drove up to where the yacht was moored. "Becky's reporter. I hate to be that way, but she's so aggressive."

"They won't let her in anyway," Val said. "Why all the cops though? Protection?"

I nodded. "Apparently people were trying to get on the boat earlier."

Val shook her head. "People are unreal. But it's extra scary given what happened." She put the car in park and looked at me. I could see the fear still in her eyes. "Jillian was strangled in broad daylight. You know that, right? With a staff full of people around."

"I know." And I didn't really want to think about it at the moment. "Let's go."

Chapter 25

We got out of the car and walked to the dock, where we were greeted by more security people. I could see cops stationed in different spots along the dock and throughout the parking lot. This had to be three-quarters of the police force. The chief must be losing his mind.

The security team, three burly guys wearing Secret Service earpieces—different guys than the first day we came out here to poke around with Damian—insisted on looking in our bags and patting us down. She seemed to have upgraded her security. Once they were satisfied we were clean, they shepherded us down the dock to a little ramp leading up the side of the boat. Up close, it was larger than it looked from even a few hundred feet away.

"This thing has, like, four floors," Val whispered as we followed the first guy. The other two had stayed behind to make sure no one else slipped past, I guess.

The guard paused at a door, pulled out his keys to unlock it, then swung it wide. "Go ahead, please," he said.

I stepped through first, Val on my heels. I heard the door shut behind us as Esther appeared, seemingly out of thin air. "Hello again. Right this way, please."

She led us up a short flight of stairs to a room that literally took my breath away. It was probably the size of our whole downstairs floor, designed for an airy, light feel—all white couches and chairs in various sizes and shapes, creating a rectangular sitting area in the middle of the room, with recessed lighting and light wood accents. Peyton waited on one of the couches. She matched the room in her breezy white sundress, but aside from her outfit she looked very unlike herself. Her hair was piled on her head in a bun and she wore no makeup. This made her look older, which I guess is the point of makeup. But it was weird to see her look . . . normal.

And today she looked sad.

"Girls," she said, rising and coming forward to hug me, then Val. "Please, sit."

I was kind of afraid to sit on one of the white couches for fear I would get it dirty. Then I noticed Rhiannon curled in a ball on one side of the smaller couch. Much like JJ, she opened one eye, surveyed the situation, then went back to sleep. I sat down next to her. Val chose one of the chairs. Peyton sat back in her original spot where she had a good view of us both.

"Can I get you anything?" she asked. "Lemonade? Water?"

"Lemonade would be great," I said. Val nodded her assent.

"I'll ask Chandi to prepare a tray," Esther said, and left the room. The white carpeting muffled her footsteps into silence.

"Thank you for coming," Peyton said. "I'm sorry about the police and all the . . . fanfare. I really hate drawing attention to myself."

That made me almost giggle out loud, considering the

size of her boat, but I managed to swallow it. "No problem. It must be scary for you, to have people trying to access your home."

"It is," she said. "Where I usually dock, people are used to me. Plus there are usually other boats much bigger with much more important people on them, so I'm a small fish. But here . . ." she trailed off, knotting her fingers together. She almost seemed uncomfortable with her own fame. "I wish people wouldn't make such a big deal."

"People love Hollywood," Val said. "And you and Marco are so well known."

Peyton didn't comment on that.

"We do get a fair amount of celebrities here but none of them show up on a boat like this," I added. I didn't want her to think our island was deprived of famous people. "Anyway, how are you both doing?" I wondered where he was, but it was a ginormous boat. He could be anywhere. Some boats this big had amenities like concert halls, underwater viewing areas, entire spas, and Olympic-sized swimming pools. You could probably go a month without bumping into anyone else who lived here too.

"Shocked," Peyton admitted. She glanced up as Esther returned with a tray. "Thank you, Esther."

Esther placed the tall lemonade glasses and a plate of cookies—homemade, from the looks of them—onto the table, then sat on the other lone chair. "What a terrible day," she said to me.

"Horrible." As images of Jillian threatened to creep back in, I sipped my lemonade to distract me. It was delicious. Definitely not from a bottle in the market. "How did you find out?" I asked Peyton.

"The police. I'm assuming they found my number in Jillian's cell phone. We actually . . . spoke this morning. I know she was meeting you two to discuss the event."

I nodded slowly. "The hotel staff were hoping you'd be there for the meeting," I said. "They were disappointed when I said you weren't coming. So you two were . . . close?"

"We've known each other for years," she said, which didn't really answer my question. "I met her on a movie set ages ago, when they were supplying some shelter dogs for a part. We discovered we were both animal people. Have a cookie. Please. Esther baked them this morning."

Val and I each took one. "Yeah, animal people usually stick together," I said lamely, not really sure what else to say, then took a bite of my cookie. It was amazing. Better than Ethan's, and that was saying something. "This is delicious," I said.

Peyton nodded. "Aren't they? In any event, I know there's been a flurry of activity on the League's part. Jo reached out this morning. So I thought it best to confer with you two directly." She leaned forward, resting her forearms on her knees. "Jo and the team want to keep going with the fundraiser."

"Yes. She called me too." I glanced at Val. "I forgot to tell you."

Val frowned. "They called to say they still want to have it?"

I nodded.

"What did you say?" Peyton asked.

"I told her I'd talk to Val. She said she'd be in touch." I hesitated. "Look, Peyton. I appreciate everything you've done already for us. I don't want you to feel obligated to see this through if you want to leave, after what happened."

She looked puzzled for a second, then smiled. "Oh, you think I'm backing out. Absolutely not. I want to do an event for you. I just want to do it a bit differently."

"Differently?" I repeated. "Differently how?"

"I don't think we need to make it such a grand affair like what Jillian was driving for. And I actually don't think we need the League's help."

"You don't?" Val asked.

Peyton shook her head. "I'm not a fan of hoity-toity events like that. Jillian and I . . . had very different opinions on how to maximize fundraising opportunities. She liked a big splash. No, I think we should do it at your café."

"You do?" I glanced at Val. That had been my suggestion at first, but Val didn't think it would work for this event.

She nodded. "I do. We can use your garage café and backyard for the bulk of it, but still have the cats available for people to see what they are supporting. I'll still be your face. We can do some fun auction items if you want, but I can get you the same price per ticket—more, actually—we wouldn't have to spend money on the venue, and we wouldn't have to give twenty-five percent to the League. Not that they don't do good work," she said, holding up a hand. "But you're a small guy and I think you need it more." She looked from me to Val and back again. "Plus, who wants to have a party where . . . such a terrible thing happened?"

I thought about her proposal, trying to see it from all sides. I had no real stake in the League, other than they had brought me Peyton in the first place. Did that mean they deserved my loyalty? What would they think if we bailed on them, then they found out we did it anyway?

On the other hand, twenty-five percent was a lot. I

knew we would still get a lot, but still. I didn't need the big party if we could make the same amount of money for the rescue operation.

"We'll keep the meet and greet we had on the calendar," Peyton said, still trying to sell her idea. "I bet we can sell out by then—I'll put my people on it today, if you agree—but if we don't, the meet and greet should put us over the top. What do you think?" She looked at us as eagerly as a child would at Santa telling him about her Christmas list. "And, we can even make the meet and greet part of the fundraising efforts. How about this." She leaned forward, her eyes sparking with excitement. "We bill it as a free event, with a suggested donation of fifty dollars to help the island's neediest residents. That's chump change to the people who summer here on the island," she said, with a wave of her hand. "And what if we start a sponsorship campaign—anyone who donates a hundred dollars or more to meet us would get to sponsor an animal in need of their choice, from the café or the animal control center."

Despite everything that had happened today, I could feel myself getting interested. "People do like to sponsor animals. If they get adopted, we can always give them another one."

Val nodded. "I like the idea. And if we have the fundraiser at the café, I'm sure I could pull it off with my own team and a couple freelancers."

"Brilliant!" Peyton clapped her hands together. Rhiannon's head jerked up from where it had been buried in her tail. She looked around, then wound her tail around her face again. "Maddie?"

"I like it too," I said. "We'd have to figure out how we'll handle the League, though."

"Let me worry about that," Peyton said. "I've known

them for a while. I'll take care of it. Oh, I'm delighted. And Esther will certainly be a help as well. She's been doing this for so long, she knows my preferences." She looked at her for confirmation.

Esther nodded. "I'd love to."

"There is one little thing," she said, once I'd picked up my cookie again to nibble on it.

I motioned for her to go on.

"I'd love if we could move the date up to this coming Saturday instead of the following. I think it's going to be tough for us to be out here that long with all this craziness going on. I don't want your police chief to run me out of town because he's tired of all his people being out here babysitting us. Will that work?"

Val and I looked at each other. I had no idea, but I was pretty sure once people heard Peyton was going to be there, I'd sell the thing out in an hour. Then it was the not-so-simple act of putting the event on. I swallowed the rest of my cookie and smiled. "Sure," I said. "We'll make it work."

"Excellent." She smiled, and I got the sense that she'd known all along this was an offer we couldn't refuse. "What do you think of a Stevie Nicks theme? Rhiannon would love it."

Chapter 26

"This Saturday?" My mother looked at us with barely disguised alarm. "Here?"

Val and I had returned from Peyton's yacht a united front to face the challenge of sitting down and telling everyone else who had a stake in this game—Grandpa, Mom, and Ethan. Luckily our mother was still there helping out in the café—she'd be the easiest to convince. Once she got playing with the cats, it was hard to get her to leave. I knew she was trying to get my dad to agree to adopt a friend for Moonshine, the cat she'd adopted when we'd first opened.

"Yes," I said calmly, trying not to let the look on Ethan's face get me agitated. "Peyton wants to leave early. People are trying to find ways onto her boat and the police are all over the marina. She doesn't think it's sustainable and doesn't want to put people out for another week."

"Makes sense," Grandpa said. "I'm sure Chief McAuliffe isn't loving having to put so many men out there round the clock."

"Val. That's kind of insane," Ethan said. "That's five days to pull this off."

"Yeah, but if it's here, it's going to be a lot easier," Val said. "I already have a setup in mind. Mostly outdoors with one of those amazing tents, with overflow outside on the lawn. The food stations will be in the garage. We can let people into the café in shifts." She looked at Ethan. "Please. I have to do this to get my mind off . . . today. Otherwise all I'm going to do is think about what happened."

Ethan sighed. "I understand." He reached over and squeezed her hand. "I'll help plan the menu."

"You're the best." She leaned over and kissed him.

"And Peyton is going to help," I chimed in. "She's got a bunch of auction items for us already—things from her personal collection she's going to donate: animal stuff, outfits from some movies, shoes . . ." I would have to watch myself so I didn't end up bidding on everything. Peyton wore amazing shoes and our feet looked to be about the same size. I'd checked.

"Yeah, she's being so generous. I have to admit, I thought she'd be harder to work with. We'd heard . . ." Val faltered a bit and I knew she was thinking of Jillian's insinuation about Peyton being difficult. "We'd heard she could be a real diva. Although this Stevie Nicks theme. How far you think she wants to take that?"

"Stevie Nicks theme?" My mother's entire face brightened at that one. She was definitely a fan of Stevie's gypsy ways. "I can definitely take the lead on that! We'll have the best decorations! And maybe we can all dress up like Stevie! That would add an element of mystique, now wouldn't it?"

I slept an unsettled sleep that night. The whole exhausting experience of the day, from finding Jillian's body to the encounter with Mish to Grandpa's story to being on

Peyton's yacht and back to party planning left my head spinning. I wasn't sure where to focus or what to do next. We had five days to plan a major fundraiser. The woman who originally had been planning it was dead—murdered—and someone walking around our island had killed her.

The whole thing was hard to comprehend. And the image of Jillian's unseeing eyes kept sneaking into the edges of my dreams. Finally at six a.m. I woke up for good and figured maybe some movement would help me get my head together. Also I needed to get ready to go to the courthouse. I really wanted to see this will that Stevie's grandmother had left that was causing so much commotion. *And possibly murder*, a little voice added. I pushed that thought aside. I still couldn't bear to think of my childhood friends as murderers. But who else hated Jillian enough to strangle her with a cat leash?

I extracted my leg from under Lucas's and slipped out of bed. JJ, who had been on my pillow, curled up in the warm spot I'd vacated and went back to sleep. Ollie, who always slept at the foot of the bed, raised his head to look at me. I scratched behind his ears, then pulled on a sweatshirt and let myself out of my room. Ollie jumped off the bed and followed. I closed the door behind us.

The house was quiet. I didn't think Grandpa was even up yet. And the coffeepot was cold and silent, so Ethan hadn't gotten up yet either. Unless he'd gotten up super early and went to do Tai Chi with Cass or something. Or else he was still mad at me for wanting to have this event.

I poked my head into the café. The residents were still sleeping. The kittens were awake and tumbling around together in their condo. I checked the schedule—our volunteer Harry was on this morning—then went to prepare the coffee and took Ollie outside. It was his favorite time of day. He loved the early morning, the dewy grass, the first kiss of summer sunlight. I did too, for that matter. I sat on the back porch and watched him trot around the yard, sniffing around like it was the first time he'd been here, tail wagging joyfully at each scent. We could all learn so much from dogs.

As I watched him sniff, I thought about Jillian. And Mish and Stevie. Given what I'd been hearing about their family drama, sure, they made good suspects. I couldn't help but think that was the easy answer, though. But that would mean there was a whole other drama playing out in Jillian's life at the same time. Unless, of course, some murdering psychopath had randomly happened upon her sitting in the gazebo and decided to strangle her. If that was the case, where would they have gotten the leash? If Jillian had brought the boxes to the hotel, depending on where she'd put them they would've been accessible. But only if someone knew they existed and where to look. Had it been a crime of opportunity, or was someone using the leash to send a message?

The only other people who would know her on the island well enough to want her dead, as far as I knew, were Chad, Peyton, and Marco. Since she didn't spend much time here, she probably didn't know many other people. Her grandmother was dead. It didn't sound like there were any other relatives, at least not close ones.

I heard the coffee maker beep inside, signaling the nectar of the gods was ready. As I rose to go in and pour myself a cup, I saw Ollie's ears perk up, then he took off around the side of the house.

"Ollie!" I yelled. Lucas and I usually let him run around the yard when we were out here because he didn't ever take off like that. I ran around the side of the house in my bare feet, completely panicked—Lucas would kill me if he ran away. And skidded to a stop when I saw him sitting in front of a woman who stood at the bottom of my front-porch steps looking like she was trying to decide if she should go to the door or not.

From what I could see from where I stood, she looked about my mom's age, carefully dressed despite the early—ridiculously early—hour. When she saw me, her eyes brightened and she waved enthusiastically, like we'd known each other forever. I approached cautiously. Ollie didn't seem to sense any danger, but he still didn't move from his blocking position.

"Can I help you?" I asked.

"Oh, I sure hope so!" She waved a piece of paper at me. "I want to buy a ticket before they're all gone."

"A ticket?" I came forward. "Ollie, come," I said, snapping my fingers. He obediently came over and sat down in front of me while I tried to figure out what the heck was she talking about. Did she think we were the ferry operators or something? That was the only ticket I could think of. Or was she trying to schedule time at the cat café? "I'm sorry, I'm not sure what you mean."

"To the fundraiser!" She thrust the paper at me. I stepped over and took it. It was something she'd printed off the computer. It was an announcement that JJ's House of Purrs—in partnership with Peyton Chandler—was hosting a fundraiser at the café this coming Saturday. *Limited spots available, $1200 per ticket. All proceeds to go to Daybreak Island animal rescue efforts.* A picture of Peyton snuggling with Rhiannon, along with a photo of JJ that I didn't even recognize, were in the middle of the text.

Apparently we were raising the price.

I looked up at the woman, confused. "Where did you get this?"

"On Peyton's fan site!" she exclaimed, as if I must be slow. "Where else?"

"I see." I studied it again. "Well, I don't actually, um . . ." I looked around the yard as if a ticket might magically appear that I could give her. I desperately needed my coffee so I could figure out a solution for this.

"Here." The woman thrust a check at me. "Twelve hundred dollars, plus another hundred for an added donation. Perhaps I can sit close to Peyton?" She looked at me hopefully.

I had to laugh. "Sure, Ms. . . . ?"

"I'm Chassie Rothstein," she said. "I know your daddy very well."

"Ms. Rothstein. Of course. Well, listen. I don't have the official tickets yet, but here's what I'm going to do." I reached for my phone before remembering I hadn't brought it down with me. "I'm going to write you out a ticket, and I'll call you when I have the real ones. Okay?"

"Lovely, dear. Just make sure you put me at Peyton's table."

"Noted. Be right back." I raced into the house and into the café, where I grabbed one of the JJ's House of Purrs postcards off the rack. I scribbled the date and place on the ticket, along with the ticket price, a note about the seating arrangements, and signed my name. I found my phone, took a picture of it so I didn't forget, then hurried back outside and presented it to her with a flourish.

"Oh, how delightful." She sighed and held it close to her chest. "Will Marco be coming too? I *adore* him."

Chapter 27

After I sent Chassie on her way, Ollie and I went inside. I poured a cup of coffee and sat down at the table with a thud. Peyton—or her minions—had apparently been busy already, since our conversation yesterday. I wondered if she'd talked to Jo, or if she'd just gone ahead and started advertising. Or if she'd leaked it to someone, who had then gone on to publicize it. I needed to google and see what was going on.

I topped off my cup, locked the back door, and went upstairs. Lucas and JJ were still asleep. I wish I could sleep like that, no matter what was going on. Ollie joined them on the bed while I grabbed my iPad and went to sit in the book nook. I curled up, tucked my legs under me, and googled the café's name first. Bones, my web guy out in California, did all my website stuff, including all my search-engine optimization, in which he was expert. I think he also did a lot of hacking, but that was a whole other story. I clicked on my website first—mostly just to see it because it was super cute—then went back to the other search results. The second hit was the announcement that Chassie Rothstein had seen. I went to that website to check it out. The "about" page told me it was a page for Peyton Chandler fans. Google told me it wasn't her official site. I read the text under the announcement.

This just in!!!!! Stolen from Peyton's official site (I added the graphics). Who's up for a trip to Daybreak Island?

Someone named Peyton_rescue_love had posted it. I wondered if people knew the ticket price.

I went to PeytonChandler.com. Sure enough, there was a "breaking news" area on her homepage, and it was all about the café event. She was nothing if not enthusiastic about this.

I flipped my iPad closed and tossed it aside. I figured I'd hear something from her soon enough, and in the meantime I needed to get ready to go to the courthouse. I had to get my hands on Marcella Cox's will and see who this executor was—and what the terms of the will were. Maybe that would shed some light on this Stevie/Mish/Jillian situation, and help clear their names.

I took a shower, put some air-dry styling product in my hair, and pulled on jeans and a T-shirt. I wanted to get to the courthouse by nine, but it was only eight. I wandered back downstairs to see if Ethan was up yet. No sign of him. Grandpa had been up sometime in between when I'd gone upstairs and come back down—the coffee was brewing—but he must've left for his walk, or some other important business. I went into the café to check on the cats. Harry was diligently sweeping cat litter. When I came in, he looked up hopefully from where he crouched down cleaning under the couches. When he saw it was me and not Adele, his crush, his face fell just a tad.

"Morning, Harry," I said.

"Morning, Ms. Maddie. These kitties sure are messy."

"I hear you, Harry." I sat down on the floor with the laser toy, which brought all the kittens and a few of the older cats. Before I knew it, I was engrossed in an active game of laser tag and lost track of time until a few minutes later when Adele burst in through the café doors, waving a newspaper at me.

"You see this story?"

I was a little afraid to see it. "No. Let's have a look." I took the paper from her hands and skimmed the front page. Which had a whole story (thanks, Jenna) on the Warner family saga right next to the more straightforward headline about Jillian's untimely death. There were accompanying photos of the Paradise and its outside area, presumably taken from the website. I doubted the police had let anyone in to take photos yesterday.

Adele whistled. "How about that. Any idea who did it? Or are they insinuating Mish and Stevie had a motive?"

"I don't know," I murmured, skimming the article, which had nothing new to report than what I'd told Ellory yesterday. Jenna's story, however, was chock-full of Warner family history. I needed to sit down and read this. "Can I keep this?" I asked her.

She shrugged. "It's yours. So what are you gonna do? The party is off, I guess?"

"No. We're having it here on Saturday. I'll explain later." I turned as Lucas stuck his head in to say good morning. "Perfect timing. Are you going to work? Or do you want to run an errand with me?" I asked.

"I can go with you," he said. "Caro can take this morning's first appointment. Let me call her."

"I'll grab you some coffee to go." I went out to the coffeepot, filled two cups and took our coffees and the paper into the car to wait for him, reading through Jenna's story while I did. She was thorough, I had to give her that. Her story was part history lesson, part family drama, part modern-day scandal. Though apparently she hadn't sniffed out anything new—yet.

Lucas opened the door and climbed in. I handed him his coffee.

"Thanks," he said. "So where are we going?"

"To the courthouse. I want to see Stevie's grandmother's will. But I need to make a quick stop at the Paradise first."

Lucas frowned. "You can do that? See someone's will?"

I nodded. "Yeah. In Massachusetts wills become public record after probate."

"So why do you want to see it?"

"Because I wanted to see what the details were about this property, since it seemed to be such a contentious thing between Stevie and Jillian. And it feels like that's the motive du jour." I slowed at the light near the ferry dock. I watched early-bird vacationers crossing the street, eager to start their day on our picturesque island. Although there were a lot of people streaming from this boat. I leaned forward, squinting a little. I saw a lot of people hauling equipment. Equipment that looked a lot like cameras. Then it dawned on me.

The media circus had arrived.

"Look at that," I said, pointing.

"What's going on?" Lucas asked.

"The media. Peyton's been linked to Jillian and the fundraiser."

I turned toward the waterfront when the light turned green, and we reached the Paradise five minutes later. I felt my heart kick up a couple of notches even just driving

into the parking lot and hoped I could handle this visit.
I parked and looked at Lucas. He too looked doubtful
about this trip.

"What are we doing here?" he asked.

"I want to find out where she'd put all the stuff for the
event. You coming?"

"Of course."

We got out and headed into the lobby. I scanned the
check-in area. No Purple Hair. She was probably traumatized too and had to take some time off. I waited until
one of the people working the desk was free and went up.

"Checking in?" the middle-aged, pleasant-faced man
inquired.

"No, thank you. I actually was hoping to talk to Marianna. My name is Maddie James. We had an appointment yesterday."

A cloud passed over his face. "Ah, yes. One moment,
I'll see if she's available." He picked up the phone, murmured something into it, and then hung up. "If you care
to wait for a few minutes, she can come down shortly."

I thanked him. Lucas and I went over to the sitting
area to wait. I had my eyes open for Chad, but didn't see
him.

Marianna didn't keep us waiting long. "Ms. James,"
she said, hurrying over, heels clicking efficiently on the
marble floor. "Marianna Huston. I'm so terribly sorry
about everything that happened."

I nodded gravely. "Yes, it's awful. Thank you."

"Did I know you were coming back today?"

"No. Sorry. I wanted to find out if the giveaway items
were here?"

"The boxes? Sure they are. Jillian had them couriered
over Saturday. We stored them in one of our event war
rooms."

"War room?" Lucas asked.

She smiled. "Event-planner terminology. We have small rooms near all our event spaces where the teams can set up computers, have meetings, troubleshoot."

"I see. Are those rooms open?" I asked. "Meaning can anyone access them?"

"The police asked the same question," she said with a small smile. "No. I mean, the hotel staff can. But the general public cannot."

"Is someone picking them up?" I asked. "If not, I can take them."

"Another League staffer is picking them up. I'm afraid I can't release them to anyone else."

"I see. Did you happen to see Jillian yesterday morning?" I asked.

"Me? No. We were supposed to have our meeting, as you know. I didn't get in until about nine thirty and went straight to my office. When I got called to come down, the . . . incident had already occurred." She glanced at her watch. "Anything else?"

"Is the woman who was working the front desk here? She had purple hair?"

Marianna shook her head. "Yolanda? She has a few days off. She was terribly traumatized by this whole thing."

I thanked her and turned to go, but she called me back. "Shall we continue to hold that date? I didn't want to assume not."

"I think you can let the date go," I said. "We'll definitely look to do another event here, though."

We got back in the car and drove to the courthouse downtown, right near city hall. The one thing I liked about it was that it had its own parking lot, so there was no wasting time circling streets looking for a spot. After we got through security, the guards directed us to the probate court.

The man behind the desk had bushy, curly hair and thick glasses. He squinted at us when we walked in. "Mornin'," he said. "What can I do for ya?"

"I'm looking for a will," I said, flashing him my best smile.

"Name?" He pushed his glasses up on his nose with his middle finger.

"Marcella Cox."

He let out a little laugh. "Popular lady, that one."

"Pardon?"

"You're the third person to come in here today looking for that will." He disappeared into the stacks behind him.

I glanced at Lucas. "Third person?" I murmured.

The clerk returned with a folder. "Forty-five dollars," he said. "It includes photocopies. Sign here." He pushed a clipboard at me.

I pulled out my wallet, handed him the money and signed the form. He handed me a receipt. "You can go right there." He pointed to a small desk. "Photocopier is over there."

Lucas and I went over to the desk with the file. I sat. Lucas leaned against it.

"Third person today to request this will," I said in a low voice. "I bet Jenna is one of them. But who else?"

"The cops?" Lucas suggested.

"Maybe." I flipped through the pages, scanning the words for anything that jumped out. Finally, after three pages of miscellany, we got to the meat of the will—the estate.

With regards to the Cox estate, all properties on Allegheny Lane West, I hereby bequeath my grandchildren,

Steven Quincy Warner and Jillian Marcella Allen, the opportunity to retain full ownership.

The *opportunity*? What the heck did that mean? I kept reading.

If either of my grandchildren proves to me that they will use the property as it was meant, to remain in the Cox family, perpetuate the lineage, and continue to be a benefactor of Daybreak Island before my death, that individual shall inherit. In the event of my death before the decision is made, I hereby appoint Leopold Mancini to have final say. If a decision isn't made within four weeks after my death, the property shall immediately revert to the Daybreak Island Land Trust and become the property of the Town.

I had to read that twice, sure that my eyes were deceiving me. It had to be the stress of the past few days. Phrases swam in my head—*perpetuate the lineage, benefactor, Leopold Mancini to have final say.* This document named Grandpa as the executor? And he failed to mention that?

"What's wrong?" Lucas asked, alarmed by the look on my face. When I didn't answer, he peered over my shoulder at the paper. It took him a minute to get to that part, but eventually his eyes widened. "Does that say . . ."

"Grandpa? Yeah. Sure looks like it. Unless there's another Leopold Mancini on the island." I grabbed the papers and went to the copier. I needed to bring the proof home when I confronted him about why he hadn't told me the whole truth about any of this.

Chapter 28

I let Lucas drive home and read the words from my photo-copied sheet three more times on the way. I didn't really know what to say or how to approach Grandpa about this. Why hadn't he mentioned any of this to me? And how could he be working for Stevie but also be the executor of Stevie's grandmother's will? And why had she chosen Grandpa? I know he'd told me she and Grandma were friendly, but were they really that close? Was it because he was the former police chief and she considered him trustworthy? It made no sense at all.

But now it meant that I had to stick my nose in and figure this out. Not only were my friends involved, but now my grandfather was too. I couldn't just sit back and plan a party.

"You had no idea?" Lucas asked, when the silence got too loud for the car.

I shook my head. "It was like pulling teeth to get him to tell me Stevie had hired him. But I don't get it. How could he be both?"

"I guess you're just gonna have to ask him, babe."

Lucas reached over and squeezed my hand as we pulled into the driveway. "Want me to come with?"

"No. It will be better if I talk to him on my own. But thanks." I leaned over and kissed him.

"I have to go to the shop for a bit. Do you want to keep Ollie here?"

"Yes. I could use some Ollie today. Thanks." I kissed him again and stepped out of the car.

A flash went off in my face. Instinctively I put my hands up to shield myself as Lucas jumped out of the car. Another flash went off.

"What the . . ." Once the silver dots cleared, I realized there were four photographers in our yard. They must have been lurking out of sight and sprang on us when we arrived.

"It's not them," one of them said.

"Not who? This is my house!" I yelled.

A woman stepped forward, her eyes glinting in anticipation. "Can you confirm the cat rumor?"

I stared at her. "What cat rumor?"

"Peyton and her cat," the woman said. "What do you know?"

I had no clue what she was talking about, and of course Grandpa chose that moment to fling the front door open.

"Private property," he yelled, jerking his thumb toward the street. "Off, now."

A couple of them tried to slink back toward the bushes, but Lucas redirected them. They grumbled a little but went out to the road. For the first time I noticed a couple of vans parked along the street. Nondescript, of course. The tabloids didn't want to announce their presence, but Becky was right. They were here.

"Jeez." Lucas shook his head. "Ballsy, aren't they?"

"They sure are," I murmured, but my mind was on the woman who'd asked me about Peyton and her cat. What was she talking about? Part of me wanted to go talk to her, but I had a feeling it would be like feeding a shark.

"You'll be okay?" Lucas looked doubtfully at where they had clustered like a pack of wolves, waiting for their opportunity to pounce again.

"Fine. I'll sic Grandpa on them again if they try anything." I looked back at the front door. Grandpa stood there, arms crossed over this chest, daring them to come back. "Go. Let me take care of yelling at Grandpa Leo."

Lucas backed away. "I don't want to be anywhere near here while that's occurring."

Once he'd backed out of the driveway, I took a breath and headed inside. Grandpa had left the doorway and was nowhere in sight. Val had AirPods in her ears, pacing around the living room talking on the phone. Ollie, thinking they were playing some sort of game, followed on her heels, tail wagging. JJ watched the whole thing from the couch with a bit of disdain.

"I'm so pleased you're able to help," Val was saying. When she caught sight of me, she flashed me two thumbs up. "Yes, I'll see you first thing in the morning. Thank you so much!" She hit the red button to disconnect the call and danced over to me. "We got the coolest caterer on the Cape to come over and do your party. How much do you love me, huh?" She leaned over and gave me a huge kiss on the cheek.

"I love you lots," I assured her. "Now where's Grandpa? He was just here."

"Don't you even want to know who it is?" Val demanded. "This is a huge get, especially on, like, four days' notice!"

"I do. Sorry. Who is it?" I pushed my hair out of my face and waited, trying not to show my impatience.

"Enchanted Dishes. I think it's a sign," she said. "Get it? Enchanted, Stevie Nicks theme?"

"Right. Yes. That's amazing, Val. Great job."

Val sighed. "You'll be happy when you taste their food. I've been researching and—"

"I'm super happy already. Swear to God. Listen, I really need to find Grandpa, okay?" I left her midsentence and hurried toward the basement door. He'd probably headed straight back down there, maybe to work on Stevie's case.

I pounded down the stairs and skidded around the game room corner to Grandpa's office door, pushing it open without knocking. He glanced up from his desk, barely arching an eyebrow at my dramatic entrance.

"Are you kidding?" I demanded, without preamble.

"About?" He pushed aside the papers he was reading and folded his hands over them.

"You're the executor of Marcella Cox's will! You had to pick between Stevie and Jillian."

Grandpa sighed and leaned back in his chair, rubbing his eyes. "Yes, well. It's unfortunate that Marcella did that. I had no idea."

"You what?" This story was getting more outlandish by the minute. All this drama—and possibly someone's life—over some stupid pieces of property and an old woman's unexplained thought process.

"I didn't know, Madalyn. Not until Marcella passed and her attorney called me."

"Ugh." I sank down in one of his guest chairs. "But why *you*? And is that normal?"

He shrugged. "People do all kinds of things with

their wills, Maddie. You have no idea. And Marcella and your grandmother were good friends. Don't you remember?"

"You guys had a lot of good friends. Why was this one so special?" My grandparents knew everyone, partly because of Grandpa's job and partly because Grandma was involved in so many things on the island it was hard to keep track. They had always been a very social couple. I had never kept much track of who was who and what their relationships were.

That said, I did remember Marcella being around a lot when I'd lived on the island. She'd been an eccentric woman who wore hats and fancy outfits, like, every single day for no good reason. I remembered her as stiff, New England old money. "I guess," I said. "So you were already working for Stevie when you found out?"

Grandpa gave me a look. "You are relentless."

"Grandpa. People are wondering if Stevie killed Jillian over this stupid property! And your granddaughters had to find her body. Are you forgetting all of this?"

Now his eyes darkened to downright stormy. "No, I most certainly am not."

"So what happened when they found out?"

He shrugged. "They weren't happy, of course. But it was hardly my fault. And I didn't meet Jillian actually until, well, until she showed up here."

My eyes narrowed. "What about the will reading?"

"She didn't come in person. She was on the phone."

"And what was her reaction?"

"I'm sure it wasn't what she wanted to hear, but she kept her opinions to herself."

"But then she showed up here looking to raise all this money for our café." Jillian's motives for helping us were starting to smell fishy. Exactly what Mish and

Stevie had insinuated. "So how were you going to make this decision, then?"

Grandpa sighed. "I hadn't really figured that part out yet."

"So does it automatically go to Stevie because she's dead?" That would definitely not look good for Stevie. Or Mish.

"No," Grandpa said. "The lawyer explained that I will still be able to make a decision based on what I feel Stevie's intent for the property is."

This sounded really complicated to me. "I would think his intent would be to live there, right? That's what he's been doing."

Grandpa didn't comment.

"What are you going to do?" I asked.

"I don't know, Maddie. And I can't really talk about this now because as you can imagine, this whole thing could be halted until her murder is solved." He left the rest of it hanging, unspoken: *In case Stevie is convicted of killing her.*

"What a mess." I stood to go, then turned back. "Did Jillian come to the café because she was trying to impress you so you'd give her the property?"

"We'll never know that for sure, Doll," Grandpa said. "But I have a sneaking suspicion the answer would be yes."

Chapter 29

I needed to get out of this house for a few minutes. My conversation with Grandpa had left me antsy and I had to think. I called JJ, slipped on his harness, and headed down the street toward Damian's. JJ would get some treats, I could get some fries, and if Damian wasn't too busy, I could run this whole mess by him and try to get some perspective.

A conversation didn't look promising when I arrived, though. Damian's place had a pretty big crowd for this time of day—meaning, between lunch and dinner. The ferries were starting to make more trips over as the summer schedule kicked into gear, and more and more tourists were catching those ferries to experience island life, even if it was just for an afternoon. Admittedly, this was all the better for local businesses. When people came out here, especially if it was for a short time, they tried to cram as much as possible into the visit. That meant eating all the food they could fit in, having ice cream, buying souvenirs—it became almost manic for some people, who wanted to say they'd gotten the lay of the land and brag about it to their friends back home.

JJ and I headed in the side door to the fish market area, which I figured would be quieter. Damian was actually in there filling up the case with fresh fish. He had a full staff manning the takeout area. He glanced up and smiled when he saw us.

"Hey, you two. What brings you by?" He came out from behind the counter to scratch JJ's head. "You looking for a snack?"

"He's always looking for a snack," I said.

"Well then let me get right on that." He went back around the counter. "And what about you? You look like you could use a treat too."

"I could. Some French fries, preferably."

"Coming right up." He pulled open the sliding window that separated the fish market area from the restaurant and called out for a double order of fries.

"Looks like you're busy," I said, gazing out at the crowd assembled at the various picnic tables.

He nodded, coming around to place a dish of what looked like assorted fish parts down on the floor. JJ attacked it, and Damian laughed. "It's been steady the past few days. Season's kicking into gear, right? And I feel like it could get really busy around here with all the . . . activity."

"What activity?"

He gave me a look. "Your celebrity friends?"

"Oh. That. Well, wait until you hear the rest."

"Uh-oh. Sounds juicy."

"Yeah." I sighed. "The woman from the League? Remember the one you saw in my driveway the other day?"

He nodded.

"Well, she's dead."

Damian's eyes almost popped out of his head. "What do you mean, she's dead?"

"I mean, she's no longer alive. As in dead. Someone killed her."

"Holy . . ." he leaned against the front of the fish counter, taking that in.

"Yeah." I filled him in on the events of the past day and a half, finishing with the will revelation. He listened without interrupting until I was done.

"Wow," he said finally. "Do they have any suspects?"

"Well, there's me and Val, Mish and Stevie, Jillian's staff, her celebrity pals . . ." I ticked off the list on my fingers.

He gave me a look. "Why would they suspect you and Val?"

"We were supposed to meet her. We found her."

"Yeah, and she was also going to get you a ton of money. That would be stupid."

"True. I don't really think they suspect us. I'm more worried about Mish and Stevie." I lowered my voice as the door opened and a family came in, exclaiming about the freshly filled case. After an annoyingly long perusal of the case and a story about how they rented a place with a kitchen and were trying their hand at cooking "real" fish for the first time, they bought some cod fillets and left.

"Because of the property stuff?" Damian asked, picking up our conversation.

I nodded. "Mish hated her. You saw her screaming at Jillian."

"Yeah. She flipped me off too," Damian recalled with a grin. "But don't you know her really well? You think she would do that?"

"I don't want to think that. But who else would?"

"You just listed a whole bunch of people. Including

your celebrity pals. Which, by the way, I'm mad at you about."

"Mad at me for what?"

"Why didn't you invite me over to meet them?" He was half teasing, but I knew he would've loved it.

"Because I didn't know they were coming?" I said.

"You had a whole photo shoot with them."

"Yeah, but I didn't know about it before it happened."

"Still. You should've called the minute they showed up." He grinned. "Actually, I think that's why I'm so busy. People got wind that they were on the street and are eating here in hopes of catching a glimpse of them."

"You're kidding."

"I couldn't kid you about something like that. Look at this crowd." He waved a hand at the full patio. "It's awesome. Early in the season to be this full." He paused. "What the heck is that about?"

I swiveled my head around to see what he was looking at, just as I heard shouting from the outdoor dining area.

"You have no right to do this. These are people's lives!" A male voice. I craned my neck but couldn't see the shouter. I heard another male voice respond, but couldn't quite make out the words.

I glanced at Damian. "You need to go see what that's about?"

"Yeah, probably should. I'll be right back." He headed outside, pulling his apron over his head as he went.

Curious, I peered out the window. I wanted to see what was going on. But when I got there, my eyes widened. One of the shouters was Chad, Peyton's agent. I didn't recognize the person shouting back, but it was a younger guy. Handsome. And a lot bigger than Chad, which meant this could be a short fight.

And Damian was now in the middle of it. I could see him trying to talk them down, while the guy I didn't know leaned around him pointing a finger in Chad's face. The rest of the diners watched in fascination, their lobster rolls forgotten.

I snatched JJ up, earning a squeak of protest, and hurried outside, coming to a stop next to Damian. "Hey," I said. "What's going on?"

"These two aren't getting along so well," Damian said, waving his hand at Chad and his nemesis. Up close, the other guy was even more handsome than I'd thought at first. And even bigger. His enormous biceps were covered in tattoos. The one closest to me was a snake, coiled around his arm with its tongue lashed out at the very top near his shoulder. His boyish face contorted in anger that shifted a bit when he turned his attention to me. His spiky black hair was tipped blond at the top.

"Chad," I said cooly. "Still looking for salmon?"

Chad had the grace to flush, but he still glared at me. He opened his mouth to retort but I held up a hand. "My friend doesn't really need this kind of thing at his place of business," I said. "Especially since this is the second time you've caused a scene here. I'm sure you understand."

"Hey. I was just getting food and this guy—"

"Don't even," the other guy warned, his voice dangerously low.

Chad's lips pressed tight together. Beads of sweat had popped out on his forehead, even though he was in the shade and it wasn't terribly hot. He finally looked away from the guy and back at Damian. "Sorry," he muttered. "Didn't mean to cause a scene." His apology sounded sarcastic at best. He reached into his pocket, pulled out his wallet, and took out a hundred-dollar bill. He handed it to Damian. "For your inconvenience."

"That's really not necessary," Damian began, but Chad dismissed him with a wave of his hand.

"I insist." And he strode over to his car, got in, and peeled out.

The other guy watched him go, then glanced back at me and Damian. "Sorry about that," he said. "Your food is really good, man."

"Thanks," Damian said. He looked down at the bill in his hand, jaw clenched.

The guy walked over to a Harley parked in the lot, climbed on, and roared away. I watched him go. Along with musicians, I'd always had a soft spot for motorcycles.

Once the dust had settled and everyone went back to their food, I looked at Damian. He shrugged and stuffed the bill in his pocket. "If he keeps coming in here and being rude, maybe I can retire early," he said.

"You know who that is?" I asked as we walked back inside so JJ could finish his food.

"No. Do I want to?"

"Peyton Chandler's agent."

"You're kidding."

I shook my head. "Wish I was. Nice guy, right?"

"So who's the guy he was yelling at?"

"Never seen him before," I said. "But Chad's only been on the island for"—I checked my watch to remind myself what day it was—"like two days. How does he have an enemy already?"

"Well," Damian said, "if he wasn't such a nice guy, I'd wonder about that too."

Chapter 30

The next morning I woke from another night of poor sleep. I'd spent most of it tossing and turning, disturbing poor Ollie and JJ—not Lucas, who could sleep through anything—and managed to stay in bed until six thirty, when I couldn't be still any longer. I was feeling restless, uneasy, and really unhappy about Grandpa's alleged role in this production that Stevie's grandmother had instigated. I was also mad at Stevie and Mish for not filling me in from the get-go, once Jillian had made her appearance. I had as much of a right to know as anyone, since my grandfather and my cat café were now involved.

Most of all, I was mad about Jillian taking me for a fool. She'd waltzed in with her money and celebrity endorsers and her charm and designer outfits and promised me the world. Or at least, a bucketload of money. And I'd gone right along with her, lapping it up like I'd just fallen off the turnip truck.

Ethan had been right. We should've stayed away.

I needed to get out of the house and I didn't feel like taking a walk, so I went down to the basement where I'd stored the bike I'd bought last year upon my return to the island. I'd decided that I needed an alternate mode of transportation given the levels of traffic here in the summer. It was a sweet bike—a seafoam green Rove 3, suitable for both street and trails. I'd only used it once since then, but hey, better late than never. And an early bike ride to the beach had to improve my mood.

I dragged the bike out through the bulkhead door and closed it behind me, hoping I'd remember to lock it when I got home later or else Grandpa would kill me. Safety first with Grandpa. He'd never dream of leaving his house unlocked, regardless of the low crime rate he was so proud of on the island.

I hopped on, popped my AirPods into my ears, turned the music up high, and pedaled around the side of the house by the café. It looked great. There were twinkling lights outlining the garage, and the new sign had come in. Just in time for our big event. It was a spinoff of the JJ's House of Purrs sign with just the word *Café* on it, but in the same cat shape. And orange, of course, because JJ was orange.

I pulled out into the street and pedaled furiously, heading toward the beach, loving the feel of the breeze hitting my face. I'd forgotten my helmet. Lucas would scold me if he saw me, but I wasn't going back. I headed toward Whistle Cove, one of the lesser-known beaches, because I wasn't too excited about seeing people right now and wanted to avoid any chance of an early morning, stake-out-my-sand crowd. I'd had enough of crowds—both the happy kind and the gawking, there's-a-dead-body-in-the-gazebo kind—and just wanted time to think.

I got to Whistle Cove in about twenty minutes. It had always been one of my favorite beaches as a kid, because there were never as many people as on the main

beaches. My grandmother and I had come here all the
time when I was young and we wanted to sneak off for
some time on the sand. It was off the beaten path and
you had to either be an islander or know an islander to
know about it. Plus it was small and not near any of
the food places or souvenir shops, and that was usually
something tourists wanted nearby when they went to the
beach.

I rode down the windy road leading to the parking
lot, veered inside, and drove directly to the bike rack to
park. I walked onto the sand, kicked my sneakers off,
and strode down to the water. Even just letting it lap
around my toes made me feel better. The ocean always
restored my energy. The salt air cleared my head, even
when the brain fog had built up to an insurmountable
level, as it was right now.

I was overwhelmed. I felt like I couldn't handle any
of this—from the party to the murder investigation. Val,
on the other hand, had done quite well compartmentaliz-
ing the stress of Jillian's dead body and was maniacally
focused on getting this party done. She was meeting
with Jo today to complete the transfer of the favors—the
dreaded cat leashes—and close things out with them. I
wasn't sure how anyone could stand to look at the stupid
things these days, although no one but us knew that a
leash had been the weapon used against Jillian. The cops
had kept that detail close to the vest. Then she and Peyton were meeting later to go through Peyton's speech.
Meanwhile, I felt like I was floundering around just
trying to get my day-to-day work done, running through
murder suspects in my mind.

I was anxious for an update from the cops. I hadn't
heard a peep since Sunday. There was no word of an

arrest being imminent. There had been a brief press conference about the murder, but they didn't really say anything except that it was an ongoing investigation, blah blah blah. I walked slowly along the shore, digging my toes into the wet sand as I went, thinking about this whole mess. Finally I sank down where the water could still reach my toes and watched the sun come up over the horizon. Out here, my head felt clear. Like my mind could actually work again. I sat and thought for a long time about what I knew, and what I'd seen and heard. I still kept coming back to five people: Stevie, Mish, Peyton, Marco, and Chad. Since I was really hoping it wasn't Stevie or Mish, I focused on the other three and what I knew about them.

Peyton seemed like a lovely person. Soft-spoken, loved animals, generous, by all accounts. More money than she could ever spend, if the yacht was any indication. She'd known Jillian for a while. I thought about the interactions I'd seen. Jillian was bossy, but she was like that with everyone. Though I had seen Peyton and Jillian arguing on my back porch the day of the photo shoot, and Peyton had sounded dangerously angry with her.

Marco Moore. Another seemingly great guy. Pleasant, down-to-earth, nice to my grandpa. Also loved animals. Very unassuming. He, however, had seemed to snub Jillian the other day. I remembered him getting on his bike and riding away while she was talking to them outside.

And finally, Chad Novak. Of my whole list, if it had to be one of them, I wanted it to be him. Unlike the others, I didn't think he was nice. I'd seen him screaming at a kid about salmon, for God's sake, not to mention the altercation yesterday at the fish store. What was it about that place? And he and Jillian seemed tight when I'd seen them together. I'd thought it was about his agent duties, but maybe not.

Were they seeing each other? Had something gone bad? I hadn't seen any evidence of any of that, but I'd spent a few hours with them in a very public setting. I wasn't going to be the best judge. Still, he'd been at the hotel when she died. Happenstance? I doubted it. So either he could have known she was there, or he was staying there too. Or they were staying there together, which brought me to my previous thought—a relationship gone bad.

But out of this whole cast, the only one I *had* seen publicly angry at Jillian was Mish. What had brought them to that point? And Stevie clearly wasn't happy with her either. I wondered if Stevie and Jillian had ever had a relationship, or had always lived separate lives. Either way, it seemed incredibly sad to think a piece of land could drive such hatred between two relatives, although I supposed it wasn't uncommon. But I kept coming back to this question: Could Stevie or his wife actually kill her over it?

Mish's timeline the day of the murder was odd. Stevie had been at the hotel. She'd denied being with him, but she suddenly popped up at my café without being scheduled, right around the same time that someone she'd been seen publicly shouting at had been murdered.

And no one was really at the café to note when she'd gotten there. Lucas had seen her, sure, but he wouldn't have paid attention to when she arrived like Adele would have. There were times when Adele's drill-sergeant nature did come in handy.

"Aargh!" I dug my foot into the sand and kicked a wad of it toward the water. I still couldn't make any of the pieces fit together in my brain. And I certainly wasn't any closer to figuring out who the killer was. I got up, took one last look at the ocean, and turned to go home. I felt better just being here, but I hadn't solved any of these problems.

I hopped back on my bike and pedaled toward the exit. As I did, I caught sight of two guys sitting on a parked motorcycle, locked in a steamy embrace. That normally wouldn't have caused me to take a second glance—but one of them was Marco Moore. I'd recognize that sexy, messy hair and scruffy beard anywhere.

Still, I had to do a double take, pedaling closer while attempting to not look like I was gawking. But that meant I wasn't paying attention to where I was going. I swerved right into a parked car, flying over the handlebars. As I hit the ground face-first, instinctively trying to protect my head, my bike skidded to a stop and landed on top of me.

Chapter 31

Should've worn that helmet.

The words, spoken in Lucas's voice, floated through my brain as I tested my limbs to make sure they were all in working order. Shoving the bike off me, I heard shouts and then running feet—and saw Marco Moore and the guy he'd been kissing standing over me, looking concerned. Marco's . . . fling (boyfriend? hookup?) hauled the bike off my leg and stood it up while Marco bent down next to me. My eyes lingered on the other guy for a minute. Even in my disoriented state, I had to note how hot he was. And young. Way younger than Peyton.

He also looked really familiar. It took my rattled brain a minute for all the pieces to fall back into place, but then I realized. The giant tattooed snake bicep gave it away.

He was the guy who had been yelling at Chad in the parking lot of Damian's restaurant yesterday.

Just as the thought registered, I had to push it aside when Marco leaned over, his face filling my view.

"Are you . . ." he began, then his eyes widened when he realized it was me. "Maddie! Are you okay?"

I had no idea if I was okay. I turned my attention back

to my body and focused on any potential injuries I may have given myself. My knee was screaming, my wrist felt sprained, and my ankle where the bike had landed didn't feel so hot, but nothing seemed broken. What a klutz. "Yeah. I think so. Aside from my pride." I managed a weak smile.

The guy watched our exchange with interest. "You two know each other?"

Marco nodded. "Maddie owns the cat café. You know, the fundraiser. Maddie, Adam. Adam, Maddie." He made the introduction with a bit of a grimace, as if he'd rather do anything but.

"Ah," Adam said, a little smirk passing over his lips. He looked at me. "I remember you. From the fish market."

It was hard to have a conversation lying on the pavement. I rolled over and accepted the hand Marco offered to pull me up. My vision swam for a second, then cleared. "Yes, that was me," I said. I dusted myself off and inspected the bloody scrape on my knee.

Marco bent down to have a look too. "It doesn't look deep," he said. "I may have a Band-Aid. Adam, can you check the bag?"

The other guy nodded and jogged back to the bike, leaving Marco and me alone. Marco focused on my knee until it became weird, and then stood to face me so we were awkwardly looking at each other. I could tell he was trying to assess what, exactly, I'd seen, and then figure out how to explain himself.

"Maddie," he began nervously. "I should probably tell you—" but I cut him off.

"Marco. Please. Don't feel like you have to explain anything to me. Honestly." I reached down and tried to brush the dirt out of my cut, more for something to do than for any other reason. "I don't even know you," I added. "Why would you need to explain yourself?"

He sighed. "Everyone knows me. And I mean that in the least egotistical way possible. I mean everyone knows who I am and that I'm supposed to be with Peyton and . . . it's complicated."

I smiled at that. "Most things are. Don't worry," I added as Adam walked back over to us. "Your secret is safe with me. If it is a secret."

"It's totally a secret. Not that I'm ashamed of myself or Adam or . . . anything. It's just, well." He cleared his throat and turned to Adam. "Thank you."

"No problem." Adam turned to me with a smile, like he was a doctor and I was his scared patient. "I found a baby wipe too. I can clean it out for you?"

"Uh, sure," I said, since he looked really eager to do it.

"Are you sure your head is okay?" he asked. "That was quite a spill. Do you want me to call an ambulance?"

"Oh God no. I'm fine. I didn't hit my head."

"You're very lucky," Adam said as he knelt down and began to tend to my wound. "You should always wear a helmet."

"Adam is a nurse," Marco said.

I wasn't surprised. "At Daybreak Hospital?"

Adam nodded. "For nine years now."

"My dad is the CEO," I said. "Brian James."

Adam looked more impressed with that than the fact that he'd been making out with *the* Marco Moore a few minutes ago, until my crash-test-dummy act. "You're Brian James's daughter? Doesn't he have a few of them?"

I grinned. "He does. But I'm the oldest, which makes me the favorite."

Adam laughed as he patted the Band-Aid into place, then stood. "I can see why. You're good."

"Thanks. I'll put in a good word with my dad. Maybe he can get you a promotion." I turned to Marco, who still watched me like I was a stick of dynamite that might blow at any moment. "Nice to see you again."

"You too," he said.

"But wait," Adam said. "Are you sure you should be riding home?"

"I'm fine," I said.

"Where do you live?"

"Over in Daybreak. By the ferry dock."

"That's too far," Adam said, turning to Marco. "Right, baby? Why don't you drive her. You said you needed to get back soon anyway and I have to get to work."

"Um. I don't think my bike will fit on your motorcycle," I began, but Adam shook his head.

"Marco met me here and we went out for a bike ride. He has a car." He pointed to a plain black Ford sedan with rental plates. "He'll take you."

Marco looked like he'd rather do anything but that, but he hid it well. "Uh, yes," Marco said. "For sure. Come on, Maddie."

Adam picked my bike up and hoisted it on his shoulder like it was a kid's tricycle. He loaded it into Marco's car and helped me into the passenger seat. "You take care, Maddie. And get a helmet!" He rapped on my window once, then went around to the other side of the car and kissed Marco goodbye. Apparently he didn't care about Marco's image.

I turned to look out the passenger window, trying to give them some privacy while they murmured something to each other. Finally Adam walked away. I heard the motorcycle engine rev a minute later, then he tore out of the parking lot.

Marco cleared his throat and started the car, pulling a baseball cap low over his head and settling sunglasses over his eyes.

"You really don't have to drive me," I said.

"I'm happy to," Marco said. "Besides, I wouldn't dare risk Adam thinking I didn't do what he said." He winked to show me he was teasing, then pulled out of the lot.

I smiled at that.

"I've been seeing Adam for a long time," he said when we were on the main road, even though I hadn't asked. He seemed eager to tell me. Or maybe he was just eager to tell *someone*. "Twelve years, to be exact. I come out here whenever I'm not working."

"Twelve? Wow. Like, before you and Peyton became an item?"

He nodded. "We met way back when I was a nobody." *He sounds a bit wistful for those days*, I thought.

"And no one's ever seen you guys together?" I found that hard to believe. Then again, Daybreak had a lot of celebs in the summer. They usually stuck to certain areas of the island where most people wouldn't treat them like circus freaks.

"We keep to ourselves," Marco said with a wry smile. "Adam understands how complicated my life is."

"So you and Peyton . . ."

"Are together for the image," he finished. "For our respective careers. We are a power couple," he said with an eye roll. "It wasn't our idea. It was Chad's." He said the name like it left a bad taste in his mouth.

"He's your agent too?" I'd figured as much, but hadn't been sure.

Marco nodded. "He said it would give us even more star power. Don't get me wrong, she's lovely, but not my type. Clearly. And she has her own interests too."

"So who knows about you guys? Like, the truth?"

"Hardly anyone. Chad, of course. It was all his idea in the first place."

"It was?"

Marco nodded. "He orchestrated the whole thing. He helps Peyton and I manage all other affairs. And I mean that literally."

"Really," I said thoughtfully. Was that why he and Adam had been fighting at the fish market? Disagreeing over something specific, or maybe Adam was tired of the whole thing in general?

"Yes. And our closest friends know, but that's it. Peyton and I are both very respectful of each other, and what it would mean career-wise if we were discovered to be, well, frauds. But life is short, you know? I've been thinking about that a lot lately." He sounded sad, and I wondered when it would become an easier decision to leave his career behind and just be with the person he loved.

There were so many people who felt like they had to live a certain way to keep up an image, and it made me sad. I thought of Lucas and how happy I was with him. I couldn't imagine what it would feel like to only be able to be with him some of the time, and always in secret. I felt terrible for Marco and Adam. And Peyton. It seemed like a crappy way to live, fame and fortune aside. I wondered if she also had someone she loved but couldn't be with.

I also wondered if Marco knew his boyfriend had been fighting with his agent. "So does Chad know Adam too?"

An odd look crossed his face and he turned to look at me before dragging his eyes back to the road. "Why do you ask?"

"Because I saw them arguing at the Lobstah Shack the other day."

That caught his attention. "You what? That's what he meant when he said he remembered you from the fish market?"

"Yeah. Obviously I didn't know who Adam was then."

Marco's jaw set, but he didn't say anything else.

"So does he know him?"

"I never introduced them. He knows I have someone who lives out here, but I try to keep Adam out of it as much as possible." He smiled wryly. "I guess I'm just naive. He's probably known all along. And I guess Adam is pretty good at keeping secrets too."

"People love you and Peyton so much." I said. "Are you sure it would matter? Sometimes we think people are going to react a certain way and they surprise us. The ones who matter, anyway."

Marco looked at me, and his eyes were so sad I felt like crying. "It's a nice thought, Maddie, but that's not how it works in our world. Maybe for the younger people coming in, you know? But Peyton and I . . . we've been a 'thing' for so long. It would kill our careers. At least that's what Chad and Jillian drilled into us."

Wait. "Jillian?" I repeated. "What did she have to do with it?"

He shrugged. "Those two colluded on a lot of things, trust me. She's been around for the past decade. She and Peyton kind of have that animal connection going. Or at least they did. I think they weren't as close these days. Esther had really been advising Peyton to distance herself from that relationship."

"What was Chad and Jillian's relationship? Were they . . . together?"

Marco sent me a funny look. "Hardly. He's her brother."

"Her . . . come again?" I asked, sure that I had heard him wrong.

"She was his older sister. Some crazy story about them not knowing about each other for a long time, then they met about ten years ago. You really didn't know? Isn't her family out here?"

"They are, but . . ." I trailed off. I had no idea if anyone knew this. It seemed like every time I had stuff straight in my head about all these relationships, something new happened. Related? Did that mean Chad was also here because of the will and the estate? He clearly wasn't mentioned in the will. Maybe Marcella hadn't even known about him, which is why he and Jillian hadn't known each other for all those years. Maybe he and Jillian had cut a deal that if she got the estate, she'd split it with him.

And maybe she'd changed her mind, and he'd killed her over it. Although if she had gotten the property, couldn't he have come along and sued her later for some of it? Killing her seemed extreme.

"Was it a secret?" I asked. "That he was her brother?" Maybe he was the one who had given Becky the anonymous tip about the family feud. It made sense.

"Not with us, but with the family?" Marco shrugged. "No idea. I wasn't tight with either of them." He didn't have to add that he didn't like them very much. His tone said it all.

"Why was Esther trying to get Peyton to stay away from Jillian?" I asked.

Marco shrugged. "I think she thought it was getting toxic. Peyton was spending most of her time doing

Jillian's bidding. She had her going to a lot of events around the country, being a spokesperson for different organizations . . . it was starting to become a full-time job and Peyton was getting burnt out." He pulled up in front of my house. "Here you go," he said.

I went to open my door and saw Stevie's yellow Subaru parked outside. I nearly groaned out loud. What now? I kind of wanted more time with Marco, but clearly he was itching to drop me off and drive away.

Before I got out, I reached over impulsively and squeezed Marco's hand. "Listen. Your secret is safe with me. But be careful, okay? There are paparazzi all over the place. They were hiding in my bushes yesterday."

His eyes widened. "You're kidding. Sorry about that."

"Not your fault," I said. "Hey, one of them said something to me yesterday, though. It made no sense. She asked me if I could confirm the cat rumor."

Marco's face literally drained of color. "The cat rumor?" he asked, and his voice sounded choked.

I nodded. "When I asked her what she meant, she specifically mentioned Peyton and her cat. You know what she meant?"

He shook his head, a strangled laugh escaping his lips. "They're rag reporters, Maddie. They come up with outrageous rumors and stuff like this all the time. How they get away with printing half of it without multimillion dollar lawsuits is beyond me."

I didn't quite believe him, but didn't want to push too hard. "Come back to the café soon, okay? You and Adam are welcome any time."

"Thanks. I'll grab your bike." He started to open his door but I shook my head.

"Please. I've got it. You stay here where it's safe," I said with a wry smile. I retrieved my bike and waved at him. He took off a little faster than necessary, turning the corner with a screech of tires. I watched until his car disappeared from view, then parked the bike in front of the porch and hurried inside, trying not to look like I was limping.

Chapter 32

When I walked into the house, I could feel the frantic energy enveloping our living room. Stevie was on the couch, his head in his hands. Grandpa sat next to him, looking grim. I could tell he noticed my gimpiness, but filed it away for later. Val hovered near the kitchen door, clearly unsure of what to do.

I raised my eyebrows at her, a silent question. She gave me a look that said *You aren't gonna believe this.*

"What's going on?" I asked, dropping onto the chair across from them.

Stevie raised his face from his hands, and I was alarmed to see his eyes were red and teary.

"It's Mish," he said, and his voice sounded utterly broken.

I froze. "Is she okay? What happened?"

"They took her."

"*Who*?" I looked at Grandpa for help.

"The police," they answered in unison, then looked at each other and looked away.

"What on earth for?" I asked, but I had a sinking feeling in my stomach that I already knew.

"They think she had something to do with Jillian's murder," Stevie said. "But that's impossible. My wife is a good person. She's sweet and kind and she would never do anything to hurt anyone. She just doesn't have it in her." His voice broke on the last words. "Just because she didn't like Jillian for what she was doing to us . . ."

I sat back, my head spinning. "Why do they think she did it?" I asked.

"Because her alibi doesn't hold up," Stevie said. "She asked me to drop her off at the Bean that morning on my way to . . . run an errand. She said she was meeting her friend Shannon."

"Because her car was in the shop," I remembered. "But I thought you dropped her here."

Stevie looked at me strangely. "Her car wasn't in the shop. She just didn't want to find parking downtown. Did she tell you her car was in the shop?"

She definitely had. "I'm probably thinking of another day," I said, waving it off. "Go on."

"That's it. She was going to have coffee then come here," Stevie said. "She said Shannon would bring her. But Shannon said she never showed. She tried to call her a couple times, then I guess she just went on with her day. When the police questioned her, she told them the truth."

"But Mish did come here. When I got home, she was here. Lucas thought she got dropped off around ten." *Right around the time we found Jillian's body.* "I can ask him. Is he still here?"

Grandpa shook his head. "He went to work."

I fixed my gaze on Stevie. "Do you have a lawyer?"

He nodded. "My grandmother's lawyer."

I wondered if that was such a good idea, but decided not to bring that up. Instead I said, "But you were the one at the Paradise that morning, weren't you? Unless you lent Mish your car."

He stared at me, the blood draining from his face, and looked nervously at Grandpa before turning back to me. "What . . . what do you mean?"

"I mean, I saw your car leaving the parking lot right after we discovered Jillian's body," I said bluntly. "Don't tell me there's another yellow Subaru like yours out here. I've never seen one. Did Mish take your car?"

"No! She did not have my car." Stevie's whole body physically drooped. His face fell back into his hands. "Who else saw me?" he asked, his voice muffled.

Probably half the island. "I don't know," I said. "I went out to the parking lot to wait for Sergeant Ellory."

He looked up again, resigned. "You're right. I was there. I was spying on my cousin." He looked sheepish. "I knew she had been telling people that she was staying with me and Mish to make it look like we all got along, but she left every night. I was trying to figure out what she was up to. I followed her there the night before—in Mish's car," he added. "It's less noticeable, as you know. Anyway, I followed her there, but by the time I got inside I couldn't find her. And I asked for her at the front desk and they said she wasn't registered as a guest."

"So she used a fake name or was she staying with someone?"

He shrugged. "No idea. I never found out. I went back that morning to try again and well . . . you know what happened from there."

It sounded flimsy to me. I looked at Grandpa, but his face gave nothing away. "Have you heard the name Chad Novak?"

Stevie thought for a moment, then shook his head. "No."

"You never asked Jillian where she was going every night? Did she really think you didn't notice she was leaving?" I asked.

"It wasn't really my business if she stayed or left," he said. "Was she staying with that guy? Is it a boyfriend or something?"

I ignored the question. "So what was your plan? What were you hoping to find out by following her?"

"I don't know, Maddie," he said quietly. "I've been desperate. I wanted her to be doing something really crappy so I could bring it to your grandfather to help my case." He looked at me pleadingly. "I know you think I'm a terrible person, but my grandmother . . ." he shook his head. "I loved her a lot, but toward the end she wasn't really . . . herself."

"That's a lie."

All our heads whipped around to find Ethan standing in the kitchen doorway, arms crossed over his chest. I'd never seen him look this angry, but it made him look taller. His face matched his fiery red hair, and he glared at Stevie.

Stevie rose and faced him. "Sorry?"

"I said, that's a bunch of lies." Ethan came forward to face him. Val went to him, but he shook her off. "Your grandmother was one of the kindest people I've ever known. She was stuck in that place all alone when you had that huge property where she could've stayed."

"She needed twenty-four-hour care," Stevie said quietly. "Do you . . . work at the facility?"

"I volunteer there," Ethan said.

"Ah." Stevie nodded. "She mentioned you. Not by name, but said she'd found a good friend who worked there who spent time with her. I was glad for her."

"Yeah. Well, she told me a lot of stories about her

family. And none of you seem like you deserve anything of hers. Did you ever even go visit her?"

"She wouldn't let me in," Stevie said, incredulous. "The last couple of times I went to see her she refused to see me."

Grandpa interrupted. "Ethan. I appreciate your fondness for Marcella, but I need to agree with Stevie. Her condition had . . . deteriorated."

"Still," Ethan said, his gaze still fixed on Stevie. "You could've let her be at home."

"There was no money to take care of her, man!" Stevie shouted, startling us all. "She froze all her assets when she got sick! What she didn't spend, that is." As fast as the fight had come into him, it went out and he sat back down heavily on the couch. "That's what no one realized. The land is worth money, sure. But the main house needs a ton of work and landscaping that place alone . . ." he shook his head. "And good home care on this island is incredibly expensive. She needed constant care. You know that, right? You were there."

He waited for Ethan to give a curt nod of acknowledgment.

"The place she was in, they let us pay in installments and I was going to pay them off once the property was mine," Stevie continued. "So yes, she was right. I wanted to sell part of it. To pay off her debts, and to keep my daughter in her school. The rest of it, I would keep and live on forever. I love it there. My cousin didn't. Jillian would have sold all of it off to the highest bidder and never looked back. And worst part? She didn't need it. Mish and I need it. The rents here for retail are insane, as you know, and Mish's store doesn't make a huge profit. And we can't keep paying for Mirabelle's school without the extra income. She needs to be in that school."

Mirabelle was their daughter. "What kind of school is it?" I asked.

"Mirabelle is . . . on the spectrum," he said quietly. "But she's a really gifted musician. She needs the extra attention and she can't get it on the island. It's why she's in a special school."

I looked at Grandpa. Why hadn't I known that? Maybe I wasn't as good a friend as I thought.

"Anyway, that's my reason for wanting the property so badly. And I know, if Grandma was in her right mind, it never would've been a question. But she'd started fixating on Jillian, and her mother, and even my mother, and then she got kind of obsessive about it. And then she got sick. Like, really sick. There's nothing I can do about that. But what I do know is, my wife had nothing to do with Jillian's death." He looked at me, deadly serious. "And if they try to go forward with charging her, I'm going to confess. I can't let her go to jail. Mirabelle needs her."

Ethan looked properly chastised. "I'm sorry," he said to Stevie. "I got very attached to her."

"Don't be sorry," Stevie said. "I'm glad she had a friend during her last days."

I reached over and squeezed Stevie's hand. "No one is confessing to anything. We're going to figure this out. I don't believe Mish is a killer either."

His eyes filled again. "Thank you, Maddie."

"Of course." Really, I was dying to drop my bombshell and see his reaction. "So this Chad Novak. He's actually Peyton Chandler and Marco Moore's agent. And I heard the strangest thing about him."

"What?" Stevie asked.

"Someone told me he's Jillian's brother that she never knew until about ten years ago."

I thought Stevie was going to pass out. His whole face

turned white. He looked at Grandpa. "Did you find this out?"

Grandpa shook his head slowly. "Where did you hear this, Madalyn?"

"I can't reveal my source, but this person heard it directly from Jillian," I said. I turned to Stevie, "Is that possible? Wouldn't you have known? Wouldn't *Jillian* have known? I would think it would be kind of obvious."

Stevie massaged his temples, ostensibly to ward off a headache. "My aunt, Deidre, was married to Jillian's father for a while—right out of high school, I think. They got divorced within a year. That was probably the last straw for my grandmother. She didn't believe in divorce." He rolled his eyes, then caught himself and glanced at Ethan. He didn't comment. "She was very prim and proper. So maybe my aunt just never bothered to tell anyone about a new relationship . . . or a kid. My mother and her sister weren't close and when my aunt and my grandmother had their falling out, my mother kept her distance as well. I haven't actually spoken to Deidre in about twenty-five years. I remember my grandmother saying she was always looking for *the glamorous life.* Whatever that meant."

"Would your aunt have given her son up for adoption? If she had gotten pregnant soon after her divorce . . ." I trailed off, trying to piece the story together in my head. "Or, maybe her mother isn't the common parent. Maybe it's the father. Since I'm assuming he is a half brother. In that case he'd have no claim, right?"

Stevie looked at Grandpa. "Can you find any of this out?"

"I'm sure I can," he said. "But why do you want to know?"

"What if he did it?" Stevie asked. "If he really is her

brother and no one knew it, what if he thought he had a claim to something she had? Like the estate?"

Exactly what I was thinking.

"She didn't have the estate," Grandpa pointed out. "And if he wanted something she didn't have yet, why would he kill her? Then he wouldn't get anything. And if it's the same father, like Maddie said, it's a moot point."

Stevie had no good response to that. He left a short time later, dejected and looking lost.

Chapter 33

After Stevie left and I explained my bike accident to Grandpa—avoiding the part about Marco of course—I went up to take a shower. My knee hurt, and my whole left side where my bike had landed also hurt. JJ, my steadfast companion, accompanied me, which I appreciated. I couldn't wait to turn on the hot water and let it soothe my aching muscles.

While I waited for the water to heat up, I turned to JJ. "What a mess," I said.

He squeaked his affirmation.

"I don't believe Mish killed her. But someone did. How do I figure out who? This is way too complicated."

JJ flicked his tail and dropped his face between his paws, clearly tiring of the conversation.

"Yeah, that's what most people think of me lately." I sighed and got into the shower.

After, I called Katrina. I figured she'd be my best way into Ellory's confidence.

"Hey," she said. "Did you hear? About Mish?"

"I did. That's why I called. I need to talk to your boyfriend and was hoping you could pave the way."

"He's coming by in about half an hour on his break," she said. "Don't tell him I told you."

"On my way."

I snuck out the back door and drove over to the Daybreak Island Animal Control Center where Katrina spent most of her days when she wasn't out doing actual rescues. I'd grabbed us coffees on the way, so I'd have an excuse to be there. A dark sedan that I recognized as Ellory's unmarked car was parked outside next to Katrina's van. I parked behind them and headed inside, ignoring the Closed sign on the door. Katrina tried to take a lunch break every day. Most days she was unsuccessful, but Ellory had been helping her with that, coming over to take her out for lunch or at least spend lunch with her when his schedule allowed. I guess since he'd made an arrest, he could do that today.

Now, he sat on the floor petting a German shepherd, who looked blissfully happy. He—or she—was the only one, though. The humans looked extremely serious. Katrina glanced up when I came in. The dog rolled over, giving Ellory more access for belly rubs.

"Hey. We were just talking about you," Katrina said casually. "I told Mick you were stopping by to see me."

"Yep. Here's your coffee." I handed her one. "Sorry, if I'd known you were going to be here I'd have gotten you one. Want mine?" I smiled brightly at him.

He rolled his eyes. "Wasn't born yesterday, Maddie. I'm assuming you heard, then?"

"About Mish? Yeah. Stevie's at my place and he's a mess. Why are you so sure it was her? Did you actually find, like, DNA or something?"

"No, Miss CSI," he said. "No DNA."

"What time did Jillian . . ." I swallowed. "Do they have a time of death?"

"She hadn't been dead long. They estimated maybe a half hour to an hour before you found her."

So somewhere around nine or nine thirty, which meant the fact that Mish had been at my place since ten didn't matter.

"Did you find out if she was staying with someone at the Paradise?" I asked.

"They didn't have her registered as a guest, but they said she'd been in and out for days. She was clearly visiting someone there, but I haven't been able to find out who yet. They did see her with a guy, having a serious conversation in the restaurant. Apparently the guy got angry and left her there."

"Was he staying at the hotel, or was he with her as a guest?"

"The woman I talked to didn't know."

"The purple-haired woman?"

"Yes."

"You got a guest list?"

"Of course I did," Ellory said. "But thanks for the reminder."

"Do you recognize any names? I can look if you want."

He looked like he was weighing that, then sighed. "Sure. Fine. It's in the car. Why, you know anyone who she might have been staying with?"

"I'm not sure," I said. "But I'm happy to look. So who else did you talk to?"

He gave me a look. "Only half the hotel, the League staff, her family. Sister, mother. They both live in Pennsylvania. Sister is out of the country on vacation. No story there. No dad—he died years ago. Your celebrity friends—let me tell you, it took a lot of work just to get on that fancy boat of theirs to talk to them."

Peyton and Marco. "What did they say?"

"Neither of them seemed that broken up about it. Said they didn't know her all that well, just through the animal events. They alibied each other. They were doing yoga together or something through some virtual class." His face suggested what he thought of that.

"Peloton, probably," I said.

"Whatever. That older woman, Peyton's . . ." he cast about for the word.

"Assistant? Esther?"

"That's it. She and one of the bodyguards confirmed their story. Which isn't saying much, since I assume they make a pretty good salary to do whatever they're told, but I have no evidence of either of them being there."

"Which bodyguard?" I asked, thinking of the Italian wannabe who'd chased me and Val off the dock.

"Guy named Joseph Francetti."

Since I didn't know any of their names, that meant nothing to me. "Okay. So what's your big evidence about Mish, then?"

"Because she was seen screaming at the victim in public—by you, among others—and her family was involved in a legal drama with her."

"Jillian was also having a disagreement with all three of the others right outside my place! If that's your only evidence—"

"Along with the small fact that no one could account for Mish's whereabouts that morning after her husband dropped her off at the Bean," he continued, ignoring me. "And she had access to the murder weapon—according to you."

I hated when my own words came back to bite me. "She and Stevie both did."

"What time did Mish get to your place that day?"

"I wasn't home, as you know," I said. "Adele confirmed she showed up just after ten."

"Stevie dropped her off at eight forty at the Bean," he said. "Which still gives her plenty of time to get to the hotel, kill Jillian, then get to your place."

"But that's assuming Jillian was just sitting there in the gazebo, waiting for someone to come along and strangle her," I said. "Mish would have to be really lucky to just arrive and have her sitting there alone like that, kill her, and get to my house without breaking a sweat."

"She's right," Katrina said. "It's a big hotel. Jillian could've been holed up in her room all morning, for all anyone knew, if she was staying there. No one would know that they'd closed off the patio for the meeting, right? No one except the guests who tried to go out there."

"Unless they had arranged a meet," Ellory pointed out.

"Sure. I'm assuming you checked her phone records for that?'

"Waiting on them," he said. "But that's my best guess."

"Stevie admitted to being there," I said. "At the hotel. He told me if the charges against Mish don't get dropped, he's going to confess."

Ellory's eyebrows shot up. "Come again?"

"He was there. I told you I saw his car."

"Right. I checked it out. He told me he thought she might be there and wanted to talk to her, so he was waiting to see if he could spot her." He rolled his eyes. "Sounded pretty unorganized to me, but what do I know about detective work. Members of the staff reported seeing him in the hotel lobby, waiting, between nine and ten. So I have witnesses who saw him at the time of her death."

"But what if he snuck out back to kill her, then came back in?" I asked.

Katrina stared at me. "Are you trying to get Stevie arrested?"

"No. I'm just trying to poke all the holes in the story now that will come out later," I said. "Their lawyers could also say they were in on it together, and the fact that you couldn't definitively say which one did it means you can't prove it." I read a lot of murder mysteries.

"I thought about that," Ellory said. "If they really were in on it together. But I'm not feeling the cousin. That guy is kind of a wuss. No offense," he said when Katrina and I both opened our mouths to protest. "I don't think he has what it takes to strangle someone. Especially a relative, no matter how much he doesn't like her. Plus I don't think he's that good of an actor. He may not have liked her, but he seemed pretty shocked that she was dead. And he was distraught when we took the wife away."

I sighed. "Much as I hate to say it, I agree with you. But you think Mish has what it takes to strangle someone?"

"I can see that more than I can see him doing it," Ellory said.

"That's all you have?" I asked Ellory.

He shook his head. "A staff member saw what she said was a woman down by the back of the property. Dressed in black, a hat, glasses, like a jogger."

I waited. "And?"

He shrugged. "And nothing. It was right around that window of time the coroner said she was killed."

Oh, boy. Police work at its finest. I tried to remember what Mish was wearing that day, although she could have changed. "That's a little weak, no?" I asked. Something about Ellory's demeanor made me think perhaps he wasn't as sold on this idea as he was trying to convince us he was.

He shrugged. "It's enough."

"It's so not! This place is crawling with joggers looking to experience all the sights. The route behind Paradise is an ocean view, for God's sake. You don't think a hundred tourists are out there every day? What's really going on, Mick?"

"Maddie. I don't have to justify our arrest—"

"It's because your chief is friends with the hotel guy, isn't it," I said. "You had to do something fast."

He said nothing.

Katrina stared at him too. "Is it? Because we all know he's quick to jump the gun."

Ellory sighed. "You know the chief hates when out-of-towners get killed. Especially in prominent establishments."

It was such a funny statement that I had to giggle. I could picture Chief McAuliffe presiding over a meeting with the department, telling them in a serious tone that no tourists were allowed to be killed. Residents, fine. Then I realized they were both staring at me as if I'd kind of lost it. Who knew, maybe I had. I cleared my throat. "Go on."

He frowned at me. "Obviously, it's not the kind of tourism advertisement we want. And we certainly don't want our residents thinking that we can't close a case."

"Okay," I said, still waiting for a better reason.

He didn't have one.

"Mick," Katrina said. "Did he order you to arrest someone? And poor Mish ended up as the scapegoat?"

"I wouldn't exactly put it that way," Ellory said. "The chief wanted to make sure that if we had enough to make an arrest, we didn't sit on it. That's all. Believe me, I want to make sure we have the right person too. And right now, it looks like Mish is it." He stood and brushed off his pants. "Come on. Let's look at that list."

I followed him out to the car. He got in, riffled through some papers, and handed me a few sheets. I scanned the list, stopping with a triumphant finger-point at Chad's name. "This guy," I said to Ellory. "Chad Novak. He's Peyton and Marco's agent. And I have it on good authority that that he's Jillian's long-lost brother. Stevie says he didn't know."

"Brother?" he repeated.

"Yep. Apparently a long-lost half brother or something that Jillian didn't know about and only found out ten years ago or so." I went back to the list, but nothing else stood out. With a shrug, I handed him back the papers. "Might be worth checking out. Just in case. If he was the one fighting with her, that could mean something. Especially if he felt entitled to whatever she was here on the island to get. And as much as I like Peyton and Marco both, something tells me they had their reasons to dislike Jillian too."

Chapter 34

"I can't believe you roped me into this." Adele tied up the last bag of trash and hauled it to the door. "You know I don't like people."

It was meet-and-greet-with-Peyton day. And Adele was dreading it. I stifled a laugh and picked up my own bag of trash. "I thought you liked Peyton." Given that we were down a volunteer (Mish), Adele was stuck with me and Grandpa today, working this shindig. And if JJ's House of Purrs' Instagram page was any indication, it was going to be a huge hit. Clarissa had been hyping it on our social since Monday—although we hadn't really needed to with the personal campaign Peyton had launched. She was all in, spreading the word on all her social accounts, Marco's accounts, and probably half a dozen places I hadn't seen.

"I do like Peyton. I just don't like all the other people who are going to show up," she grumbled.

"I know. But it's a good thing." I patted her on the back. "Our campaign really resonated." Katrina and I had taken the sponsorship idea Peyton had floated and gone a step further, using a "by the numbers" theme to break down the number of cats that had already passed through the café, our adoption rate, and what it cost to care for one kitty who resided here. With Ellory's and Lucas's help, we'd even created posters with photos of all the animals in the café and a few facts about each of them.

I was really good at throwing myself into stuff like this, but the whole Mish-being-arrested thing was like a cloud over everything. Even Adele had been very subdued since she'd heard. There were some people she pretended indifference for, but I knew deep down she really liked. Mish was one of them. I had a strong feeling that anyone Adele didn't like wouldn't last here at the café. If you passed her test it usually meant something.

So it was safe to say neither of us were convinced Mish had killed Jillian, but despite staying up half the night trying to piece the puzzle together, I still wasn't any closer to figuring out who was the next best option on my list. The police didn't seem to be concerned at this point—they'd made their arrest, the chief was happy, at least according to the press conference they'd held yesterday, and apparently the hotel business was now able to thrive again.

It didn't sit well.

But I had to push it out of my mind, at least for the moment, if we were going to put out a positive vibe for the day.

"You know what kind of people we're gonna get crawling all over this place today? All those Kardashian-follower types." Adele made a face and fluffed one of the cat beds that had been flattened by too many kitties sitting on it at once. "They give me a headache."

I had to laugh. She was probably right. "Still, they're all probably going to give a donation to get to sponsor a cat or buy some swag or something. And, tickets to the fundraiser if it hasn't already sold out."

"We're at eighty-nine percent sold out!" Val yelled from the next room. "We'll definitely hit our numbers today. And if we have more demand"—she poked her head around the corner—"I'll set up chairs outside the tent. I mean, I'm going to have a second tent on standby anyway in case it rains. Actually, I should use the tent anyway. I'm going to open up more seats. Mom! We're going to add more tables." She disappeared again.

Adele and I looked at each other and burst out laughing. "Is she always like this when she's planning a party?"

"Mm-hmm," I said. "But it looks like she's embraced this whole idea. Which is a little ambitious. If I had to plan this thing in like four days I may have jumped off the nearest bridge." I turned as the doorbell in the main house rang. "Who's that?"

"Probably some rabid fan wanting to be first," Adele grumbled.

I ignored her and headed out, meeting up with Val, who was also on her way to the door. "Expecting someone? It's early," I said.

She made a face. "I hope it's not Esther. Man, she's so involved in this planning. She's like a micromanager. I hate it. But Peyton asked that she be involved so . . ." Val shrugged and pulled open the door. "Oh! Jo. Hi. Are you here to bring the favors?"

Jo stepped inside, carrying a box. An older man stood behind her holding two more. "Yeah. This is all of them," she said, indicating the boxes.

"You can just drop them," I said. "We'll take care of it."

The guy literally dropped his and went back out onto the porch without a word. Jo put hers down too, glancing over her shoulder in annoyance. "Sorry about him. He's annoyed that he made the trip out here," she said.

Guess he and Jillian weren't close, if that's what was on his mind. "No problem," I said. It felt a little awkward and I glanced at Val.

"Thanks for being so understanding," she said.

Jo shrugged. "Yeah, well. What are you going to do."

"Are you guys leaving soon?" I asked.

"Soon," Jo replied, somewhat evasively. I wondered if the cops had asked them to stick around. But if they'd arrested Mish, that couldn't be the case.

"Well, thank you for everything," I said. "Maybe we'll get another chance to work together down the road."

Jo smiled, something I didn't think I'd seen her do yet. "Maybe."

After they left, I turned to Val. "I think they might be upset about the event."

"Yeah. Well, we can't do much about that." Val bent down and hefted one of the boxes. I grabbed the other two and we took them into the café. "Here okay?" she asked, indicating the area behind the counter.

"How about over—" I started to say, but Val's phone rang so she dropped hers and forgot about me.

"There," I finished to the empty space. I moved the boxes myself. Once they were piled behind my counter, I grabbed a pair of scissors off my desk and cut through the tape. I took a breath and pulled up the cardboard sides. Neatly coiled leashes were piled up in the box, all secured with a clear piece of plastic. They looked so benign, not like something that could be used to murder another human being.

Since no one else knew that, I was pretty sure everyone coming to this thing would be delighted to have a

Rhiannon-inspired cat leash. I lifted one out, still encased in its plastic sleeve. There was something about it that seemed off to me, but I was distracted by Ethan coming in.

"Hey," he said. "People are already lining up outside. I'm going to open the café."

"Sounds good," I said. "I'm going to get ready now." I tossed the leash back into the box and closed it. "Are you okay?"

"I'm fine." He still looked troubled, though.

I reached over and squeezed his hand. "I'm sorry," I said. "I know Marcella's death was hard on you. I wish you would've told me."

He shrugged. "I thought it might sound silly. I didn't know her that well, right? Only a couple months. We just . . . connected."

"Doesn't matter how long you knew her. If you connect with someone, you connect with them." I paused. What I was about to suggest wasn't really my business, but we were friends and that's what friends did, right? "Maybe you should go home for a visit. See your grandma. It's been a year, after all."

Ethan thought about that, then nodded slowly. "You may be right."

"I'm always right." I winked at him. "Now I'm going to shower so I'm ready for this shindig."

I headed back inside, leaving Ethan sitting on the steps. At least he'd finally told me what was bothering him. As I headed upstairs, I called Becky.

"You heard?" I asked when she answered. "About Mish?"

"I guess you haven't been to our website," she said. "We got the tip last night. The cops didn't want the nationals to get it first."

"You believe it?" I asked.

"I just report it," she said, though she sounded subdued as well.

"I feel awful for Stevie. He was here yesterday talking to Grandpa. He swears she didn't do it, and that he'd confess if they tried to make this stick."

Becky whistled. "Really?"

"Yeah." I let myself into my bedroom and shut the door behind me, then dropped onto the bed next to JJ, who was sprawled out on his back. "Hey. Speaking of tips. I got one yesterday too."

"About?"

"I heard from someone . . . close enough to Jillian, that Chad Novak is, like, her long-lost brother."

"Who is Chad Novak?" Becky asked. I could hear her flipping pages in a notebook to write this down.

"Peyton Chandler's and Marco's agent. And Jillian might have been staying at the Paradise with him when she was killed."

"Hmm. So what do you think? He did it?"

"I don't know. He's not the nicest guy I've ever met. I'm not sure what it means, but maybe it means something. I told Ellory too. He said one of the hotel people saw her fighting with some guy in the restaurant. He got mad and left her there. It could be him."

"I will check it out. Thanks, girl."

"Anytime. Oh, and something else weird happened that I meant to tell you about." I'd almost forgotten about it, but being in the café with my cats had reminded me.

"Hit me. You know I love weird stuff."

"The tabloid people were hiding in my bushes."

Becky snorted. "You're lucky they weren't hiding in your house. That's not weird."

"You didn't let me finish. One of them came up to me

and asked me to confirm the rumor about Peyton's cat. Did you hear anything about her cat in your travels?"

"Her cat?" Becky sounded truly baffled.

"Yeah, you know how her cat is as famous as her? If not more? Rhiannon?"

"So what would the rumor be? That it's not really a cat? It's a computerized stuffed animal?" Becky laughed at her own joke. "You're the cat person. What could that mean?"

"I don't know. I just hoped maybe you'd heard something."

"I haven't. But I can ask around, I guess. Now that we're not technically investigating a murder anymore."

Chapter 35

An hour later the line outside our place reached almost down to the ferry dock. Adele was probably losing her mind. My mother and Lucas were helping out in the café, because Ethan was slammed. Becky had sent Jenna and Kevin to cover the event, and they were outside talking to people waiting in line. While I was grateful for the coverage, I wasn't sure her motives were entirely about the cats, but I'd managed to deflect her so far. I was sure she would corner me at some point to ask about Mish, and I didn't want to deal with it.

At ten, Grandpa went out to greet Peyton and Marco, who arrived on the down-low in a black suburban with Chad and some handlers who were going to manage the line of people and the amount of time each guest spent with the stars. Of course, anytime someone picked a black suburban as the car, it was obvious that they were trying to be stealth. So there were a few screaming fans running behind the car into our backyard. Luckily Peyton's people intercepted them and led them back to the line while Grandpa brought the two stars in through the back door.

But when he came in, he had a weird look on his face. "Here are our guests of honor," he said to me, holding the door open. Peyton stepped through—no Rhiannon—and smiled at me. "Hi, Maddie. Good crowd," she said.

"It's amazing," I said, going over to give her a hug. As I reached her, she stumbled forward and I had to grab her arm to steady her. I thought she'd tripped, but then I realized Marco was behind her and he'd fallen into her, shoving her forward. Grandpa reached out to steady him as he grabbed for the doorframe, trying to regain his balance.

"Sorry, baby," he said, and I was shocked to hear his voice slurred almost to the point of being unrecognizable. I looked at Grandpa. He shook his head, miming someone drinking.

Jeez. Marco was drunk and it was barely ten a.m.?

"Watch what you're doing," Peyton muttered, shoving him off, almost causing him to lose his balance again.

He caught himself, then looked at me. It took him a moment to focus, but then he lurched forward, reaching for me. "Maddie! So good to see you. How's that knee?"

Peyton's head whipped around, first landing on him, then sliding to me. She looked suspicious.

I avoided her gaze. "It's fine," I said. "Thank you. Can I get you some coffee?"

"Nah." He patted his pocket. "I brought my own refreshments."

Peyton looked like she wanted to hide. "Go sit," she hissed at him. "And stop talking."

He shot her a look then stumbled over to one of the chairs, sitting down harder than necessary.

"I'm so sorry," she said to me and Grandpa. "He hasn't been himself lately."

"He's drunk," Grandpa said flatly.

"I know," Peyton said. "He's been struggling. I didn't realize that he'd been drinking until we were already on our way here."

Chad walked in. It was the first time I'd seen him since Sunday, on the steps at the hotel. He looked rough—hair tousled, a couple days' worth of five-o'clock shadow, eyes red. He met my gaze, mumbled a greeting, then turned to Peyton. "I'm sorry. I should've smelled it on him. I'll take him home."

"There's a ton of people here waiting to meet him," Peyton said doubtfully, but I could tell she was worried about him actually meeting anyone in this shape.

"It's really not good publicity if he's drunk," Grandpa said. "We can say he's not feeling well. People will understand. They have you."

"And we don't want there to be fallout for you because he's drinking too much," Chad said to Peyton. "I'll take him back to the boat. Don't worry about it." Without giving her a chance to answer, he went over to the couch and grabbed Marco's arm, hauling him up more roughly than was probably necessary. "Let's go."

"Go where? I just got here." Marco tried to wrench his arm away, but he lost his balance and almost fell again. Luckily the couch was there so he didn't hit the ground. I looked away, embarrassed for him.

"You're causing a scene and we're going. Come on." Chad jerked him back to his feet and dragged him to the door. But Marco was surprisingly quick for someone so drunk. He wound up and clocked Chad on the side of the head, not hard, but hard enough that he yelped and let go.

"Whatsa matter?" Marco jeered at him. "Am I ruining your perfect image? Or hers? Lemme tell you, none of our images are lookin' good these days."

Chad angrily advanced on Marco. Grandpa stepped in front of him. "Not here," he said, and in an instant I could see how formidable he'd been in his prime.

Chad glared at both of them. "Come on. I'm taking you back," he said to Marco, grabbing his arm again.

Marco tried to wrench free, but Grandpa took his other arm and said something to him that I couldn't hear. Whatever it was seemed to calm him down and Grandpa patted him on the back, then they both led him outside.

"What did you say to him?" I asked Grandpa when he returned.

Grandpa shrugged. "That if he went quietly and slept it off, he could come here and stay for a few nights when he felt better. That I'd make it a B&B just for him."

Chapter 36

Peyton was clearly bothered by Marco's drunken show, even when Chad returned and assured her he was sleeping it off, but she covered it with grace as soon as we opened the doors to her clamoring fans. I was kind of worried that it would be too much for her solo, but she was in her element once she started meeting people. And Val helped her handlers move everyone through with no-nonsense precision. I could see why she was good at this event planning stuff.

At the front of the line was our very own Leopard Man. He was decked out in full leopard gear and tail today. His girlfriend, Ellen, accompanied him. "Peyton's my favorite," he confided in me. "And my love here is worried I'll run off with her."

Ellen laughed, but I noticed how tight she held on to Leopard Man's arm. Their relationship was fairly new, but I thought it was adorable. Since I was a child, Leopard Man was an enigma on the island, between his unique clothing style and his penchant for speaking mainly in Shakespeare. When we learned his true identity last year—including that his name was actually

Carl, which I didn't think fit him at all—it was finally
an opportunity for him to let people in a bit more, even
though he was still quite intent on preserving both his
privacy and his eclectic status. "I'm not worried," she
said. "You wouldn't get very far very fast on that giant
boat."

I laughed. "True story. Oh, you should talk to Val,"
I told him. "She has a job for you at our fundraiser on
Saturday." As far as I knew, Val was still looking for
Leopard Man to be auctioneer, even with the limited live
items we were planning to have.

"Lovely," he said. "'How far that little candle throws
his beams! So shines a good deed in a weary world.'"

"*Merchant of Venice!*" I said, snapping my fingers.

"Very good," he said.

I'd gotten rusty on my Shakespeare after I left college,
but I needed Leopard Man to know that I could keep
up with his literary references, so I'd had to brush up. I
would say I got three out of five references.

"I'm always happy to do a good deed for the cats," he
said. "And Peyton Chandler, well, she's the icing on the
cake." He winked at Ellen. She slapped his arm.

"I'll make sure you get some special attention," I told
them, and went off to tell the handlers.

Five hours later, we saw the last guests out and locked
the café doors behind them. The kittens were the last ones
standing—the rest of the cats had all gone to their pre-
ferred hiding spots after the first few hours. While we'd
kept the amount of people in the café at one time man-
ageable, the traffic had been steady the entire time. The
good news, however, was plentiful: my shop shelves were
empty, we'd gotten sponsors for all the cats with a waiting
list to sponsor the next arrivals, and we'd collected more

than two thousand dollars in spontaneous donations. Five cats had adoption applications. Our event was officially sold out, including the extra tables Val had added on the fly this morning, and Leopard Man was looking forward to being our auctioneer.

And I was exhausted.

"Would you like any coffee, or iced tea or something?" Grandpa asked Peyton, who was on the couch snuggling Ashley. "You were a trooper today."

"Please. I love this stuff," Peyton smiled. "I'll have to pass on the iced tea, though. I should go see how Marco is doing."

"I'm sure he's sound asleep," Chad muttered. "Either that or he went out on another bender."

Peyton gave him a filthy look.

"I hope he's feeling better," I said brightly. "Give him our best. And thank you so much for today."

"It was a huge hit, right? I'm so glad we've got a full slate of guests for our event."

"We are too," Val said. "Busy week, but it's all coming together."

"Excellent." Peyton stood, reluctantly letting Ashley go. "Oh, and by the way. I'd like to adopt Ashley. That is, if she didn't find her home today." She looked at me hopefully.

I found myself hesitating, for just a second. A couple days ago, I wanted nothing more than for this celebrity to adopt one of our cats. But I couldn't shake that reporter's question from my mind. And not knowing the answer was giving me pause.

I smiled. "I had someone who inquired about her, but nothing is final yet. If they don't come back by tomorrow, we can do the paperwork."

"Amazing." Peyton clapped her hands together, much like a little kid. "I can pick her up Sunday before we leave."

"Lovely." I took a deep breath. "Peyton, the other day, the tabloids were here. Waiting in the yard when I got home."

"Oh, my. I'm so sorry," she said, her hand flying to her mouth. "It's all our fault."

"No, not at all. We got rid of them, but one of them asked me an odd question. They asked me to confirm if the rumor about your cat was true." I paused. Chad, who had been gazing out the window, snapped to attention. "Do you know what they were talking about?"

Peyton's face went dark. In the moment it took her to regain her composure, Chad snapped at me. "Why were you talking to them anyway? You have no authority to speak on her behalf."

"Watch it," Grandpa said, before I could even respond. "They accosted her, not the other way around."

"Chad, please," Peyton said, before turning to me. "I don't have a clue what she meant," she said with a little laugh, but it sounded forced. "Those people make their living on making things up. I'm so sorry they bothered you, Maddie." She glanced at her watch. "We should go."

Chad hustled her out to her car.

I looked at Grandpa. "What do you think of that?"

"No idea," he said thoughtfully. "But her people are certainly protective of her. What do you think it meant?"

"I wish I knew." I went out to the café. Ethan, Lucas, and my mom looked as exhausted as I felt, but they also looked happy. "We sold out of everything," my mother said triumphantly. "Pastries, yogurt parfaits, sandwiches. The coffee is also running pretty low. We had to make a new pot every hour!"

"That's awesome," I said. "We also sold out the event."

My mother jumped up and hugged me with a squeal. "That's so great, honey."

"You're kidding! Way to go, babe. I'd kiss you but I'm too tired to get up," Lucas said. "I haven't worked this hard in years."

"Sorry about that, man," Ethan said. "Congrats, Maddie."

"Yeah, Val is psyched." I glanced down at my phone as it started buzzing on the table. Damian. I picked up. "I'm sorry I didn't call you for the meet and greet," I started, but he cut me off.

"The cops are at my place."

"Why? Are you okay?"

"I am. But someone's not. They found someone hurt out on my beach."

Damian's place backed up against the water near the ferry docks. There was a small area down there to sit, along with a path you could walk along the water that started all the way at the other end of our street. "What do you mean, found someone?" I asked, jumping to my feet.

"A guy walking along the water found someone unconscious down there and called the cops. But Maddie, it's not just anyone. It's Marco Moore. And it looks like he didn't just pass out. They think someone assaulted him."

Chapter 37

Ten minutes later I was inside Damian's place, watching the cops milling around down on the little beach. Marco Moore had, in fact, been the guy unconscious on the beach and had been transported to the hospital. I imagined my dad's day had just gotten complicated. Luckily, he'd been alive, but pretty badly hurt. He had been hit over the head and left there.

"Do they have any idea how long he was out there?" I asked Damian.

Damian shook his head. "They wouldn't tell me anything. Just asked if I saw anyone down there. I hadn't—it's been a busy day. My staff either. None of us have had time to go to the bathroom, never mind take a walk on the beach."

I stared outside. I didn't see Craig or Ellory out there, or I would've gone down to ask them. I wondered how long after Marco went back to the boat that he'd wandered out here. Had he randomly picked a fight with someone? Had someone recognized him and tried to get his autograph and he'd lost it? He hadn't been a happy drunk, from what I'd seen this morning.

Or had Chad dropped him off on the beach and hit him over the head on the way back? I tried to shake off that dark thought, but couldn't. What if this was related to Jillian's murder? If it was, that meant it sure hadn't been Mish.

I grabbed my phone and texted Craig.

The assault down by Damian's. What do you know about it?

He texted back immediately.

Not much. Guy had a decent head injury when they found him. Unconscious and taken to the hospital. May need to be airlifted to Mass General.

You think it's connected to the murder?

Silence. Then again, he couldn't say yes without admitting they might have the wrong person in custody. I got back in Grandma's car and called my dad. "What's going on over there?" I asked.

He sighed. "Crazy day. I'm assuming you know and that's why you're asking? Your actor friend?"

"Yeah. How is he?"

"Still unconscious."

"Will he be okay? Are they keeping him there or moving him?"

"Maddie. You remember a little thing called HIPAA?"

I sighed. "I just want to know if he's going to be okay."

"Well, you aren't a relative."

"Do you know if anyone is there with him?"

"His girlfriend. The other actor," my dad said. "We had to give him a private room and clear the floor. She requested police as well. It's creating a bit of a stir, if you can imagine."

"I can. Hey, Dad. There's a nurse who works there. A guy named Adam."

My dad waited. "Okay. There are a lot of nurses here, Maddie."

"I know, but I need to know if he's working today. Any way you can find out for me? Please?"

"I'm not even going to ask why. Give me a bit, Madalyn. I'll try to find out and call you back."

"Thank you, Daddy. Love you." I hung up and leaned back in the seat. I wanted to text Peyton but I didn't want to intrude. I didn't want to pretend I knew them well enough to invade their privacy during such a terrible time. I wondered if Peyton would pull him out of the hospital. With their money, Peyton could afford to put up a whole team of private doctors on her boat. That way they could get out of here.

But my mind kept wandering back to that dark place and taking it a step further. What if Peyton and Chad were in on this together? What if they both knew Marco's patience for the whole charade of their "relationship" was wearing thin—it had certainly seemed that way to me the other day—and they decided he'd become a liability? Did Peyton believe in Chad enough to let him completely drive her life this way? And what did that mean about Jillian? Had they conspired together to kill her too? But where did she fit in?

I couldn't figure out how Peyton felt about Chad. Either she felt obligated to stay as his client because of what he "had" on her, or it could be kind of like the whole Stockholm syndrome thing, where she actually felt a connection to him. If so, could she be orchestrating this whole thing and using him to do the dirty work? Had he convinced her Jillian was the mastermind and Marco was unreliable, and convinced her she needed to get rid of them?

Maddie. Those are awful thoughts, I chided myself. What if it was as simple as, something had happened with Adam and Marco? Maybe they'd met down by the water and had an argument. I was certain that the way they were living had to be stressful for both of them. Maybe Marco had come across Adam with some other guy and a fight ensued. After all, Chad had returned pretty quickly from dropping Marco off. Would he have had enough time to take him to the beach, clock him, clean off his shoes, and come back to the event?

Impatiently I checked my phone. It shouldn't take my dad that long to find out if someone on his staff was working, should it? I guess if you were the CEO, though, you didn't really get into nurse schedules.

I leaned back against the seat and opened Instagram. Impulsively I typed in Jillian Allen's name. I'd been meaning to look up her social accounts all week, but there had been so much going on. I found her right away. Her profile picture showed her in one of her fancy outfits, laughing at someone off camera. Probably at some League event. I scrolled the photos. Mostly they were of her with well-dressed people at seemingly fancy events. None of her with animals. I checked Facebook, but her account was locked down to the public. I was trying to think where to look next when my phone rang in my hand. My dad.

I answered it eagerly.

"Adam DeSantis," he said without preamble. "He's the only nurse named Adam on the payroll. He is off today."

"Thank you, Daddy," I said, blew him a kiss through the phone, then hung up and googled Adam DeSantis.

Adam DeSantis, according to WhitePages.com, lived in a small house downtown on Mulberry Street. It was close enough that he could walk anywhere worth getting, but far enough removed from the action that he wouldn't hear every party that was going on. His little yellow house was cute, with rose bushes out front and a purple front door. I didn't see his motorcycle in the driveway. He also didn't appear to have a garage. The house was also super close to his neighbors on both sides. The older gentleman who lived to the right sat out on his stoop and glanced at me curiously when I walked up. I smiled in what I hoped was a nonchalant fashion and rang the doorbell.

Silence from inside. I tried to peer into the little side window without actually looking like that's what I was doing when the guy next door called over.

"He's not home."

"Thank you," I said. "Any idea where he is?"

The guy shrugged. "He has Thursdays off. I would try Shady's Tavern."

The motorcycle bar. Made sense for a Harley guy. That was the place where all the local bikers hung out. I thanked the neighbor and hurried back to my car.

Shady's Tavern had lived on Bicycle Street for fifty-plus years, down at the less-fancy end. I pulled up out front and found a parking spot a ways down the street. All the front spots were taken up by motorcycles. I scanned them for Adam's, but really I couldn't tell the difference. I hadn't gotten the best look at his, given that I'd been too busy face-planting in the beach parking lot when I'd seen it.

I pushed the door open and went inside. It had a typical biker bar feel—dark, boozy, rock music. I paused, letting my eyes adjust to the dim lighting. There were about twenty people or so in there, scattered between the bar and the tables. It was early still—barely five—so that wasn't unexpected. I didn't see Adam at the tables, so I headed to the bar.

The bartender, a guy with a beard that grazed his

chest, biceps the size of watermelons, and a receding hairline, gave me a long look as I approached. "Help you?" he said warily.

I recognized him. Grandpa knew him. Which wasn't notable in and of itself because Grandpa knew everyone on this island for the most part, but because Grandpa had brought me and Val in here in the past. He'd wanted his girls to be exposed to all kinds of environments and not have that fear-based reaction that so many people were taught about various groups. I knew for a fact he'd been more comfortable with the bikers than some of the allegedly upstanding businessmen on the island. Thankfully I had a good memory for names.

I smiled. "You're Ax, right?"

He cocked his head at me, trying to place me, clearly wondering how I knew his name. "Who's asking?"

"Maddie James. Chief Leo's granddaughter."

Now his eyes widened and he broke into a giant smile. I thought he was going to jump over the bar and hug me. "Maddie! You're all grown up! Where's the chief? He with you?" He scanned the room over my shoulder.

"I'm sorry, he's not today. But he's doing well and I'll tell him you said hi."

"So what can I do for you? Here for a drink? Whatever you want, it's on the house."

"Actually, I'm looking for someone." I slid onto a stool. "Adam DeSantis?"

"You've come to the right place. He's here most nights." He glanced at his watch. "Unless he's with that boyfriend of his." He winked at me.

My eyes popped. "You know about him?"

Ax shrugged. "Sure. This is the only place they can really go without worrying about *exposing* him." He used air quotes around the word, punctuated by an eye roll.

"You ask me, no one gives a crap, but to each his own. Maybe it makes everything more exciting."

"Is Adam here now?"

"He was. He got a text message a while ago and took off like someone was chasing him. Hope he's all right."

"Had he been here long?" I asked casually. Although the point was likely moot. I had no idea how long Marco had been down on that beach unconscious. He could've easily come here after the altercation for an alibi, maybe had someone text him to pretend he'd gotten the emergency call.

But my gut instinct really wasn't feeling it. If he'd legit gotten a text that had spooked him, someone had told him about Marco. Maybe Peyton had texted him.

"He was here since about two. He didn't have a lot to drink, though. Just a burger and a beer. Mostly he was just hanging, watching the baseball game."

"Thanks, Ax. Hey, if he happens to come back here tonight, can you tell him I'm looking for him? I can leave you my number."

"Sure. For the chief's granddaughter? Anything." He pulled out a notepad that had drops of what appeared to be lemon juice on it and posed his pen over a clean page. I recited the number.

"Got it. I'll be on the lookout."

As I turned to go, he called me back. "Send Leo down for a drink one of these days, would you? It's been way too long."

I promised I would, then turned and headed back to my car. If Adam had heard about Marco, chances were he'd gone straight to the hospital.

Chapter 38

I called Lucas on my way over to the hospital.

"What's going on?" he asked.

I told him about Marco. "He's at the hospital. I'm going over there now."

"You think they're going to let you in?" He sounded doubtful.

"Of course I do. I'm going to shamelessly use my dad's position if anyone gives me a hard time."

Lucas sighed. "You need to be careful, Maddie."

"I will. But I really need to know if this is related to Jillian, or if it had something to do with Marco's mood earlier today."

"But if he was that drunk and went back to the boat, how did he get over to Damian's?"

"No idea. Unless he took a nap, then went out for some food and found himself some trouble. Either way I'll let you know what I find out. Hey, can you give JJ his dinner?"

Lucas promised to, and I hung up. Becky was texting me but it would have to wait.

I drove around the back of the hospital and parked, then hurried to the special entrance that led to the administrative offices. When I burst through the door of my dad's office, his longtime assistant Anne Marie looked up and broke into a smile.

"Well hello there!" she exclaimed, coming over to wrap me in a hug. "It's been way too long!"

I squeezed her back. "So good to see you too."

"You're looking for your daddy?"

I nodded.

"He went downstairs for the press conference."

"Press conference?"

Anne Marie nodded. "That poor handsome actor who's down on the fifth floor. The media got wind of it and it's been a little busy around here." Despite this, Anne Marie looked like she was enjoying the action.

"Fifth floor, huh?" I said. "Listen Annie, I need to go down there and see him. Can I get through?"

"Of course you can. If anyone gives you a hard time you tell them to call me." She puffed out her chest importantly. I didn't doubt her. Anne Marie held as much clout as my dad around here, if not more. That's what happened when you were the CEO's right hand for so many years. She worked not just with my dad, but with multiple CEOs. No one questioned Anne Marie.

I gave her a kiss on the cheek. "Thank you!"

"Should I tell your dad you'll be back?" she asked.

"No. I don't want to ruin the surprise." I left her office and found the nearest stairwell, heading down two flights to get to the fifth floor.

When I stepped into the hallway, it was quiet. My dad hadn't been kidding when he said they'd cleared the floor. I walked down the empty hall, stepping lightly, afraid to disturb the silence. I felt a bit like I was in a horror movie.

The first wing I walked through was completely empty. When I turned the first corner, I found the activity.

Two uniformed officers were positioned outside a room directly across from the nurse's station. I wondered if they were there because he was a celebrity, or because they were worried about his safety. There were two people behind the desk. Other than that, all was quiet.

I took a deep breath and walked down the hall like I owned the place, stopping in front of the door. The cop looked at me. "How'd you get on this floor?" he asked.

"I'm here on behalf of my father. The CEO," I said. I felt only a twinge of guilt using his name this way.

Still, the cop shook his head. "Sorry. Strict orders. No one allowed in the room except family."

I wondered what that meant. Peyton wasn't technically family—they'd never gotten married. I tried to peek in the window to see if she was there, but the curtain had been closed tight.

I glanced over at the nurses. I didn't recognize either one of them, unfortunately. They couldn't even vouch for me. I'd have to ask Anne Marie after all. But when I got back upstairs, my dad was there.

"Absolutely not," he said when he saw me. "I can't believe you came here for that purpose!" He sounded really mad, which wasn't like him. Anne Marie was still at her desk, trying to pretend she wasn't listening to our fight.

"Dad. Don't be mad. I'm just trying to find out his condition for . . . a friend of his."

My father looked at me suspiciously. "What friend?"

"It doesn't matter. That's the only reason I wanted to go see him. Honestly. But if you can get me just a general update—"

"Madalyn! Have you forgotten everything I've ever

taught you about etiquette?" My father's voice had
started to rise, a sign that I was really pushing him to his
limits.

Before I could open my mouth again and make it
worse, Anne Marie stuck her head in. "Cool your jets,
Brian," she said. "She's telling the truth."

Both of us turned and gaped at her. I'd never heard
anyone—aside from my mother—speak to my father like
that, especially someone who worked for him.

She ignored him and focused on me. "You're looking
out for Adam, aren't you."

"How . . . how do you know that?"

She laughed. "I know everything about this place, remember? Adam is a good boy. We have lunch together
every Wednesday. He chose a hard path," she said with
a nod. "But he deserves to at least know how Marco is
doing."

"Anne Marie. What on earth are you talking about?"
my father asked.

"Marco Moore's boyfriend is a nurse here," she
said. "He can't get in to see him without blowing this
whole concocted story about his relationship with that
actress. So he's sitting outside on a bench hoping to
hear something before the news goes public."

"He is here?" I asked.

"Yep. I went out and brought him a coffee a few minutes ago." Anne Marie looked at my dad. "Get her an
update, Brian."

Chapter 39

Twenty minutes later, I went down the back stairwell and outside. Sure enough, Adam sat alone on a bench, a cup of coffee in his hand and an untouched sandwich sitting next to him. He looked deflated, like a balloon whose air was slowly seeping out of a pinhole.

I slid onto the bench next to him. He looked at me, but didn't seem to recognize me at first.

"Hey, Adam. Maddie James. We met at the beach the other day," I said.

It took him a second, but then it registered. "Yeah. The CEO's daughter." His voice was flat, as if his entire personality had emptied out of him and all that was left was this robotic voice and some jerky movements. "What are you doing here?"

"Anne Marie sent me. I thought you might like some news on Marco."

He looked at me sharply. I could see the inner battle of hope and defense playing out behind his eyes as he tried to predict what I was about to tell him. "How do you . . . right. The CEO's daughter." He clutched the coffee cup so hard the lid popped off. "So . . . ?"

"He's not awake yet, but the scans show normal brain activity. No swelling or bleeding. They are cautiously optimistic." I repeated the words I'd memorized upstairs in my dad's office. "At this point they aren't airlifting him elsewhere."

Marco let out a breath that sounded almost like a sob then looked away, blinking back tears. "Thank you. Is anyone in there with him?"

"I think Peyton was, but she's going home to rest. So in twenty minutes, you should go up to the fifth floor by the back stairs, and my dad will personally escort you to his room." I smiled. "You can stay as long as you like."

He looked at me like I'd just told him he'd won the lottery. "You're . . . you're serious?"

I nodded. "I told my dad. Actually, Anne Marie did. She convinced him it was the right thing to do. I hope you're not mad."

He broke out in a big smile, tears now running down his face. "Mad? You're an angel." He leaned over and hugged me. "Thank you, Maddie."

"Of course. I know Marco is worried about people finding out, but something tells me he would want you there."

"Yeah." Adam's face clouded over again. "He always felt he had so many things to hide, you know? That everything about him had the potential to derail his career. And Peyton . . ." he grimaced.

"What about Peyton?" I asked.

"She's the same way. The two of them were, like, conspiracy theorists. It was paranoia city. They acted like Russian spies were tracking their every move."

Maybe not Russian spies, but certainly American paparazzi, I thought, but kept my mouth shut. "Why do you think that is?" I asked. "I mean, they're both big stars in their own right. Why on earth would it matter if they weren't together?"

"You don't get Hollywood, do you?"

"I don't, actually. Never had the opportunity to learn the inner workings," I said wryly.

"Well. I'll spare you the gory details. Let's just say that you dangle enough money and status in front of people and then act like it could be snatched away at any second, you have a lot of power over them. And Peyton and Marco have been in that place for a long time. That guy has so much control over them it's sick."

"What guy?" I asked.

"Their illustrious *agent*." He said the word like one it was a disease.

"Chad."

"Oh yeah. He's been pulling their strings for years."

I knew this, of course—Marco had basically told me as much. But it was interesting to hear it from Adam's perspective.

"Then after Peyton did that rescue mission and Jillian came onto the scene things just . . . snowballed," he went on.

"So why did Marco still need to be part of her image after that? Sounds like her career shot right back to the top once the whole cat thing came to fruition. The Cat-woman franchise alone, right?"

He shrugged. "Chad had them brainwashed. I swear, it's like a cult with its charismatic leader. Although he's not that charismatic. And most everyone else can see right through him. Then with Jillian putting her two cents in, there was no getting through to them. Chad kept telling Marco all his secrets were going to come out and he'd be nothing again."

"You mean his relationship with you?"

"Not just that. Marco didn't want anyone to know how he started out."

"How did he start out?"

Adam smiled. "I met him in California. We were both trying desperately to become actors. Doing penny-ante commercials, anything to get a break. Well, his first big break was a dog food commercial," Adam said.

I waited. "Okay. So what?"

"He ate the dog food. It was supposed to show that the food was natural and fine for human consumption. It wasn't," he added dryly. "This was way back before natural food was cool. But he did a whole dog-food-eating campaign and that's how he first started acting."

There had to be more. I mean, that was gross, but on the scandal scale it had to rate pretty low. "So what? I'm sure tons of actors and actresses get their starts that way, no? Maybe not dog food per se, but something equally as embarrassing?"

"You have no idea," Adam said. "But he'd done other things too, which I won't get into. If you know what I mean."

"Oh," I said. I could make a good guess.

"Yeah. He used a different name and he looked . . . very different back then, so it hasn't come back to bite him yet. But Chad spent so much time drilling it into his head that all of this would come out and tarnish his teenybopper god image and he'd be finished. Marco let himself get swept away by all this. He is literally terrified of people finding out. It's really sad."

"And you?" I asked. "How'd you get here?"

"I cut and run. Decided I wasn't cut out for the Hollywood life and came home. I'm much happier here."

"Smart choice. So what's the cat rumor about?" I asked casually.

"What cat rumor?"

"One of the tabloid reporters asked me to confirm the rumor about Peyton and the cat. Do you know what that means?"

Adam's gaze slid away from mine. "No clue," he said, but I knew he was lying as sure as I knew my own name.

I decided to try a different tact, if he wouldn't tell me anything about Peyton. "So how well did Marco know Jillian?" I asked.

"Enough to hate her guts as much as anyone," Adam said.

I stared at him. "Seriously?"

"Of course. She was pulling a lot of the strings. And as long as she had Peyton under her thumb, Marco was still going to do what they said. The whole thing was a cluster." He paused. "But if you're asking me if he killed her, the answer is no."

I blew out the breath I'd been holding. "You're sure?"

"Could he have? Maybe. Did he? No. And I'm not just covering for him. We were together that morning. At my sister's house. She had a small party for us the night before and we stayed over." He smiled sadly. "It was our anniversary. We made breakfast together that morning. Brunch, actually."

"Wait." I grabbed his arm. "You were with Marco? He wasn't on the boat?"

"No. I just told you he was with me. Why?"

"No reason," I murmured.

Other than, he and Peyton had alibied each other. And two other people had been complicit in that alibi. The assistant and the bodyguard. This took Marco out of the running for the murder, but it still left the question of who'd done it wide open. And time was running out for Mish.

Chapter 40

I tossed and turned for most of the night, waiting for news on Marco. I'd texted Peyton after I left Adam, to tell her I'd heard and to offer my sympathies. She hadn't responded. Adam had promised to let me know when Marco regained consciousness, but so far, nothing. I'd caught up with Craig after I'd gotten home, and they had nothing new. Members of the police force confirmed Chad had brought Marco back to the yacht and left again alone. No one noticed him leaving out through the main cabin door—or at least they weren't saying anything if they had. The only other possibility that made sense, according to Craig, was Marco leaving the boat perhaps by a back entrance farther down the dock, which was less monitored, and walking along the beach all the way to the ferry docks and Damian's, where someone had clocked him.

But why?

If . . . *when* . . . Marco woke up, he could tell someone who'd done it. If he'd seen them. There was always the possibility he'd been hit from behind.

I waited until six a.m. before I called Becky. She

sounded wide awake when she answered. It didn't surprise me.

"Hey," she said. "I was just about to call you."

"About Marco Moore? Did you hear something?"

"Nothing new. We have a reporter outside the hospital waiting for news. I've gotta tell you, Maddie, since you've come back to the island things have been way more exciting. We've gotten a lot of good stories because of you."

I had to laugh. Leave it to Becky to find the silver journalist lining in all of this. "Glad to help. Listen. I feel like this has to be related to Jillian."

Becky was quiet. I could hear the wheels turning. "Tell me more," she said finally.

"Can I come by the office? Maybe we can put our heads together."

"Yeah. I'll be there in an hour. I'll bring coffee."

I jumped out of bed and went to get dressed, already feeling better. I was buoyed by the thought of talking everything through with Becky. We had always been good at figuring things out as a team, from back when we were kids. I thought about waking Lucas up to tell him where I was going, but as usual he was sound asleep. I'd spare him and just text him.

I hurried downstairs for coffee, but Val intercepted me. "Hey. You're up early. Have you heard anything?"

I shook my head. "Nothing."

"Do you think Peyton will bail?" she asked.

"Out of town or out of the event?"

She shrugged. "Both."

"I honestly don't know, Val. The event probably isn't top of mind for her right now." I glanced desperately at the coffeepot—so close but so far away.

"I know. I feel awful. But meanwhile, the tent is being delivered today," Val said. "We're just going to proceed as if we're moving forward. Ethan is closing the café early so we can start setting up. Oh, and you should see what's going on outside." She nodded at the back door. "Grandpa's out there with Jo."

I frowned. "Jo from the League? She's still here?"

Val nodded. "She came to the door and Grandpa went outside with her. I tried to tell him he didn't need to talk to her, that we'd sorted it out, but he didn't want to hear it."

I went to the back door and peered out. Sure enough, Grandpa and Jo were outside, having what looked like a serious conversation. But they weren't alone. Sergeant Mick Ellory had joined the party.

I went outside, curious now. "Hey," I said. "What's going on?"

The party of three stopped talking and stared at me as I walked over. I searched Grandpa's face, then Ellory's. Nothing. Cop-faced, the both of them. I sighed and looked at Jo. "Are you still here because of Jillian?"

"Sort of." Jo pulled a wallet out of her jeans pocket, flipped it open, and held it out to me. I glanced at it, then did a double take. I met her eyes, a silent question.

"FBI," she said. "Special Agent Janice Wong."

Why on earth was the FBI at our door? "So you're not . . . Jo. And you don't work at the League."

She tipped her chin slightly, an affirmation.

"So what are you doing here?" I asked, but I had a sinking feeling I may have an idea about the answer.

"Your grandfather was looking into someone I was also investigating." She glanced at Grandpa Leo. "I asked him if we could compare notes."

"Jillian?" I asked Grandpa.

He nodded.

I looked from him to Ellory. "So what did you find out?"

"She was receiving large sums of money into her account," Grandpa said. "It's been going on for a couple years. I hadn't been successful in tracing it before she died."

"So you were investigating her," I said. "On Stevie's behalf. Even after you told me you'd stopped when she engaged with us."

"I did," Grandpa said. "That's why I didn't get any further."

"Oh. So, what, she was embezzling or something? Like, from the League? She wouldn't." Would she? Despite her quirky personality and love for expensive things, I felt like Jillian had really taken her job seriously and wanted to help animals.

"We don't know where it was coming from," Ellory said.

"Okay," I said. "So do you think it could be related to her death?"

"As we said, we don't know," Ellory said.

"Well, I thought you already had her murderer?"

"It's an ongoing investigation," Jo—Agent Wong—cut in.

"But wouldn't it be over now that she's dead? Unless you think if she was getting money from someone and it had something to do with her death." I waited for her to confirm. She didn't.

"We aren't sure yet what she was involved in," Wong said. "We were investigating her because there were suspicions that she was using the League's fundraising activities as a payday opportunity. We're trying to figure out if there were others involved or if she was acting alone."

"You're kidding."

"Unconfirmed, as I said. This stays between this group." She eyed me. I gathered that her demeanor I'd been silently wondering about it was just her agent demeanor. It didn't look like she ever cracked a smile.

"You can't mention this to your sister," Grandpa said.

"So does the rest of the staff know? About you?" I asked her.

Wong shook her head. "No. I've been 'working' there for a while now. Trying to get her to trust me enough to bring me in."

This still wasn't making great sense to me. "I don't mean this to sound . . . harsh, but why does the FBI care about someone taking a few thousand bucks from a non-profit? It seems a bit low profile for you."

That hard stare again. But instead of answering my question, she said, "Did Jillian ever follow up on all those conversations with a formal proposal?"

"No," I said.

"And the League's cut? Did you ever nail that down?"

I nodded. "I think she said twenty-five percent." I tried to remember, but Jillian had tossed out a number in passing and we'd never gotten it in writing, which I guessed should have been a red flag for me and Val, but we were apparently too fixated on the amount Jillian had promised we would raise.

"No paperwork?"

"No."

"And you didn't think that was odd?" Her tone confirmed my naivete.

I shifted my weight from one foot to the other. "I figured we'd get to it. She was . . . kind of a whirlwind."

"You can say that again," Wong said. "This has been one of the most tiring jobs I think I've ever had, just trying to keep up with her."

Chapter 41

I went back inside to wait for Grandpa to be done. Luckily Val had gotten distracted with something and wasn't waiting in the kitchen.

I poured myself coffee and glanced impatiently at my watch, tapping my foot. I wanted to get going, but I wanted to talk to Grandpa first.

He came in ten long minutes later. He didn't look surprised to see me.

"What the heck is going on?" I demanded. "Jillian was stealing money?"

"Apparently so," Grandpa said. "But she was also getting money from somewhere else, it seems. They can't trace that money back to the League. But there was definitely skimming going on, according to our friend outside. And Jillian did a lot without contracts."

"But why is it an FBI case? Like I said, it seems really minor league for them."

"Embezzlement is a federal offense, no matter the amount. But let's just say they think it spanned further than a few thousand bucks from events."

Jeez. "Could this help Mish?"

Grandpa poured himself a cup of coffee. When he turned back, he seemed to weigh his words. "Well. I found out something about Mish."

"What? Something that will get her released?"

"Mish hired her own PI to get information on Jillian. Her lawyer passed along the message to me, asked me to get in touch. I haven't been able to reach him yet, but she told the lawyer that he'd found out something about Jillian that might point to her real killer."

"Do you think it was about her brother?"

"I guess we'll know if he gets in touch with me. But that's the other thing I meant to tell you—Ellory confirmed Chad Novak has an alibi for the time of the murder."

I froze. "He does?"

Grandpa nodded. "He was with his personal trainer from eight thirty until ten. They were working out in the hotel gym, and a number of guests and staff verified that."

"Did you find out anything about him? Like which half is related to Jillian's family here?"

"I did. It's on the father's side. So Chad would have no claim to Marcella's property."

"Unless Jillian had promised something to him if *she* got it," I said.

"Right. But she'd have to be alive to do that."

And just like that, it was back to the drawing board.

I got all the way to the *Chronicle* before I remembered I was supposed to pick up coffees for us, and had to drive back over to the Bean. I got lattes and a bunch of pastries and donuts for Becky and the staff and drove back over. The office was buzzing for this early in the day, but when you had a murder and a celebrity assault all in the space of a week, it made for a busy newsroom.

"Finally," she exclaimed when I came up the stairs. "What took you so long?"

Before I could put the boxes of goodies down she dragged me into her office and shut the door.

"Jeez," I said, shaking the spilled coffee off my hand. "Glad to see you too."

"So get this." Her excited voice was low, like she was trying to tell a secret in a crowded room. "The thing you mentioned to me. Good tip, Maddie. We did some digging."

"Tip?" I was drawing a blank, too focused on the whole FBI drama.

"Yeah. About Peyton Chandler and the cat. It's probably bigger news in your world, to be honest, but it could have repercussions for her career since her whole persona is built around it—"

"Becky," I interrupted. "What?"

"This rescue cat of hers? Not really a rescue."

It all came flooding back to me. I remembered I'd mentioned the journalist's question to Becky the other day. Seemed she'd taken it seriously after all. "Rhiannon?" I asked slowly. "What do you mean, not really a rescue?"

"She's from a breeder. Actually, she's like the second or third Rhiannon. Allegedly. She's no rescue from a hurricane zone. The original one was, but she's been replaced."

Replaced? What on earth? "How did you find this out?" I asked.

Becky smiled. "People think reporters at small papers are slouches. We've got some relentless staff here."

Jenna, no doubt.

"We found the breeder who sold her the two subsequent Rhiannons," Becky continued. "The woman said Peyton's . . . representative was very specific about what they wanted, showed her pictures and everything to get the cats as close to the original as possible. Talk about a bait and switch for your dedicated fans, right?"

"You're *kidding.*" I dropped my head into my hands. That would not go over well in the rescue community. Adele might personally throw Peyton into the ocean when she found out. Avid rescuers couldn't stand the thought of going to breeders, considering all the adoptable pets left in shelters, often to die there. It seemed like such an odd story to concoct. I mean, everyone would've sympathized with Peyton if Rhiannon had died. She could've adopted other rescue cats and everything would have been fine. Maybe they would've had to change the brand around a bit, but they could always still sell Rhiannon-branded stuff. They could've made a killing off it. Her fans would've wanted a piece of the iconic cat's line of clothing or accessories.

Accessories. Rhiannon's brand. Something was firing in my brain, trying to connect, but I couldn't quite grasp it.

"I'm not," Becky said. "Actually, the woman didn't sell them to her directly."

I raised my head. "Let me guess. Chad Novak." If he and Jillian were intertwined in this whole scheme of getting Peyton and Marco to do whatever they wanted, it had to be Chad. But what was Jillian getting out of it? Chad as their agent was obviously living a sweet life off their movie-making celebrity status. Was he sharing with his sister? But if he was doing so well, why would he need her property if she got it? No, there had to be more to the story. Perhaps it had to do with Jillian's own standing in the rescue community, her position at the League, her ability to influence if Peyton was her go-to person.

Becky shook her head. "The woman was supposed to look up the name of the person and get back to me. I'm assuming it was some lackey who just did the deal to keep Peyton out of it. "Why do you think it was Chad?"

"Because not only is he Peyton's and Marco's agent, he's also Jillian's long-lost half brother." I felt like I'd told this story a million times by now. I filled her in on what I'd learned about Jillian's family drama.

She listened with rapt attention. "Wow. This chick was living on the edge, huh? No wonder someone offed her. So this really had nothing to do with Mish."

"I don't think so, no. I think the person who clubbed Marco was also Jillian's killer. So I was down to two main suspects: Peyton or Chad. Then Grandpa just told me that Chad has an alibi for Jillian's murder. The cops verified it with the hotel staff. Which leaves me with . . . Peyton. God, I hate to even say it," I said, rapping my knuckles against my forehead. "She seems so sweet."

"She's an actress," Becky pointed out.

"True." I sighed. "Peyton obviously didn't do the dirty work, but maybe she had someone do it. There are also two people who covered for her and Marco. Marco definitely has an alibi for Jillian—he was at his boyfriend's sister's house sleeping off his anniversary party—and he didn't cave his own skull in, so it's not him. But she and Chad could still be in on it together. He just didn't kill Jillian. Because she was his sister?"

She was scribbling furious notes in columns on her page, trying to keep this all straight. I knew the feeling. My own brain felt like a jumbled mush of facts, rumors, and some threads of the truth.

Becky finished writing and looked at me, tapping her pen against her desk. "You know I have to break the cat story, right?"

"Yeah. I figured as much. But hey, the fundraiser might not go on anyway, depending on what happens with Marco. So do you want my tip now?"

"Wait. The brother story wasn't it?"

I shook my head. "There's more. Completely off the record," I added, waiting until Becky gave an impatient nod and motioned me to continue. "The reason I was late today. Grandpa got a visitor this morning. An FBI agent."

Becky's eyes widened. "What?"

"She was undercover in the League, posing as Jillian's second-in-command. They suspected she was embezzling funds from the rescue. She and Grandpa bumped into each other during their respective investigations of Jillian. But Grandpa found other payments going into Jillian's account. He hadn't gotten to the bottom of it when everything blew up."

"Wow." Becky thought about that. "So how is all this connected?"

"Beats the heck out of me. The only thing that makes any sense is that Chad and Jillian were in on this whole idea that they had to keep both Peyton and Marco under their thumb. They knew secrets about them, right? So maybe they were actually blackmailing them. For money. Maybe that's where those payments were coming from that Grandpa found?"

Becky picked up the thread. "Maybe they were funneling them through someone else. To keep the eyes off them."

"So they were both greedy. And Mish and Stevie got caught in the crossfire. But if they had this paycheck, why was she so fixated on the estate?"

"If you're greedy like that, there's never enough," Becky pointed out. "And maybe Peyton and Marco had threatened to stop paying. Maybe they'd decided that enough was enough."

I thought of Adam. "Maybe. And they couldn't risk it. And then Marco threatened to call it all off and expose Chad and he hit him? Tried to kill him? Chad was alone with Marco that day he was assaulted. He took him home from the meet and greet because he was drunk. Granted, there are witnesses acknowledging he dropped Marco off, but who knows what happened or who was making stuff up. The cops have no idea how long he was there on the beach."

My phone rang, distracting me. A number I didn't recognize. I answered. "Maddie James."

"Maddie. This is Chad Novak." *Speak of the devil.* "Peyton wondered if that cat was adopted? Ashley?"

I raised my eyebrows at Becky, trying to telepathically alert her to this phone call. "I don't think so, but I have to check with my front-desk person. I think we gave the people until today to let us know."

"Can you do that now?" Was it my imagination, or did he sound more angsty and short than usual? "She wants to get her today, if she's available."

"Today?" What was up with this? "I can find out. Um, how's Marco?"

"No change," he snapped. "Call me back as soon as possible. On this number." He disconnected.

I put the phone down and looked at Becky. "Something strange is going on. That was Chad. He wanted to know if Peyton could adopt the cat she was looking at and take her today."

Becky frowned. "Today? Why?"

"No idea. Either she wants to be able to snuggle with

two cats because she's upset about Marco, or she's planning to run. Maybe she's afraid someone can trace something back to her." And just like that, the missing piece clicked.

I jumped up. "I have to go. I'll call you later."

Chapter 42

I flew home, nearly running over a few tourists on the way. I needed to confirm the suspicion that had been brewing in the back of my mind. And then I had to figure out what to do about it if I was right.

I pulled into the driveway on two tires, jumped out of the car, and ran over to the café/garage. I could see the tent set up in the back and presumed that Val had already gotten to work in here too.

I checked there first. The door was unlocked but it was empty when I burst inside. The place looked amazing. Aside from the counter, one would never know that it was a café, never mind an actual garage. It actually looked like a glamorous witch had swept through here with a magic wand. The Stevie Nicks theme had definitely come to life. Everything was pink and black—Rhiannon's pink, of course—with silver sparkles. Sheer drapey fabrics covered the walls and hung from the ceiling with moons, stars, and paw prints dangling every few feet. Whatever she'd done with the lighting gave everything a midnight-sky feel, which I assumed would be even more impactful at night. High tables for socializing were interspersed with food stations for both hot and cold food.

It looked beautiful, and for a moment I just stopped and appreciated how great it was going to be.

I ducked back outside and went to the tent. It was empty too—they hadn't started setting up in here yet. It must've just arrived. But boxes were piled up in one corner. Val had apparently started bringing things out. I went over and looked, hoping that what I wanted was out here.

It was. I used my car key to slice into the top box and pulled out one of the infamous Rhiannon-branded leashes.

I held it gingerly, almost expecting it to burn me. It didn't. It was just a plain old piece of faux leather. I used my key again to slice through the thin plastic wrap holding the leash together and unwound it.

Amazing how such a benign object could be used to take a person's life. I ran my fingers down the length of it, then looked more closely. Aside from the changes to the sparkles, it looked exactly the same as the one I'd seen on Rhiannon that day, way back in the beginning.

With one exception. There was no dangly paw print on this one. I grabbed another one out of the box and checked it as well. It was gone. The design was different.

Still clutching the leash, I pulled my phone out of my pocket, cursing myself for not noticing this before. I dialed Ellory's cell. He answered on the first ring.

"It's Maddie. Listen, odd question. But the leash you got at the crime scene. There was a little charm right? That had fallen off? I saw it on the bench that day. Next to . . . her."

"Hold on." I heard something clanging, like a metal

drawer, then papers shuffling. Finally he returned to the phone. "I'm looking at the photos. Yeah. A paw print, on the bench. The little charm was still on the leash but it must've popped off during the attack."

I let that sink in. "Are you at the station? I need to show you something."

Ten minutes later I stood in the lobby of the Daybreak Harbor police station. I wondered if Mish was being held here still. Hopefully she'd be going home soon.

"Maddie?" Ellory stuck his head out the door leading back to the offices. "Come on."

I followed him to his office and placed the leash on his desk. "You have the photos of the weapon?"

"I do," he said, sitting down and motioning for me to do the same.

I did. "Can you compare them to this one?" I held up the leash.

He gave me a long look. "What's this about?"

"Please. Just look at them."

He sighed and pulled a folder out of a pile on his desk, opened it, and flipped through it. He pulled out a couple of photos and laid them on the desk. "What am I looking at?"

"The colors, and the place where the charms should be."

He looked. Then he picked up the new leash and studied it from a couple of angles. Looked at the photos again. "The color is lighter."

I nodded. "What else?"

"There's no charm."

"Right! Not even a little hook for it." I sat back triumphantly.

"So?" he asked.

I leaned forward, indignant. "What do you mean, so?

The leashes are different. This," I said, stabbing his photo with my finger, "is a prototype. They got the real ones later. Saturday, to be exact. The day before Jillian died. She had the boxes delivered to Stevie's, then took them with her to the Paradise."

Ellory picked up the new leash again. "So you're saying . . ."

"Only one other person that I know of had this leash: Peyton Chandler. Her cat was wearing it."

He tipped his chair back, still studying the leash. "That you know of."

"They had a sample sent to her. She was using it. But she didn't love the color of the sparkles, so she wouldn't have let anyone else use it. I'm telling you, she's getting ready to bail. Chad already called me today asking for the cat she wants to adopt. It sounded urgent, which tells me she wants out. And Mish is not the killer. You have to help me." I hated to beg, but I really needed him to listen.

"So what do you want to do, Maddie? I can't just go barging in there and accuse her of murder. Her lawyers would be down our throats in a second."

"You're right," I said thoughtfully. "You can't, but I can try to get her to talk. With your help."

"What exactly are you suggesting?"

"Let me go over there. I can use the cat as my excuse. Maybe I can get her talking."

"Absolutely not."

"You have a better idea besides letting them sail away into the sunset?" I asked.

"Who's sailing into the sunset?" Craig leaned against the doorjamb.

"No one," Ellory said at the same time I said, "Peyton Chandler and whoever on that boat really killed Jillian."

Craig raised his eyebrows. "Come again?"

"I think it was her. She orchestrated it, maybe with Chad, and got one of those bodyguards to do it," I said, filling him in on the leash differences and my thought process. "And she's getting ready to leave. Chad called me earlier looking to see if we could bring over the cat she wants to adopt. It's the perfect way for me to get on the boat." I turned back to Ellory. "You know they're just going to stonewall you if you try. Especially since you already theoretically have the killer."

"She's right," Craig said.

I spun around, amazed. "I am?"

He shrugged. "Yeah. They're never going to let us anywhere near them. We have no concrete evidence, aside from the different leashes, and someone already in custody. But I think you're right. I think this Hollywood bunch had something to do with it." He held Ellory's gaze. Ellory looked like he'd swallowed something nasty, but said nothing. Craig turned back to me. "So what do you suggest?"

I repeated my idea. Craig looked at Ellory. "It's worth a shot. Look, we already have cops crawling the marina to *protect them*." He used air quotes and an eye roll to accentuate this. "We can send her in with a wire."

"Lucas can come with me," I offered.

"Great," Ellory said. "Let's endanger two citizens instead of one. And what happens if Maddie gets her talking and they realize it's a setup? They can motor that stupid behemoth boat right out of the harbor."

"Yeah, at five miles an hour," Craig said. "They won't get far. Plus we can alert the Coast Guard to be on standby."

"Her grandfather will kill us," Ellory said. "You of all people should know that." He pointed at Craig.

"Not if we involve him," Craig said. "Actually, maybe we send him in with her instead."

"He's still a civilian," Ellory snapped.

"A highly trained one with thirty-five years on the force," Craig said dryly.

Ellory's inner struggle played out on his face as Craig and I waited. In the end, thankfully, he must've decided that the danger of putting the wrong person on trial outweighed a careful sting operation. "I guess I'm out-voted. Okay, let's get this in motion. Maddie, call Novak back. Tell him you can bring the cat over at"—he checked his watch—"four o'clock. That will give us time to get in place. Tomlin, call Mancini and get him on board. I'll pull a team together and let the chief know."

Chapter 43

"Maddie. Can you hear me?"

Craig's voice came through clear as day in my ear. "Copy," I said. "Or should I say 'Roger'?"

I pretty much heard Craig roll his eyes on the other end of the line. "Don't worry about it. You won't be on this thing long enough to need to know the lingo."

Grandpa and I were in Grandma's old car with Ashley in her carrier, waiting for the patrol officer's signal to turn into the marina. Of course I had no intention of giving Ashley to Peyton at this point, but if I tried to waltz on to the yacht with no cat, it would be apparent that something was off.

"Now you listen," Grandpa said, turning to me. "You stay close to me and let me take the lead. Okay? This isn't a TV show."

He hadn't been sold on my idea, but Craig and Ellory—once I'd convinced Ellory—had done a good job of convincing him and letting him be unofficially in charge of putting the plan together. I also got the sense their chief hadn't been a huge proponent. Ellory had to go to his office with all the theories and do the whole song and dance to convince him. In the end, the chief must have weighed the consequences of letting me and Grandpa leverage our relationships with the consequences of sending an innocent woman to jail and decided to give it his blessing. I imagined Ellory would pay dearly if things went south, though, so I wanted to make sure nothing went wrong.

"Got it," I told Grandpa, aware that a whole bevy of cops were listening.

"Good. Mick." He spoke to his wire. "Do we know how many security people are there?"

"The team this morning reported two out on the dock. No idea who is on the boat."

The officer at the gate waved us in. I drove to a spot near the dock and parked, then took a deep breath. I hoped I wasn't wrong here. But my gut was telling me that I wasn't. Someone on this boat had committed these crimes. Most likely Peyton herself. And if Ellory didn't think I could be right, he wouldn't have signed off on this.

"Remember what I said," Grandpa told me as we got out of the car.

"I got it." I grabbed Ashley's carrier, squared my shoulders, and marched toward the docks. Chad must have cleared us with the goons out front, because they waved us through. I went up to the little door on the side that Val and I had used the other day and knocked once, then pushed it open.

"Hello," I called, using my brightest voice. "It's Maddie."

Grandpa followed me through the little foyer into the giant living room. Chad was in the room, alone. He looked kind of . . . off. But that was to be expected if he had committed murder or assault and was trying to get out of Dodge.

"Hi," I said.

"Hey."

Esther appeared in the doorway.

"Hello, Leo. Maddie." She nodded at us.

"I'll take her," Chad said, reaching for Ashley's carrier.

I held it out of his reach. "Unfortunately I can't do that. Peyton needs to sign the paperwork as the adopter. We have an agreement that we need in writing for all our adoptions. Is she here?"

He looked like he wanted to punch me in the face. "No," he said through gritted teeth. "Obviously she's at the hospital with Marco."

"Oh. How is he doing, by the way?" I asked. I could feel Grandpa getting stiff beside me. He didn't want me talking, but I felt like taking this conversation through its natural course was the only way this was going to work.

"No change."

"That's unfortunate," Grandpa said. "Have they made any progress on the investigation?"

"They don't report to me," Chad said.

"And no one has any idea how he ended up out on the beach after you dropped him off that day?" Grandpa asked. "I would think with all the people guarding the boat that someone would have seen him coming or going, no? Don't they both have security that follows them when they go out?"

Chad shook his head. "Marco never wanted it." He looked like he was about to say more, but then he clammed up.

"Why don't I sign for Peyton?" Esther broke in, "I do most of those things for her anyway. And I live with her, so it would be like she's my cat anyway, right?"

"I'm sorry," I said. "I really need the formal adopter to sign the paperwork. Do you want to call me when she's back and I'll come back with her?"

"No," Chad said. "She really wants the cat to be here when she returns."

"And my granddaughter just told you that isn't going to happen," Grandpa said smoothly, putting his hand on my shoulder.

"Honest to goodness," Esther said with a sigh. "Why does everything have to be so difficult?"

I turned, wanting to ask her what she meant, and it took me a second to process what I saw. Esther held a small pistol in her hand, pointed straight at us.

Chapter 44

Grandpa shot a warning look my way. He didn't need to. I was still trying to reconcile Esther holding this gun.

"All of you. Out here." She motioned toward the sliding doors that led out to the deck, unfortunately on the side of the boat facing the water, away from the plethora of cops out in the marina. "I'm sorry, Leo. I do think you're lovely, but now you're in my way." She motioned to Chad. "You too. Out there."

Grandpa took my elbow, giving it a reassuring squeeze as Esther shepherded us out the door and closed it firmly behind us. I noticed that there was a cat carrier out here too, by the railing. And Rhiannon was inside. Next to the carrier there was a suitcase.

Holy crap. They were going to try to escape on the lifeboat. Without Peyton? Was she really at the hospital? Did this mean she was innocent?

"Why is she out here?" I asked, pointing to Rhiannon. "It's too hot!"

Esther chuckled. "That's the least of your worries, my dear. Chad. Get the boat ready."

Stiffly, Chad went over to the railing. I could see the

top of the lifeboat, mounted to the side of the yacht. Chad began fiddling with the ropes. I wondered if he even knew what he was doing.

"Esther," Grandpa said calmly. "Are you going to try to ride a lifeboat out of here? You aren't going to get far. The Coast Guard has already been alerted. Everyone knows what you've done."

I gaped at her. "You? You killed Jillian and tried to kill Marco?"

"Yeah," Chad said. "She killed my sister."

Esther gave him a withering look that suggested he shut up. "I had to. That woman was going to destroy Peyton. Peyton kept letting herself get in deeper and deeper over her head. All those favors, all the endorsements, all the events in exchange for her *keeping her mouth shut*. And this one wasn't stopping it," she said, jerking her gun in Chad's direction. "Making her go along with the nonsense about Rhiannon. Tipping off the breeder so she could hold it over Peyton's head too. And the poor cat." She gazed at the carrier. "It's not Rhiannon's fault. She's as much a victim of this as Peyton is. I should just shoot him now and get it over with, but I figure I'll wait until we're out further." She smiled a chilling smile at Chad. "Hopefully there will be some sharks out there."

Wow. I'd never really thought of Esther as a sweet old lady—I'd never thought much of her at all—but she looked truly frightening at this moment. And Chad looked murderous. I wondered if he was afraid, or if he had a plan that he was waiting to put into action. I hoped Mick was listening to this and they were going to send in reinforcements.

"So you killed Jillian," I repeated, trying to keep her talking. I had no idea what she planned to do with us if she was going to shoot Chad and feed him to the sharks.

"I did. It was quite easy," she said. "I knew where she'd be. I knew everything about her. It's one of the benefits of being invisible to most people. They can't see what's right under their noses. So I left early that morning, took the walking path all the way up the beach and over to the hotel. I knew she'd be outside. She went out there every morning. My plan was to get her alone to talk. But they'd cleared the patio for your meeting." She smiled at me. "Quite thoughtful of them and they saved me some trouble."

"You brought Rhiannon's leash with you to do it?" I asked.

"Actually, I brought it with me to make sure she was handling the revisions. It was one of the things I wanted to talk to her about. I really did go there to talk. But as usual, she was impossible. And she dismissed me like . . ." Esther's jaw set and she shook her head. "I started to leave, but then she sat down and turned her back on me. And before I knew it . . . well. Let's just say it happened fast."

"And Marco? Was that you too?" I could see Grandpa out of the corner of my eye, inching away from me, sliding just out of Esther's peripheral vision. I hoped he knew what he was doing. I hoped he had a gun, although I was pretty sure he did. He usually did. Not a lot of people realized that he still carried, but he'd told me once that he did. I imagined it was an ingrained habit, and at the moment I was grateful for it. Not that I assumed he'd want to just shoot Esther, but at least he could defend us.

She sniffed with disdain. "He was going to ruin it all. Throw it all away for that nurse. I don't care about his reputation. Peyton is more important than him anyway. But that means she has more to lose. He was easy too. Drunk as a skunk, as usual. I told him we were going to get some breakfast. The security team was used to him going out on his own so they didn't even blink an eye. Walked him right down to the beach and clocked him. I would've made sure I got the job done, but then I was interrupted by some tourist." She sniffed.

"Where is Peyton really?" I asked. "She's not at the hospital, is she." I looked at Chad. He gave a slight shake of his head. Had Esther done something to her? Was she about to? Or was Peyton in on this and getting ready to make her grand exit too?

"That's it. Stop talking," she snapped, advancing on me.

After that, everything happened so fast I barely had time to think.

Chad leapt forward, grabbed Rhiannon's cat carrier, and in one awful move flung the carrier off the side of the boat, shouting something about how all the problems had started because of the cat. Esther screamed. At the same moment, Grandpa came up behind Esther, striking her head with the butt of his own gun. With a cry, she went down.

And I didn't even think twice—I raced to the railing and flung myself over the side, one thought screaming in my mind: *Save the cat.*

Chapter 45

The shock of the water left me gasping. I'd thought it would be warmer. Still, I didn't think twice. Once I resurfaced and opened my eyes, I cast around to see where the carrier was. I could just see the top of it floating about ten feet from me.

I dove under and swam like our lives depended on it—Rhiannon's did—and reached it, yanking it out of the water and holding it above me, tilting it so the water would drain out, while treading water furiously to keep myself afloat as I gauged the distance to the shore. The boat was so long that I was all the way out at the end of the dock—and I wasn't sure I should try to head back there. It felt safer to head straight to shore, which wasn't far, but looked like a mile right now. I was a good swimmer, but this carrier full of soaking-wet cat was heavy. And poor Rhiannon must be so terrified. I heard her furious meows and was grateful—I hadn't been sure if she'd inhaled any water.

Seriously, how was I supposed to swim with this cat? I could hear shouts and sirens all around me and really hoped that meant someone was coming to help.

But I couldn't wait. Holding the carrier high with one hand so it skimmed the water, I used my other arm to slowly start swimming, cursing myself for wearing jeans today. They were weighing me down and making me colder. Gritting my teeth, I forced myself to keep going.

And then I heard a motor behind me. Praying it wasn't Chad or someone from their sphere, I turned around, still kicking my feet to stay afloat. And almost cried when I saw it was Craig and another cop in a little orange boat. They pulled up next to me. Craig reached over and grabbed the carrier, placing it on the floor of the boat. Then he grabbed one arm while the other cop grabbed my other arm, and they hauled me up and over the side.

"You okay?" Craig asked.

I nodded, feeling my legs and arms go completely weak, and collapsed on the floor.

Craig motored the boat to the shore. The other cop jumped out and helped pull it onto the sand. Someone ran up to the boat with a towel. Craig took it and wrapped it around me, then helped me climb out of the boat.

"Is Rhiannon okay? Can you bring her to a vet? What about Grandpa?" I asked anxiously.

"Everyone's okay. They have Esther and Chad. It's over, Maddie."

Thank God. "What about Peyton?" I asked.

Craig shook his head. "They found her on the boat. They think she's okay, but still waiting to hear. Come on, let's get you out of those wet clothes."

Chapter 46

"Thank you all so much for coming. You have no idea how much this means, not only to us, but to all the animals on the island who need help, like Thurber." Katrina snapped her fingers, and the dog who had been patiently sitting at her feet sprang up onto the dais and gave her a kiss.

The crowd in the tent applauded. We still had a full house—all the people who'd bought tickets honored their purchase and had come together as scheduled to help our animals, despite the cat scandal that Becky's team had broken last night on the *Chronicle*'s website, with a more detailed story in the print edition today. Val and I had assumed the event would be dead in the water, but we'd started getting phone calls first thing this morning that the community was still supportive of the event. In fact, the very first call was from Lilah Gilmore, one of our influential island elders, which was basically an invitation to others to jump on board. So they did, much to Katrina's elation.

I stepped back up to the mic. "So while we don't have

our official guest of honor tonight, she asked me to convey her thanks and much love for all of your support, and she's asked for our guest list. She'll be sending each of you a gift of her appreciation, and she wanted me to tell you all that she has committed to a monthly donation to JJ's House of Purrs of ten thousand dollars a month."

The audience cheered again. There had been pockets of discussion about the whole cat scandal at the beginning of the event, but I'd put my best public-relations hat on and spun it to make Peyton sound like a saint who had lost her beloved cat and didn't want to disappoint her fans—which of course was all true.

"Did she adopt the other cat?" someone else called out.

"She did. And what's more, she pledged to add more rescue cats to her household this year." I smiled as the audience cheered and toasted her. Peyton really did love cats, and she'd been horrified when she heard what Chad had done to her precious Rhiannon. And she loved Ashley—that was undeniable.

What we hadn't shared with the crowd was the fact that her own agent and his sister—Chad and Jillian—were blackmailing her for obscene amounts of money to keep this secret that they'd somehow convinced her would make or break her career. Same as they'd done to Marco. It was incredibly sad to me that they'd had such a hold over both of them—two of the biggest stars in the world who couldn't figure out how to remove themselves from their grasp. But luckily, Chad was going down too. While he hadn't been part of the murder and had only found out about Esther when she decided they all needed to leave the island so she didn't get caught, he'd been just as guilty of his own crimes. Jo and her team of agents had been more than happy to take him down for blackmail as part of this operation. And, she'd even stuck around for the party. I saw her in the back, leaning against the wall, observing the crowd as if she were still searching for a criminal mastermind.

The whole thing still felt a bit surreal. After the event on the yacht had played out yesterday, the police had moved in and swept the whole boat. They'd eventually found Peyton, drugged with something and locked in one of the master suites. The captain of the boat had also been drugged. Esther hadn't thought that part through very well—she needed him to drive the boat, but she knew he wouldn't cooperate with anyone but Peyton. But she'd been more intent on keeping Peyton quiet because, as she'd admitted to the police, Peyton "wouldn't have been pleased with my methods for protecting her."

Peyton, who remained innocent in the whole mess, had started to get a bad feeling about Esther's actions after some comments she'd made when Marco had been hurt. Peyton had tipped off Grandpa that she thought her longtime friend may have had something to do with the murder and the assault. Peyton had also confessed that Chad and Jillian had been blackmailing her and Marco for years now, and Esther had been pressuring her to stand up and shut it down. And it turned out she'd had an alibi for the murder after all—she'd set up a meeting with her lawyer and Stevie Warner's lawyer to see how she could help him keep his home and property. She'd gotten wind of the family rift that was going on and wanted to make it right. Plus, I assumed, any way to retaliate against Jillian would be satisfying for her.

Leopard Man stood up. "How is Rhiannon?" he asked.

"She is perfectly fine," I said. "The vet checked her out yesterday after the . . . incident, and gave her a clean bill of health."

"Thanks to your quick action," Leopard Man said.

The crowd cheered again.

I felt my face turn red. "It was nothing."

"A toast to Maddie," Cass Hendricks, our island guru, called out, raising his glass.

The crowd joined him. My face turned even redder.

"And a toast to Leo," Mick Ellory added. "Who set up that sting operation on the boat like the pro he is."

Now the crowd really cheered. Grandpa accepted their applause with grace, standing up and thanking them all. I had to laugh. Grandpa had known all along what we were walking into on that boat, and the way he'd handled it made me think he'd had no business retiring as chief.

"Now, please, enjoy your evening. We have lots of food, music, and kitties and puppies to snuggle," I said. Along with the café cats, Katrina had brought along a few of her dogs to mingle too in hopes of getting them homes. "Thank you all for coming!"

As the crowd turned back to their food and conversations, I stepped down from the little stage and went to join Lucas, who stood off to the side. He slipped an arm around me. "Nice job," he said.

I smiled. "I'm just grateful people still came."

"Everyone loves the café and you and Katrina. Of course they'd be here to support you."

"Yeah." He was right. It was one of the good things about home. For all the faults of living on a little island like this, there was a lot of great stuff. Like community.

"I can't believe we pulled this off." Val and Ethan came over to stand with us.

"I had no doubt." Ethan leaned over and kissed Val. "I'm going to get us a drink. Maddie, Lucas, what'll you have?"

"Martini," Lucas and I said in unison, and then burst out laughing.

When Ethan walked away, Val turned back to me. "He asked me to go back to California with him to meet his grandmother," she said.

My eyes widened. "Wow. That's huge, Val."

"I know." She smiled. "I'm looking forward to it."

Katrina came over with Thurber. She looked decidedly lighter, as if a thousand-pound weight had been lifted from her chest. "Ten grand a month. Plus the proceeds from this event." She shook her head. "I can't believe it. We're going to have to strategize about how we handle it."

"Already on it," I said. "We have an appointment with a financial advisor next week."

"I should've known," she said with a laugh. "So what do you think this will mean for us? I feel like this is going to open a lot of doors."

"Oh," I said, "I have a few ideas."

7-30-21